STAMP of FATE

NESSA L. WARIN

Dreamspinner Press

Published by
Dreamspinner Press
5032 Capital Circle SW
Ste 2, PMB# 279
Tallahassee, FL 32305-7886
USA
http://www.dreamspinnerpress.com/

Stamp of Fate

Cover Art by Shobana Appavu
bob@bob-artist.com

ISBN: 978-1-61372-656-3

Printed in the United States of America
First Edition
July 2012

eBook edition available
eBook ISBN: 978-1-61372-657-0

To Elisa, who stuck with me on this from day one.

# CHARACTER GUIDE

## LEAD CHARACTERS

Mortal Identity: Tadd Leventis, CEO Omega Industries
Immortal: Ares, god of war
Identity Symbol: Spear

Mortal Identity: Declan Anagnos, CEO of Alpha Wing Communications
Immortal: Hermes, messenger of the gods
Identity Symbol: Kerykeion

## OTHER OLYMPIANS

Mortal Identity: Adara Lambros, owner of Lovely Hearts matchmaking service
Immortal: Aphrodite, goddess of love and beauty
Identity Symbol: Dove

Mortal Identity: Arion Xylander, traveling musician
Immortal: Pan, god of the wild
Identity Symbol: Pipes

Mortal Identity: Bront Karalis, owner of Olympus Casino
Immortal: Zeus, king of the gods
Identity Symbol: Thunderbolt

Mortal Identity: Cal Pagonis, owner/operator of Devilish Angels
Immortal: Eros, god of sexual love and beauty
Identity Symbol: Quiver and arrows

Mortal Identity: Denis Varela, owner of Ambrosia Vineyards
Immortal: Dionysus, god of wine
Identity Symbol: Grapes

Mortal Identity: Egan Sideris, owner/operator of decorative iron business
Immortal: Hephaestus, blacksmith of the gods
Identity Symbol: Anvil

Mortal Identity: Flavian, actor
Immortal: Apollo, god of the sun
Identity Symbol: Sun

Mortal Identity: Hermione Demos, agricultural researcher
Immortal: Demeter, goddess of the harvest
Identity Symbol: Ear of wheat

Mortal Identity: Karlyn Spiros, interior designer
Immortal: Hestia, goddess of the hearth
Identity Symbol: Crane

Mortal Identity: Lukas Gallo, CEO of Pyrois Automotive
Immortal: Helios, personification of the sun
Identity Symbol: Sunrays

Mortal Identity: Mona Doukas, "Whale" at Olympus Casino
Immortal: Hera, queen of the gods
Identity Symbol: Peacock

Mortal Identity: Phylicia Baros, CEO of Olympus Casino
Immortal: Tyche, goddess of fortune
Identity Symbol: Cornucopia

Mortal Identity: Selene Ganis, recruiter
Immortal: Artemis, goddess of the hunt
Identity Symbol: Hunting bow

Mortal Identity: Seth Mundis
Immortal: Hades, ruler of the underworld
Identity Symbol: Scepter

Mortal Identity: Sofia Tavoularis, museum curator
Immortal: Athena, goddess of wisdom and strategic warfare
Identity Symbol: Owl

Mortal Identity: Tabitha Rubis, tour guide
Immortal: Persephone, queen of the underworld
Identity Symbol: Pomegranate

Mortal Identity: Zale Glaros, deep-sea fisherman
Immortal: Poseidon, god of the sea
Identity Symbol: Trident

## MORTALS

Gabe Lawson, Tadd's assistant
Rachel Chambers, Declan's assistant
Ian Burke, museum director

# ATHENA

SHE'S beautiful even now, her dark hair spilling out in a halo around her head and her olive skin flawless and smooth. The white of her dress stands out starkly against the dark stone of the tiles, but it's the small tattoo of an owl on the inside of her right wrist and the bronze dagger protruding from her stomach that Declan notices.

"She was taken by surprise," he says, glancing over his shoulder as he crouches down for a better look. "If she'd had time to plan—"

"She never would have been killed," Tadd finishes, crouching down next to Declan. "Whoever did this knew where she was going to be."

"And who she really was." Declan reaches toward the dagger, but Tadd stops him with a hand on his wrist, his thumb brushing over the silver kerykeion tattoo there.

"Don't."

"I need to—"

"Declan." Tadd emphasizes the name. "We can't."

"She's one of us. It's my job."

"Not anymore." Tadd yanks Declan away from the body with enough force that only Declan's speed lets him stay on his feet. "We left that behind."

"Not entirely." Declan looks pointedly at Tadd's right wrist, where a small silver spear tattoo matches the owl on the woman's and the kerykeion on Declan's.

"Enough," Tadd says, shaking his head. "We don't even know who she is now. She doesn't look like someone who can just disappear. If we handle this and it causes problems—"

"You want to involve mortals in this?" Declan arches his eyebrow smoothly. "Really?"

"No!" Tadd snaps, tightening his grip on Declan's wrist. "I want to hurt whoever did this. But I can't. Not if we're going to keep these lives." He calms himself with visible effort. "We left that behind, so we have to deal with this as who we are now, not as who we were."

"We're still who we were." Declan pulls his wrist free. "Maybe we never should have pretended otherwise."

"It's a little late for regrets, don't you think?"

"No." Declan shakes his head as he moves toward the door. "I'm going to tell the others."

"That's an even stupider idea than involving mortal authorities."

Declan swivels with Tadd to face the new arrival, a petite brunette with her hair swept up in a loose braid. She's dressed professionally in a black A-line skirt, a white button-down shirt with three-quarter length sleeves, and a gray argyle sweater vest. Her shoes—low, wide loafer-style heels—manage to look both practical and professional, and the badge clipped to the exposed hem of her shirt reads Selene Ganis.

The tattoo peeking out from behind the silver bracelet on her right wrist is a small hunting bow.

Tadd crosses his arms over his chest as he looks her up and down. "What are you doing here?"

"Hunting. What else?"

"Here?" Tadd snarls as he steps forward, stretching up to his full height and using the fact that he towers over her by more than a foot to loom menacingly. "Why?"

Selene rolls her eyes and glares defiantly up at him. "I'm following a trail." The word *idiot* goes unsaid, but they all hear it. "And it's a good thing for the two of you that I am. You'd have gotten yourselves killed otherwise. Just like her."

"What do you mean? And why are you stopping us?" Declan keeps his voice calm as he steps up behind Tadd and rests his hand on the small of Tadd's back. "You don't care what happens to us. You don't like us."

"No, I don't. But whoever did this killed my sister, and the two of you are about to mess up my hunt. That I do care about."

2

"How will passing on the message about what happened mess up your hunt?"

"Who do you think did this? A mortal? That blade killed a god. It was wielded by a demigod at least. If you tell everyone, the killer will know you're aware of what happened, which might make you the next target."

Tadd steps away from Declan and curls his fingers into fists. "Let him come. I'll take him."

"Wouldn't he already know?" Declan paces back over to the body. "He left her here. That has to be some sort of message for us."

Selene rolls her eyes. "And this is why someone else is going to die before I catch my prey. She wasn't dumped here. She was attacked in her own home and fled here, looking for help, I guess, though I can't imagine why. You two weren't any use."

"We just got home."

"Calm down." Selene holds up a hand as she steps around Tadd, looking at him disdainfully.

Tadd clenches his fists tighter as he stalks over to stand next to Declan. "Trust me, sweetheart, if we'd been here, we would have helped. And whoever did this wouldn't have survived the encounter."

"I'm not your sweetheart," Selene says in a cool tone as she steps carefully around the body, her gaze fixed on the ground, looking for clues. "And I know you would have killed whoever did this, Ares." She looks pointedly at Tadd. "That's why Athena came here. If her killer managed to catch her in a position where she couldn't defend herself, this is the most strategic place to flee. You're the best fighter," she starts, "and you're the fastest," she finishes, swinging her gaze to Declan. "If she needed help defending herself, she would come to you. Everyone would," she adds, bitterness coloring her tone. "Did you know who she was?"

"You mean other than the obvious?" Declan casts a glance at the woman's tattoo as he asks.

"Yes. Other than the obvious. How did she know where to find you?"

3

"We can always find each other if we really want to. You know that. We haven't made any effort to keep ourselves concealed from those who know what to look for."

"Well, maybe you should have."

Tadd tenses under Declan's hand. "You aren't."

"I can take care of myself."

"And we can't? Is that what you're saying?"

"Tadd." Declan takes Tadd by both shoulders and spends a minute looking straight into his eyes. "Try to calm down. Please."

As Tadd sucks in a deep breath, Declan whirls and speeds over to Selene. "Stop goading him. If you want to hunt whoever did this, fine, I won't stop you. But don't come into our home and antagonize us. You're the guest here. If you dislike us that much, leave."

"Maybe I will." Selene bends down, peering intently at the woman's face and tattoo, and spends several minutes examining the dagger from every possible angle. Twice she almost touches it, bringing her hand within a hair's breadth of brushing against it, but she stops short both times. Finally she pulls back and glances coolly at Tadd before squaring her shoulders and looking at Declan. "I trust you can handle disposing of the body?"

She doesn't give him a chance to answer before she vanishes, leaving Declan staring at the empty space she'd occupied and wondering what, exactly, they'd done to deserve that.

Tadd snarls at the empty air where Selene had last been. "Well, that was pleasant."

Declan is by his side in a second. He rests his hand on Tadd's shoulder and slides it up to rub the tense muscles at the back of his neck. "Did you expect anything else?"

"No." Tadd crosses his arms, still glaring at the empty air, but his tone is slightly less sullen and he leans into Declan's soothing touch. "Not once I saw who she was. Bitch."

"Tadd." Declan withdraws his hand and steps around so he's facing the other man. "Be nice."

"I'm not nice."

"You're nice to me."

4

"You're different."

"Not that much." Declan smiles fondly and squeezes Tadd's arm. "She wanted to irritate you. Don't give in."

"Easier said than done." The moroseness in Tadd's expression is fading, though, and he uncrosses his arms and bumps his shoulder into Declan's before stepping closer to the body. "I'm easy to irritate."

"Well, yes, but that's part of your charm."

Tadd scowls again. Declan flashes a small smile as he moves to look down at the body as well. He lets his smile fade as he takes in the details, noting the bent knee and the broken heel of her right shoe. She's lying with her left hand tucked under her, nestled underneath her bent leg. When Declan bends down to take a closer look, this time investigating the body instead of the dagger, he notices something wedged under her knee, hidden in the folds of her dress.

Taking care that he doesn't touch anything, he pulls a pen from his pocket and teases the object out from under the flowing skirt. It's a white purse with a small wrist strap, tiny enough it could easily have gone unnoticed by anyone chasing her, and it's dwarfed by Declan's hand as he picks it up and curls his fingers carefully around the soft material so he can pull the zipper back.

"Declan." Tadd lays a heavy hand on his shoulder. "Don't touch it."

"We need to know who she is." Careful to touch as little of the material as possible, Declan looks inside and pulls free a tiny billfold that contains twenty dollars in cash, three credit cards, and a driver's license. "Sofia Tavoularis," he reads as he pulls the license free to show Tadd. "Her address is on the other side of town. We should leave the body there."

"Leave the body?" Tadd doesn't take the card, but he does peer at it over Declan's shoulder. "What do you mean?"

"We can't leave it here."

"But—"

"Tadd." Declan turns around and looks the other man in the eyes. "We can't leave her here. Mortals aren't going to solve this."

"And we can't be linked to a murder, even circumstantially. Not if we want to continue living these lives."

They've spent decades building their current personas and the companies that support them, changing their mortal personas every fifteen years or so to avoid arousing suspicion. They built their firms from the ground up, taking them from small businesses to the large corporations they're CEOs of today, and they did it all the mortal way.

It's not something they're willing to give up without a fight.

"We'll need to get rid of that before you move her." Tadd crouches down next to Declan, balancing himself with one hand on the tiles as he focuses on the bronze dagger protruding from her stomach. When wielded by the right hands, it's a weapon capable of killing a god. They can't let it fall into mortal custody.

Tadd eyes the protruding hilt carefully for a moment before he pushes himself back up. "I think I have something that will work."

Declan snorts quietly as Tadd heads back into the house. Of course he does.


THE heavy chimes of the doorbell echo through the foyer as Declan curls his fingers around the graphite hilt of the dagger Tadd is holding out. It's a perfect match for the size and shape of the bronze dagger, though this one has a blade of steel and lacks the magical energy that imbues the one Tadd pulled from Sofia's stomach. This one would not have killed Athena, not even if wielded by Zeus himself, but it's exactly the kind of blade a mortal assailant would use.

Declan freezes, his fingers touching Tadd's along the hilt of the dagger and his eyes wide as he tries to fathom who could be visiting at this hour. This was supposed to be a quiet evening at home, just the two of them and a bottle of red wine. Visitors—and dead bodies—were not on the agenda.

Tadd pulls the dagger back and shifts around so he can slide it into the wound. "Go," he tells Declan, carefully setting the removed bronze blade on an old towel he brought out for the purpose. He'll have to dispose of the towel later, along with anything else that might link

6

Sofia Tavoularis to Tadd Leventis or Declan Anagnos, but for now, it prevents the wet, sticky blood on the bronze blade from getting on their floor. "I'll take care of this."

Declan looks at him for a moment, then allows his eyes to roam to the myriad of weapons spread on the floor next to the body. Tadd had brought out multiple daggers so they could find the best match, and it had taken several minutes of comparison to determine they had a perfect equivalent.

"I'll send whoever it is away."

It's not going to be that easy. He knows it even before the doorbell rings again, but it's not for nothing that Declan is known for his speed and diplomacy. He flies to the door, wraps his fingers around the knob before the chime stops sounding, and twists, pulling the door open just enough he can stick his head through the crack. He's all fake smiles and pleasantries until his eyes alight on the short, slightly scruffy-looking blond man standing on their front porch.

"Lukas," he says, stepping through the narrow opening and pulling the door shut behind him. "What are you doing here?"

The smaller man looks taken aback at Declan's rudeness. "Uh, dinner? Tonight? Six o'clock?"

Declan blinks blankly. "Dinner?" He sounds as dumb as Selene implied he is, but he can't remember anything about dinner with Lukas tonight.

Then again, his mind is currently occupied with far more serious matters.

Lukas's eyebrows slide smoothly up his forehead. "We were going to discuss our business deal?"

"Business deal?" Declan can't remember that either. It's worrisome, but he'll focus on it later. Business deal or not, he can't have dinner with Lukas tonight.

"Are you all right?" Lukas tilts his head to the side and looks at Declan appraisingly. "You seem... stressed."

"Yeah. Just, uh...." Declan waves his hand vaguely as he tries to think of a suitably diplomatic reason to keep Lukas out of their foyer. He would likely understand the situation, and Declan is tempted to invite him in just to spite Selene, but she was right. They can't let anyone else know about Athena without endangering themselves.

"The housekeeper got sick all over the foyer," he says with a glance back toward the door. "It's a huge mess, and…." He flashes a strained smile. "Can we reschedule?"

"Of course. Call me when you're free."

"Thanks." This time, Declan's smile comes easier.

Lukas pats Declan on the shoulder, briefly exposing the sun rays on the inside of his right wrist, and heads off. "We're going to do big things together, man!"

Declan shakes his head and watches as Lukas climbs into the Bronte sport model sitting in the driveway. He waits for him to drive off before slipping back though the door, again taking care to only open it as far as necessary for him to get through. He can't see anyone around, but there's no point in taking needless risks that could expose what they're doing or who they really are.

Sofia is still sprawled on the floor exactly where Declan left her, but the knives are gone, put back into their places in Tadd's study, and Tadd is sitting on the bottom of the staircase that curves its way up to the second floor. He's lounging back in a casual pose with one leg extended to the floor, the other folded up on the step below where he's perched, and his elbows resting on the step behind that, but tension radiates from him, filling the foyer and making Declan's nerves jingle.

"Who was it?"

Declan joins Tadd on the steps, relaxing against the polished wood with his back to Sofia's body. "Lukas."

"What did he want?" Tadd's dislike of Lukas dates back to their glory days on Olympus, and Declan has never been able to convince him to play nice, despite numerous attempts. Tonight, though, he's inclined to agree with Tadd's opinion of the man. A visitor was the last thing they needed.

"He said something about dinner and a business deal."

"Tonight?" The accusation is blatant in Tadd's flat, unforgiving tone.

"Yeah." Declan rubs his hand over his face and pinches the bridge of his nose as he sighs. "I didn't schedule it. Maybe Rachel did and forgot to tell me, I don't know. I thought tonight was going to be just us."

"That worked out well."

Declan's lips twitch. "As always." He pushes himself up, his shoulders tensing as he turns back toward the body. "Is everything set?"

"She's all ready." Tadd climbs to his feet as well and follows Declan over to stare down at the body. "Be careful not to touch anything."

"I know."

"Hurry back."

"I always do."

"Don't look into things. Let Selene handle it."

"I—"

"Declan." Tadd steps in front of Declan and cups his chin in both hands. "This isn't your job. Let her handle it."

Declan stares at Tadd for a long moment before he nods. "All right."

"Thank you." Tadd steps back, his hands slipping from Declan's face, but before they reach his sides, Declan catches them and holds them loosely between his own as he closes the distance between them once more.

"You're welcome," he whispers, then tilts his head and leans in to brush his lips against Tadd's.

The kiss isn't romantic. It can't be with a dead body less than five feet away, but it's heartfelt and full of promise. When they break apart, Tadd reaches up to touch Declan's cheek briefly before stepping back again and jamming his hands in his pockets. "Go."

Declan pulls a pair of black leather gloves from the shelf in the closet under the stairs and slips them on before scooping Sofia into his arms and carefully arranging her so he doesn't get any blood on his dress shirt or suit pants. "I'll be right back."

9

Tadd nods and opens the front door, holding it ajar so Declan, calling on his true speed for the first time in centuries, can fly out the door and carry the body across town. When mortals find it, they will never associate it with Declan Anagnos and Tadd Leventis.

TADD goes straight to the bedroom after returning the extra knives to his study and securing the dagger that killed Sofia. He intends to just change and meet Declan downstairs for dinner, but when he glances at his phone as he pulls it from his pocket, he realizes it's been longer than he thought. Declan should already be back. Worry twists in his gut, and he sits on the edge of the bed, his phone clenched tightly in his hand as he stares at the clock on the screen.

He relaxes his grip on the tiny device twenty minutes later as Declan steps into the room. When Declan crosses to him and pulls it gently from his hand, he lets it go easily, his worry drains away. "It took you longer than I thought it would."

"I'm sorry." Declan tosses the phone toward the head of the bed and sinks down next to Tadd. He loosens his tie with one hand as he rubs at the back of his neck with the other. "There was a festival going on in the park. I had to find an out of the way spot."

"No one saw you?"

"They couldn't have. I only stopped for a second."

"Cameras?"

"Not that I saw."

"So there could have been."

"Tadd." Declan turns so he's sitting sideways, one knee pulled up on the bed and his body angled toward Tadd. "They wouldn't have caught me. I was moving too fast."

Declan looks sincere, and Tadd knows he thinks he's right, but that doesn't stop the nagging concern in the back of Tadd's mind. "A fast camera still might have caught you. If someone is diligent enough—"

"Then you can unleash your wrath on them." Declan squeezes Tadd's wrist as he yanks at his tie and pulls it completely off. "Stop worrying."

Tadd snorts, but he relaxes a little as he pulls off his tie and unfastens the top few buttons of his shirt. "That's not exactly easy."

"You're the one who was telling me to calm down before I left." Declan pulls his shirt off and tosses it into the bin in the corner. His undershirt follows, and he has his buckle undone and his pants unbuttoned before he stands and turns so he's looking down at Tadd. "What happened?"

"I had to wait a half an hour with no word from you." Tadd lets his residual worry seep into his voice. He yanks off his shirt as he stands, crowding into Declan's personal space. He slips his fingers into Declan's belt loops, yanks him closer, and pushes up on his toes so his lips are against Declan's ear. "You're supposed to be fast. That's not fast."

"I got across town, dumped a body without being seen, and got back." Declan's protest is mild and perfunctory, but it's clear he can't resist giving one. "That's a lot faster than you could have done it."

"Not the point." Tadd thrusts his hips forward, rubs their groins together, and starts sliding Declan's pants down. "It wasn't fast enough."

Declan gasps and presses into Tadd's touch. He moves his hands to Tadd's waist, fumbling with Tadd's belt and buttons and shoving Tadd's pants down as soon as they're loose enough to move. As the material falls free, he pushes forward, moving with enough speed to knock Tadd to the bed, and pulls off both their shoes, freeing them from the confines of their clothing before pinning Tadd down.

Tadd allows it for a moment, letting Declan nuzzle at his neck as his weight settles, and then he moves, using a speed that gets an impressed smile from Declan and relying on his strength to pin Declan to the bed. "No."

He doesn't give Declan a chance to respond, just leans down and nips at Declan's collarbone as he slides his hands up Declan's arms and pins them to the pillow above his head. He holds them there with one hand, sliding the other back down Declan's body to tease at his nipples and ghost against his side. "My turn," he growls as he leans in and captures Declan's lips in a searing kiss.

Declan agrees wordlessly, opening his lips as Tadd thrusts his tongue in, taking what he desperately craves. His kisses escalate into bites and nips that leave red marks on Declan's skin, and his soft strokes turn into hard and fast thrusts that make Declan writhe beneath him.

When they finally come together, it's fast and dirty, Tadd pinning Declan to the bed as he thrusts inside him. He leans down just as he's about to come, smashes his lips against Declan's, and slides his tongue into his mouth one last time as he pushes forward and they climax together, their cries swallowed by their kiss.

Tadd shudders his release and collapses on top of Declan, boneless and spent, his anger and frustration gone. "Don't do that again. Ever."

"I won't." Declan rolls out from under Tadd, fetches a damp cloth from the bathroom, and snags two pairs of pajama pants from the dresser on the way back. "I promise," he adds once they're cleaned and dressed. He tosses the cloth toward the hamper, slides back into bed, and pulls Tadd close.

"Good." Tadd lifts his head from its place on Declan's shoulder and presses his lips to the underside of Declan's chin as Declan reaches over and turns out the light. Sleep claims them quickly.

IN THE morning, Tadd skims the headlines on his phone as he pours coffee and carries the cups to the table. Their favorite local news site is already pulled up on Declan's laptop, a full color, high-resolution image of Sofia's body taking up half the page, bright in white and red and green under the headline.

They read the article together, Tadd leaning over Declan's shoulder, his coffee held loosely in one hand and the other resting on the back of Declan's chair. As they read, he slides his hand up to Declan's shoulder, gently rubbing at the tense muscles.

## Museum Curator Killed

Sofia Tavoularis, curator of the Museum of History and renowned academic in the field of ancient Greece, was fatally stabbed last night. Her body was found by a groundskeeper in the park near her home, and she was pronounced dead on the scene. Police have no leads.

Tavoularis, 29, was instrumental in expanding the Greek wing of the museum, nearly tripling the size of the collection in the four years she worked at the museum. Colleagues describe her as intelligent, direct, focused, and "an asset to the museum." She was "an expert on everything, but especially on ancient Greece," says one colleague, while another describes her as "the person you could go to with any question and get an answer."

In addition to her work in the local museum, Tavoularis was also heavily involved in academia, often guest lecturing on ancient Greece at various universities. She had intended to travel back to Greece this fall in hopes of expanding her lecture material and the museum's collection.

Her family is not releasing any details about funeral services, but both the family and the police have asked anyone who has any information regarding Tavoularis's murder to come forward immediately.

A few quick clicks reveals the story has broken on almost every local news site and a few national ones, and not all of them are as straightforward and respectful as the first story. *Historian Becomes History* and *Curator Cover-Up?* are only two of the ones that makes Tadd cringe as he sips his coffee. Finally, Tadd has seen enough. He shuts the laptop and sets his phone face down on the far end of the table, where he'll have to get up to grab it. "Enough. We know what happened. No need to harp on it."

"I should have hidden her better," Declan mumbles, poking at his eggs with his fork.

"And taken longer to get home?" There's a dangerous note in Tadd's voice he hopes makes it completely clear that would not have been an acceptable scenario. "You did what you needed to do. Besides," he adds in a slightly softer tone, "we wanted her found. Remember?"

"Yeah."

The sullen note in Declan's tone quenches any desire Tadd had to respond, and he eats in silence, not really tasting the eggs and toast as he mechanically shovels the food into his mouth. Declan stares at the closed laptop while he eats, looking as though he thinks it will reveal the secrets of Sofia's murder without being opened, and Tadd's fingers twitch toward his phone with every bite. He can't let it go, and it's clear Declan can't either.

"When Selene finds whoever did this—"

"*If* Selene finds whoever did this," Declan interrupts, bitterness tingeing his tone.

"Fine," Tadd continues with aplomb, only a little of his irritation creeping through. "If Selene finds who did this, I'm going to kill them. Multiple times." He clenches his fist hard enough around his fork his knuckles turn white.

Declan brushes the tips of his fingers over them. "Do you really think she'll give you the consideration of telling you?"

Tadd tightens his fist further. His nails cut into his palm and the pain helps ground him a little. "No."

"Then stop worrying about it." Declan pulls Tadd's hand to his mouth and kisses each of the knuckles.

"I'm trying."

"I know." Declan releases Tadd's hand when his fingers relax slightly, and pulls the fork free. He carries it over to the sink with the rest of their breakfast dishes, and as he's rinsing them off, he glances back over his shoulder. "Who do you think they meant by family?"

"I don't know." Tadd joins Declan at the counter and moves the rinsed dishes into the dishwasher. As far as he's aware, Sofia hadn't taken any mortal companions. "I can't think of anyone, unless—" He breaks off, his eyes widening and the plate in his hand almost slipping free as the thought solidifies.

Declan stares back, equally frozen, a fork in one hand and the dish brush in the other. "You don't think—?"

"It couldn't be," Tadd tries to convince himself. "We would—"

A jolt of electricity shoots through Tadd's body as both their cell phones ring. He knows there won't be anyone on the other end, just as he knows Declan is feeling the same electrical current. It's a summons he can't ignore.

"—know."

OLYMPUS CASINO is gaudy, glitzy, and completely over the top, with a touch of elegance on the side and true comfort to be found within the guest rooms. In short, it's everything a Las Vegas casino should be, and it carries with it the added bonus of being run by three Olympians. The guests don't know they're in the home of Zeus himself, Hera can often be found presiding over the craps tables or the high-stakes poker games when she's not indulging in the spa, and Tyche is using her innate luck to both run the show and make sure the house always wins. They're content with the kitschy columns and statues that line the walls of the lobby and game floor, the Greek-style togas and dresses worn by the staff, and the occasional gyro to add to the "authenticity."

Declan walks through it as quickly as possible, Tadd right beside him. They'd materialized outside immediately after being summoned, and as they stride through Zeus's domain, Declan has to suppress shudders at the garish way the individual elements clash.

"Now would be the perfect time to make use of your speed," Tadd mutters, without looking up. The carpet, at least, is relatively inoffensive, and Declan's gaze is fixed there as well.

"I would if I could," Declan replies in an even lower tone as he slips his fingers through Tadd's and gratefully pulls him out of the lobby and down a much more tastefully decorated hall. It grates on him that he can't, and not because of the risk of being caught. Anywhere else, he could have pulled them both through the lobby so quickly no mortal would have seen, but here, in the casino, he can't. Zeus doesn't allow it.

He and Tadd both are forced to function as the mortals they pretend to be.

"I know." Tadd squeezes Declan's hand as they head toward the conference room at the end. They've only been here once before, but they'd visited the same room Zeus has requested they come to this time, and blocked from his powers or not, Declan hasn't forgotten its location. He remembers every step, though this time he traces the path much less willingly.

The room is occupied when they reach it. A man sits at the far end of the table, his work boots propped up on the polished wood and his hands folded behind his messy short-cropped hair. He peers out at them with bright blue eyes highlighted by the navy of his tight T-shirt, and when he drops his feet to the floor with a thud, his jeans rustle. "Declan! Tadd! Come in!" He beckons with one hand. "Close the door, would you?"

"Zeus," Declan acknowledges, nodding his head as he pushes the door shut.

"Bront," Zeus corrects, his mouth twitching up at the corners. "Bront Karalis, since we're all maintaining this charade."

"Bront, then," Declan acquiesces. "Good to see you."

"You too! You're looking better than ever!" Bront is overly exuberant as he gestures to Declan's black slacks and pale-green button-down shirt. He hadn't yet put on his jacket or tie when they'd been summoned, and he'd come as he was, his sleeves rolled up for doing the breakfast dishes and his floppy brown hair falling in his eyes because he hadn't gelled it back for the day yet.

"Thanks," he says dryly, casting a brief glance down at himself before letting his eyes roam over Tadd, where they linger longer. He can't help but notice the way Tadd's dress pants hug his body in all the right places, or how the light tan of Tadd's shirt brings out the gold flecks in his green eyes.

16

It would be easy to get lost staring at his husband like that, and it takes Bront clearing his throat and leaning forward to rest his forearms on the table, revealing the gold lightning bolt on the inside of his right wrist, to get them to stop staring at each other. "I'm glad the two of you are still deeply in love, but there are more pressing matters at hand, don't you think? Athena is dead."

"You know about that."

"Yes, Ares"—Bront emphasizes the name as he stares at Tadd—"I know about that. Helios told me."

"Lukas?" Declan quickly thinks back over their encounter. "How did he know?"

"He said he saw her body at your house. Seemed to think the two of you might be involved somehow."

Tadd sneers. "Only in that we own the location where she was found. We would never—"

"Wouldn't you? God of war? Don't you miss the thrill of the battle?"

"What of it?" Tadd crosses his arms and looks at Bront defiantly. "Even if I did, why would I go after Athena? I can think of much more challenging targets."

"On a physical level, maybe, but she is the only one who would be able to devise a strategy to defeat you."

"And you really think—"

"Stop." Declan lays a gentle hand on Tadd's arm. "Both of you," he adds, directing his glare toward Bront. "You know he didn't do this."

"I don't, but I highly doubt it. There's no reason for him to, and he's not so stupid he'd kill someone right in his own home, particularly not with the risk of you finding out so great."

"So if you don't think Tadd did it, why did you summon us here?"

"Because where one of you goes, the other follows." Bront leans forward again, this time resting his elbows on the table and cradling his chin in his hands. "I need you to be Hermes again, Declan."

"I am Hermes."

"Really Hermes. My messenger and spy."

"You want him at your beck and call again? Doing everything you want him to and carrying messages that destroy people's lives?"

"Still bitter about that one, Tadd? It seems like it turned out pretty well in the end."

Tadd and Declan both direct glares at Bront this time. "Don't," Declan grits between clenched teeth. "Just tell me what you want and I'll give you your answer."

They stare at each other, almost at an impasse, as the seconds tick by into minutes. Finally, Bront sighs. "I want you to investigate this, Declan. Find out who killed Athena. Help me bring them to justice."

"Artemis is already investigating."

"How? Why did she know when I didn't?"

"She started hunting as soon as she felt it, I think." Tadd doesn't need to elaborate on what "it" is. Declan vividly remembers the overwhelming sensation of terror and pain that shot through his body yesterday afternoon, and he's certain Bront and Tadd do as well. There's no need to rehash it. "She found us when she found Sofia's body."

"She ordered me not to investigate." Bitterness colors Declan's tone. "She said I'd mess up her hunt, and believe me, that's one of the last things I want to do." He looks up from the table to meet Bront's eyes once again. "I'm not investigating this while she still is."

"I'll stop her." Bront meets Declan's gaze head on. "I want you on this, Hermes. I need my spy, not my huntress. Artemis won't find what you will."

"You promise she'll stop?"

"I give you my word."

"Then I'll do it. But I'm not going to mete out justice the way she would have. I'll bring the evidence to you, but I'm a spy, not a killer."

"I am," Tadd snarls. Declan puts a hand on his knee, hoping to calm him.

"That's why I need you both, Tadd. When the killer finds out Declan is investigating, he'll be in danger as well. I need you to keep him safe."

18

Declan wants to protest that he's perfectly capable of taking care of himself, but Tadd nods solemnly and slides his hand to cover Declan's. He squeezes gently as he twists his head just enough to catch Declan's eye, and Declan swallows his protest. He wouldn't be able to fight it anyway, and when Tadd looks at him like that, there's no point in trying.

"Obviously," Tadd tells Bront as he shoots an annoyed look to the head of the table.

Bront nods, his solemn expression morphing into a grin that's not at all reminiscent of the stern god who used to rule them all with his iron fist and unpredictable temper. "Good!" he exclaims, banging one fist on the table hard enough to make it move. "Get on it, then. I'll handle Selene."

Tadd and Declan nod and rise, but Bront isn't done. "Oh, and Declan," he says, his grin fading back into a stern expression, "be careful. I don't want any more of us to die."

"Of course." He inclines his head in agreement, and when Bront returns the nod, granting permission to leave, he curls his fingers tighter around Tadd's and heads out. He moves as quickly as he can manage without calling on his true powers.


TADD breathes a sigh of relief the moment he and Declan step out of Olympus Casino's front doors. The heavy bronze swings shut behind them, cutting them off from Bront's zone of power, and their own abilities come rushing back, leaving Tadd feeling momentarily heady.

The rush fades quickly, and without a word, they head home, vanishing from behind one of the columns that front the casino and appearing back in their starkly clean foyer. The housekeeper has been through, and the few almost invisible remaining traces of what happened the night before are gone, cleaned away with bleach and soap, the tiles of the floor polished to a shine.

Tadd heads straight for the back room, where he collapses with a groan on the large plush couch. "Well, that was a marvelous way to start the day."

"Oh yeah. Best ever." Declan flops down next to him and stretches his legs out across the coffee table so his feet are hanging off the far side. "Reading news stories about the goddess we found dead in our foyer followed by a trip to Olympus? I wish we could do that every day."

"I thought I was supposed to be the sarcastic one."

Declan rolls his head to the side so he can raise an eyebrow at Tadd. "You weren't doing this morning justice. I had to step in."

Tadd's lips twitch into a small smile despite his effort to stop them. "Really?"

"Yeah." Declan sighs as he turns back to stare at the blank big-screen television mounted on the far wall. "So what do you think?"

For a second, Tadd is tempted to ask what Declan means, or give some other equally smartass response, but he glances over, sees Declan's furrowed brow, and sighs. "I'm not sure."

"Me either." Declan sighs as well. "I'm not even sure where to begin."

Tadd nods and slumps further into his seat as he mulls over the events of the night before and tries to make sense of that morning. "What I don't understand," he says eventually, "is how Lukas knew to tell Bront. He didn't come inside."

"I kept him from seeing in too." Declan frowns as he sits up and swings his legs back so his feet are flat on the floor and his elbows are resting on his knees. "Maybe he saw through the window?"

"Maybe," Tadd admits dubiously. "It's possible, I guess. Why would he look, though?"

"Curiosity?" Declan shrugs. "We didn't take long to answer the door, but it was longer than usual, and if he really did have an appointment, then—"

"Did he, though? I thought you said you didn't schedule anything with him?" His suspicious tone is gone, replaced by curiosity and confusion.

"I didn't, but Rachel might have."

Tadd sits straight up. Finally, something easy about this mess. "Well, that's easy to determine. Let's go ask her."

Declan nods but doesn't move. "We can, but I think I should talk to someone else first."

Tadd doesn't like the look on Declan's face. "Who?"

Declan hesitates. "Sofia."

DECLAN isn't quite to Cerberus yet when Hades steps out from behind a rock, stands directly in his path, and forces him to stop. He blinks once as Declan comes to an abrupt halt in front of him and rocks back on his heels. "I thought you might stop by."

"Hades." Declan nods in greeting. "I'm here to see Sofia."

"Sorry." Hades looks anything but. "I can't let you."

Declan takes a deep breath and draws his innate power around him like a cloak. As he does, his clothes change from business attire to his more traditional garb of short toga, helmet, and winged sandals. It feels like armor settling in over him. "As Zeus's messenger, I have the right to enter the Underworld."

"You do," Hades agrees, but he makes no move to get out of Declan's way. "But you have no message for Sofia Tavoularis, and I don't have to let you speak to her."

"I need to see her. She should have a message for me to carry a message back to Zeus."

"You mean you *hope* she can give you a message to carry back to Zeus." Hades sticks his hands into the folds of his robe. "There's a difference."

"It's still a message." Declan insists. He concentrates again and his caduceus materializes in his hand, ready for him to wave as his right of passage. "You have to let me in."

"In, yes. To talk to her, no."

Declan wants to wipe the smug smile off Hades's face, but that won't get him closer to Sofia. "Then I'll go look for her." It could take some time to find her, even in the limited area of the Elysian Fields, but he couldn't give up without trying to find her.

21

"Go." Hades steps aside and gestures down the tunnel toward Cerberus. "Enjoy your visit to Tartarus."

"Tartarus?" Declan freezes, then turns slowly to look at Hades. "Why is she in Tartarus?" Given what he knows of Athena and the life she lived after giving up her immortal identity, she should spend her afterlife in the Elysian Fields, or at the very least the Asphodel Meadows.

"I put her there."

Declan takes one careful step forward and draws on his power. He's not a warrior god, but he got in his fair share of skirmishes in his role as messenger, and he knows how to defend himself. He's even picked up a few skills from Tadd, though he doesn't generally admit that. His strength likes in stealth rather than strength. "This is *Athena* we're talking about, Hades."

"I'm well aware, Hermes." Hades leans forward into Declan's personal space. "It made putting her there all the sweeter."

"Why?" Declan resists the urge to step back. "What did she do to you?"

"The same thing you all did." Hades drew himself up to his full height, a few inches taller than Declan. "She got to live her life up there, on earth and in Olympus, while I was stuck down here. Why shouldn't I make her suffer?"

"She doesn't deserve it!" Tartarus would be torment, particularly for Athena, whose strategies in war had led to the death of many of the shades there.

"And I do?" Hades loomed over Declan, exuding a menacing aura that made Declan, used to standing toe to toe with the god of war, tremble a little. "I have to let you in, Hermes, but I do not have to help you, and I do not have to let Athena out of Tartarus. I have determined that is where she deserves to spend her afterlife, and that is *my* decision."

"But—"

"Are you challenging me?"

Declan seriously considers it, but the urge passes after a moment. He couldn't win, never could. The years he's spent living as a mortal while Hades has never relinquished his true self will only have widened that gap. He can't do this alone. "Not today."

Hades nods and steps back. "If you change your mind, you'll probably be able to find me in my throne room." He smiles as he turns to walk away. "Give my regards to Ares."

The threat isn't subtle. Ares isn't guaranteed safe passage like Declan is, and if Hades won't meet them before they pass Cerberus, Tadd might not be able to leave. Declan will be forced to choose between speaking to Sofia and keeping Tadd safe.

He manages a terse nod and stalks back out of the Underworld, his garb transforming back to the business attire he was wearing when he arrived. Resuming his mortal persona does nothing to calm the anger boiling inside him, and as he heads back home, he thinks he might finally understand how Tadd often feels.

DECLAN stalks inside when he gets home, snatches his car keys from the hook by the door, and catches Tadd's eye. "Let's go." He's in the car, garage door open and engine running by the time Tadd makes it out, and the moment Tadd's door closes, Declan throws the vehicle into reverse and careens out of the driveway.

He's halfway to his office before Tadd shifts in his seat and clears his throat. "So, Sofia didn't know who killed her?"

"I didn't talk to Sofia." Declan jerks the car around a corner, making the tires squeal, and smiles slightly as the harsh noise eases his tension a little. "Hades has her locked in Tartarus and wouldn't take me to her." He yanks the wheel to the left, sending the car skidding around another corner. "I can't challenge him on his territory. We have to do this the hard way."

"We could—" Tadd starts, but Declan cuts him off before he finishes the sentence.

"No. He won't let you leave if you come with me. That's a last resort."

"All right." Tadd holds up his hands, clearly taken aback by Declan's vehemence. "We'll try the hard way."

"Thank you." Declan eases back on the gas a little as he merges with traffic. Most of his anger is gone now and he relaxes his grip on the steering wheel as he maneuvers the car into the pattern of moving vehicles.

Tadd fiddles with the radio, flipping through all of Declan's presets before turning it off. "Can you tell me what he said? I'd rather be prepared if we have to go back later."

"There isn't much else, but sure." They're still a few miles from the office. Declan fills Tadd in on the entire conversation with Hades, answering all of Tadd's questions and finishing just as he pulls the car into his assigned parking spot. "Perfect timing." He climbs out, waits for Tadd to follow, and hits the remote lock as he leads the way into the building.

Rachel Chambers is sitting in her usual spot when they reach Declan's office, an earpiece in her ear and her computer screen showing Declan's calendar as well as the memo she was typing. A PowerPoint presentation is minimized to her taskbar, and Declan has a brief flash of worry before he remembers he asked her to edit the presentation he gave the board last month so it could be used in pitches to other companies. It's nothing he has to do, which is good, because he strongly suspects he won't be able to take much of a hands-on approach to running the business for the next few weeks.

"You're late," Rachel says, pointing her pen at him with one hand as she presses the disconnect button on the phone with another. "I've had to reschedule two appointments already, and I was starting to think I'd have to reschedule your lunch meeting too. Where have you been?"

"With me." Tadd steps in before Declan has a chance to formulate a response. Rachel always manages to make him feel uncomfortable, like he's the clueless mortal and she's the god, and he's never quite sure how he's supposed to respond when she scolds him like that. She's his administrative assistant, but Tadd hired her for him when they first orchestrated the switch from being their "fathers" to being themselves, and he's not sure he can fire her. Tadd would probably just hire her right back.

"Mr. Leventis." Rachel lets a small smile slip through before she directs her stern gaze at Tadd as well. "I should have known you'd be at fault here." Her gaze narrows, and she purses her lips as she stares at him.

She looks so ridiculously serious that Declan has to step in. "He actually wasn't. It was personal business. Something came up unexpectedly. I'm sorry." Declan sits on the edge of her desk and directs his most winning smile and widest eyes at her. "Can you forgive me?"

"Is it over?"

"Unfortunately, no." Declan's reluctant sigh is only half-fake. "I'm not going to be able to be around much for the next several weeks, at least."

"What should I tell your appointments? I can't just ask them to keep waiting on their bids because you don't know when you'll be back. The business will go under. I'll be out of a job!"

"Like Tadd would ever let that happen."

Behind Declan, Tadd shakes his head, a small smile playing on his lips. "I'd find something for you to do, Rachel. I promise."

"Well," she huffs, "that's better than him."

"Hey!"

"Well, you wouldn't find something for me, would you?"

"I wouldn't have to, Tadd would!"

"Not the point."

"Fine." Declan assumes his most put-upon expression. "I would find you a better job than Tadd would. Happy?"

"I will be once you tell me what to do with all these meetings I have you scheduled for."

Declan closes his eyes for a minute, trying to think. Running the business can't take top priority right now, not with Bront expecting him to solve this mystery, but he can't let the business sink, either. He and Tadd have worked too hard to get things the way they are. Declan Anagnos, CEO of Alpha Wing Communications, and Hermes, spy for Zeus, must remain separate entities. "Give as many of them to the directors as you can. If there's anyone I need to handle personally, forward it to me, and I'll find time."

25

"Will do." Rachel nods. "Anything else?"

"One thing." Declan waits until he has her full attention. "Did you schedule me for a dinner meeting with Lukas Gallo last night?"

Rachel blinks twice and then her hand flies to her mouth. "Oh my God! I didn't tell you!" She sucks her bottom lip into her mouth with a hissing noise. "He called yesterday while you were at lunch! I was going to tell you, but you had that conference call, and then you rushed out like your office was on fire. I'm sorry!"

"So he did have an appointment?"

"Yeah. That's what I just said." Rachel tilts her head to the side. "Was that wrong? You didn't have anything on your schedule, and I thought...."

"It's fine." Declan flashes a smile at her and squeezes her shoulder as he slides off the desk. "I was caught up with this personal business last night and he surprised me, that's all. I'll call him to reschedule."

"Okeydokey."

Tadd laughs as he takes Declan's hand. "Thanks, Rachel."

"Bye, Mr. Leventis." She wiggles her fingers in a tiny wave as they walk out the door.

As soon as the door shuts behind them, Declan turns to Tadd, a mischievous grin on his face. "Sometimes I think Rachel likes you better than me."

"What can I say." Tadd grins back at Declan. "I'm irresistible."

"Good thing you're mine, then." They get into the elevator, and Declan pushes Tadd against the wall and pins him there with his slightly larger frame. He slides his hands up Tadd's sides to cup his face and leans in to kiss him deeply. As the elevator goes down from the top floor, people start to get on but stop short when they see Declan and Tadd inside and universally decide to take the next car. Declan ignores them, instead concentrating on kissing Tadd, his tongue sliding between Tadd's lips as he presses their bodies together.

When the elevator is close to the bottom, Declan pulls his keys from his pocket and uses one of them to override the elevator controls.

Once it's locked down, he yanks Tadd's shirt from his pants so he can slide his hands under it.

"Careful," Tadd murmurs, pulling back from the kiss just enough to talk. "Don't pop the buttons."

"I like popped buttons. They're a good look on you."

"You think everything's a good look on me." Tadd puts his hands on Declan's chest and pushes firmly, making Declan take a step back. "We can't, though."

"Why not?"

"We're in the elevator at your office building! While investigating a murder!"

"So I'll be fast." Declan leans in as close as he can with Tadd's hands in the way and smirks. "I'm good at fast."

"Oh, well, that's just what I want." Tadd rolls his eyes. "A quickie in the elevator. You're almost as classy as Eros."

Declan winces as he straightens. "Ouch. That hurts."

"Truth often does." Tadd pats him on the chest as he leans up and kisses him softly. "I still love you, though, classy or not."

"Love you too." Declan's scowl transforms into a grin, and he kisses Tadd deeply before pulling back and turning the key to return the elevator to the ground floor. He kisses Tadd again as he tucks Tadd's shirt back into his pants, and when the elevator doors slide open, they step out, their hands entwined once more.

AFTER dropping Tadd back at home so he can take care of his own business, Declan heads over to Lukas's offices. His car—one of the sportier ones Lukas's company makes—fits right in with all the other cars on the lot, which are all produced by Pyrois. It's like a showroom in the parking lot of the company headquarters, just about every model, style, and color present, and Declan shakes his head at the display as he walks in.

He's shown right up when he introduces himself, and less than five minutes after he walks through the front door, he's sitting in

Lukas's office, waiting as Lukas finishes a phone call. It's another three minutes before he's done, but when he hangs up, he breaks into a big grin. "Declan! I didn't expect to see you today!"

"Yeah, well." Declan shrugs depreciatingly. "I wanted to apologize for last night. Rachel never had a chance to tell me you'd called yesterday."

"Hey, no problem." Lukas leans back in his chair, his hands behind his head. "I know how things can get. Sometimes I don't see my assistant for days. I'd think she's not coming in, except she leaves me sticky notes on my computer screen." He leans forward across the desk, looking around comically before grinning and lowering his voice. "She says it's because I don't know how to check my e-mail, but really, I ignore most of hers. She thinks I need to know every little thing. I'm sure you know how that is."

Declan agrees even though he really doesn't. He likes Lukas, always has, even back when they were Helios and Hermes all the time, instead of just when Zeus called upon them to be. He'll let a few lies slip for the sake of doing what Bront asked—Lukas doesn't look quite so suspicious now that Declan has talked to Rachel, but he's still the best lead Declan has—and to maintain his relationship with Lukas if he ends up being a dead end in the investigation.

Lukas laughs. "No you don't. I'm sure Rachel doesn't bother you with things she can handle herself."

"No, but she didn't tell me about our appointment last night. And she likes Tadd better than she likes me."

"Is your husband trying to steal your assistant, or is your assistant trying to steal your husband?"

"Neither." Declan rolls his eyes at the insinuation. "Rachel is happily married, and Tadd would kill her within a week if she worked for him." He shudders at the thought of Rachel seriously scolding Tadd the way she sometimes scolds him. Their clashes would be epic, but they wouldn't be pretty.

Lukas laughs, throwing his head back and rocking in his chair. "I might pay to see that."

"I think a lot of people would." Not that Declan will ever let anyone have the chance to.

"True." Lukas stands and walks around the desk. "But that's not why you came. Come over here."

Declan joins him at the round table in the corner of the office. Lukas is already sitting in a chair, his phone resting on the otherwise clear surface of the table, and Declan pulls his phone out as he sits and looks at Lukas expectantly.

"Here's the thing," Lukas starts, and he launches into a spiel about what he wants Declan's help with.

It turns out Lukas wanted to talk about something Declan is interested in and needs to pay attention to—he wants Declan's company to design communication solutions for Pyrois, with an eye to eventually putting systems in the vehicles he sells—and Declan finds himself intrigued despite his other agenda. He takes copious notes on his phone and is thinking about who to assign to the project when Lukas suddenly stops talking. The silence catches Declan's attention, and he looks up from his phone, blinking. "Sorry. I got lost in my own thoughts. What did you say?"

"Nothing." Lukas leans in close, his brow furrowed. "Are you sure you should be doing this now? I didn't want to say anything, but you seem distracted."

"No, I'm not." Declan shakes his head. He should be; he shouldn't be able to focus on business at all right now, not with everything that's happened in the last twenty-four hours, but he's thinking about this with no problem. It's almost too easy to focus on business instead of what he needs to be doing. He's not as anxious to don the mantle of Zeus's messenger and spy as he felt last night when he and Tadd first found Sofia. "I'm fine."

"Are you sure?" Lukas looks at him hard for a moment and then sits back with a sigh. When Declan nods, Lukas pinches his lips together and leans forward once more, his fingers flexing as he looks straight into Declan's eyes. "I know what happened last night."

"What do you mean?" Declan knows exactly what Lukas is referring to, but he's not going to pass up the opportunity to find out how Lukas knew to tell Bront.

"You know what I mean," Lukas says softly. He looks at Declan with a sympathetic expression. "I saw you last night, through the window, while I was waiting for you to open the door. I saw Sofia too," he adds. "I know she died in your foyer."

"How did you know it was Sofia?" That's another thing that's been bugging Declan. Neither he nor Tadd knew who Sofia was until they pulled her bag out from under her. Lukas wasn't close enough to see the owl on her wrist, so there was no way for him to know she was Athena unless he had already known her mortal identity.

"The paper." Lukas picks up his phone and, after pressing the screen a few times, hands it over to Declan. Sofia's picture is on the screen, though this time it's a picture of her alive, smiling, and happy as she poses in front of a display in a museum. In the background, Declan can see the vases and coins of the Ancient Greek display and the story beneath is about Sofia's plans to expand it. It's from a few weeks ago, in the part of the paper Tadd and Declan seldom read unless someone calls their attention to it, but it explains how Lukas knew it was Sofia.

It doesn't explain how he knew it was Athena.

"Ah." Declan hands the phone back to Lukas with a nod.

"I met her not too long after that. There was a fundraiser at the museum, and after seeing the article, I had to go. We recognized each other immediately, of course. We exchanged a few words and I thought that was the end of it. I never thought the next time I'd see her, she'd be dead." Lukas looks genuinely disturbed at the thought.

"Yeah." Declan sighs. "Tadd and I got home and she was there. We didn't—" He shakes his head sadly. "I think that was what we felt yesterday. And why I didn't know about the meeting you'd scheduled," he adds ruefully.

"You ran out as soon as you felt it?" Lukas shudders. "So did I."

"Yeah." Declan leans forward and lets the worry he's been feeling show on his face. "We don't know how she got there, or who killed her, or anything, really."

"I have a theory if you're interested in hearing it."

Declan definitely is, but he makes sure to casually raise his eyebrow and does his best to look only mildly curious instead of avidly interested. "Oh?"

"Cal Pagonis. Eros." At Declan's blank look, Lukas shakes his head. "He was at that museum fundraiser too, probably because he wanted to see the naked statues or something, and I overheard him arguing with Sofia. Apparently he learned something about her on, um, what's it called? His phone sex line."

Declan furrows his brow as he thinks about it. It takes a minute before the name pops into his head. "Devilish Angels?"

"Yeah. That's it." Lukas snaps his fingers. "Anyway, Cal learned something about her on the line, and he confronted her about it. She didn't take it too well."

"Wait." Declan blinks. "Sofia? Athena? What could anyone have to say about her on a phone sex line?"

"Beats me."

"Yeah." It's almost impossible to fathom, but it is a lead, and it occupies Declan's mind for the rest of the time he's sitting in Lukas's office. It's a good thing he already took most of the notes he needed for Lukas's project; he's not thinking about it at all, not even when the conversation returns to the subject. Instead, he rolls the information he got from Lukas over in his mind, trying unsuccessfully to consolidate it with what he already knows. By the time he leaves Lukas's office, there's only one thing on Declan's mind.

He needs to talk to Cal.

TADD swings by his office before he goes anywhere else. Even if Bront hadn't specifically instructed him to keep Declan safe—which he's still trying very hard not to be offended about—he would be working closely with Declan on this and thus needs to arrange for an extended time away. His assistant, Gabe Lawson, will handle everything as competently as Rachel handled Declan's affairs, without the snark, but Tadd still needs to stop in to let Gabe know and make sure there's nothing that needs his personal attention before he leaves.

Gabe is sitting at his desk in Tadd's outer office, his feet propped up on a stool under his desk, a phone earpiece slung over his ear, and a game of solitaire pulled up on the computer screen. He flashes an easy grin as Tadd walks through the door, but he doesn't sit up, nor does he bother to minimize the solitaire window.

"Goofing off again?" Tadd asks as he sits in the chair across from Gabe's desk. He doesn't slouch the way Gabe does, but he is still in shirtsleeves and sans tie and rumpled from Declan's ministrations in the elevator, so he doesn't sit up quite as straight as he usually would.

"No." Gabe hits a button on the phone and drops the earpiece on the desk. "Just keeping myself amused between calls. If I was goofing off, I'd be trying to set a new high score in Free Cell."

Tadd's not sure if it's funny or sad that Gabe really isn't joking. Gabe is a wonderful assistant when Tadd needs one, but when there's nothing to do, Gabe slacks off with the best of them, and he's quite proud of his Free Cell scores. Tadd is pretty sure if he wants to keep Gabe around—and there's no way Declan will let Tadd get rid of Gabe any more than Tadd will let Declan get rid of Rachel—he's going to have to get some new games installed on his computer.

Today Tadd chooses not to debate the issue and nods. "Anything important?"

"Well, they all think they're important, but no, nothing needs your immediate attention. You have meetings scheduled for this afternoon and tomorrow, though, and the board thinks we should put in for some more government contracts, so they'll be pushing for a proposal soon."

"They'll have to wait."

Gabe arches his eyebrow and waits patiently for Tadd to elaborate. It's one of the things Tadd likes about him—he never pushes Tadd, even when Tadd is raving. He shrugs Tadd's vagueness off the same way he shrugs off the rants Tadd can be prone to when things aren't going well and the bursts of anger Tadd occasionally forgets to hold in. Gabe's laid-back attitude would likely cause him problems at most other businesses, but he's the perfect antithesis to Tadd and keeps him calm when Declan is at his own office and can't be around.

He's as perfect for Tadd as Rachel is for Declan, and not for the first time, Tadd is glad they agreed to pick the other's assistants. It's worked out far better than he could ever have hoped for.

"I need you to reschedule my appointments," he tells Gabe.

"All of them?" Gabe's second eyebrow joins the first in creeping up his forehead.

"All of them."

"For how long?"

"Indefinitely. I need to take some personal time."

Gabe nods, jots a note down on the calendar that acts as his desk blotter, and then looks up with his bottom lip caught between his teeth. He straightens as he leans closer to Tadd, and he's almost hesitant in the way he catches Tadd's eye. "Is everything okay at home, sir? Is Mr. Anagnos all right? I heard from Rachel that—"

"Everything's fine." It comes out shorter than Tadd intended, but he's not in the mood to talk about this. He has other things to take care of. "We have a few things we need to deal with. If anything urgent comes up, you can call me."

"Sure thing, boss."

Just like that, Gabe is back to his carefree self, and Tadd is glad that if this had to happen, it happened now, instead of a few generations ago. Back when he and Declan were first building up their businesses, when they were pretending to be Tadd Leventis and Declan Anagnos's grandfathers, Tadd wouldn't have been able to take off to keep Declan safe if he wanted to keep the business growing. Declan wouldn't have been able to take off to do Bront's bidding. They both would have suffered, and they wouldn't have ended up with the lives they have now.

Tadd shudders as he remembers what life was like when he wasn't able to be as close to Declan in the public mortal world as he was in the privacy of their home. Even when they were living as the fathers of their current identities and had established the families were inseparable friends, they didn't get to spend nearly as much time together as they would have liked. Now they're married, a darling couple of the business world, and able to spend as much time together publically and privately as they want. Tadd isn't going to give it up for anything.

Not even murder.

"Thanks, Gabe." Tadd doesn't bother to check his office before leaving. There's nothing in there that can't wait, and if something comes up while Tadd is out, he's confident Gabe will take care of it. Declan chose him well, after all.

"No problem, Mr. Leventis."

Tadd manages a grin as he leaves, his next destination already in mind. He can't follow Declan yet, not while Declan is talking to Lukas, but he can do something else that should speed the investigation along.

Declan isn't the only one who can dig into things.

DECLAN finds Cal exactly where he expected, exactly where he didn't want to go—a strip club. When he hones in on Eros's location, he takes his car home to drop it off so it's not sullied by being driven and parked on the streets surrounding the Titties and Tassels Club, and changes into his oldest jeans and the thinnest, rattiest T-Shirt he can find. It's not exactly a prime outfit for anything, but Declan is going to look out of place there no matter how he dresses, so he figures he might as well wear clothes he can burn later without any regrets.

When he's ready, Declan leaves a note for Tadd on the counter so he won't worry and materializes in the alley outside the Titties and Tassels Club. It smells awful: the scent of rotting garbage mixed with dried spunk and covered by piss and vomit. Never before has Declan been so glad he only has to use his speed to get somewhere fast when he's carrying something large or heavy. Simply showing up here is bad enough; he doesn't want to imagine what it would be like to actually have to travel through the areas, no matter how quickly he moved.

Declan isn't going to accomplish what he needs to standing here in the alley, and he won't get anything out of Cal if he lets his revulsion show, so he squares his shoulders and rounds the corner to step inside.

The interior of the Titties and Tassels Club is almost exactly what Declan imagined. There's a stage with a pole on one side of the room, a bar on the other, and several cages along the back wall occupied by mostly naked girls gyrating their hips. A neon sign points to the bathrooms, and a slightly less obvious sign points to the back, where private dances can be had for a minimum of twenty dollars. There's a bouncer, but he's a fat, tattoo-covered guy who barely manages to lift an eyelid to glance at Declan as he walks through the door, and the bartender is a scrawny kid who looks barely old enough to be serving drinks.

There aren't many patrons—unsurprising, given the quality of the club and that it's a Wednesday night—and Declan has no problem getting the bartender's attention to order a stiff Crown and Coke.

He has no problem spotting Cal, either, and he downs his drink before ordering two more and carrying them over to join Cal at the foot of the stage. "Your mother is a bitch," he says, then takes a large gulp of his drink. He settles onto the chair next to Cal and slides the untouched beverage in front of him. "This love thing is crap."

Cal curls his fingers around the glass and tears his eyes away from the girl twirling around the pole in front of them. "Problems in paradise?" he asks, running his right hand through his short-cropped blond hair and exposing the shimmering quiver and arrows on the inside of his wrist. "I can probably do something about that, you know."

"No, you can't." Declan huffs, playing up the drama as he starts griping about the curse Aphrodite put on him, Ares, and Helios so long ago. Though being unable to find sexual release with anyone besides the other two cursed gods had seemed harsh at the time, Declan is very happy with how it worked out and has to fight to keep from smiling. "Tadd and I will be fine. I just had to get away from him for a bit." He scowls and sloshes his drink, letting some of it spill to the table. He downs the rest of it while spinning an entirely fictional tale of an ongoing argument with Tadd that has driven him to seek refuge in the last place Tadd would think to look for him.

"You're hiding from him here?" Cal shoves the Crown and Coke back at Declan. "Dude. You can't even get anything out of Starla here." He gestures to the girl on stage and leers appreciatively.

Declan winces. That's not something he likes to think about. "Because Tadd will think the same thing you do—there's no point in coming—and won't look for me here."

Cal eyes Declan for a minute and then nods, impressed. "Huh. Devious."

"Yeah. Something like that." Declan turns his gaze to the stage, staring up at the girl swinging around the pole. He watches her for a while, but there's really nothing very aesthetically pleasing about the way she's moving or the way she's yanking her clothes from her body, and he can't stop himself from turning to Cal with a puzzled look on his face as he downs his third drink of the night. "You really spend all day watching this stuff? Why?"

"Dude." Cal grabs the dancer's panties from where they've fallen close to the edge of the stage and tosses them back toward her along with a ten-dollar bill. "It's not all like this. I mean, the fantasies I get to hear on my phone line…." He closes his eyes and lets out a deep sigh that's practically a moan. "Ooooh."

Declan is positive he'll be happier not hearing any of them. He doubts Cal would consider whatever he overheard from Sofia to be among his favorite fantasies, anyway, so he feels safe in returning the subject to strippers, where, sadly, he's probably going to get more information. "Yeah, I get that, but this? Really?"

"All right." Cal leans in close and lowers his voice as he casts furtive glances at the stage. "I know this isn't the best joint, and Starla could use, well, a lot of pointers, but they're not all like this. Man, yesterday I was at The Red Queen across town, and Zeus help me, there was this girl there, Mindi or maybe Mandi or Candi, I don't know. Doesn't matter. Point is, she had the most spectacular tits I have ever seen. And I have seen a lot of tits in my day."

"So why are you here if Candi is over there?"

"Well, we were having this amazingly special moment in the back, right? And she'd just taken off her bra—and seriously, dude, these tits would make even you cream your pants, I am not joking—when whatever-the-fuck that was yesterday afternoon happened." Cal sits back in his chair with a pout. "One minute I'm leaning forward and my lips are millimeters away from the best tits in the universe, and the next I'm frozen solid like I'm freakin' having a seizure or something." His pout morphs into a grimace as he shakes his head. "I was fucking terrified, dude. I couldn't move, couldn't think, couldn't breathe, and then it hurt like nothing I've ever felt before. I ran out of there after that. I was late for dinner with my mother, and I thought it was her throwing a fit and summoning me or something. I'm sure Mindi complained, and I'm going to have to beg and grovel before they'll let me back in the door."

"But you were with her when you felt that? And for some time before?" He's going to have to talk to Aphrodite and go to yet another strip club to confirm what Cal's saying, but assuming he can, Declan is left with no leads. He's about as pissed as Cal was that he didn't get to finish with what's-her-name.

"Yeah." Cal grabs the remainder of Declan's drink and downs it all in one go. "Wait, you felt that too?"

"We all did, I think."

"What do you mean? What in Hades was it?"

There's no harm in telling Cal now. Either he's lying and he already knows or he's innocent and Declan is about to give him the shock of his life. Either way, Declan's game won't be any more exposed than it is at the moment, so he takes a deep breath and looks Cal straight in the eyes. "Athena's dead. That was her being killed."

"What?" The surprise on Cal's face comes too fast to be faked. "Dead? Like, for real dead?"

"Like only Hades himself can talk to her now dead, yeah."

"Fuck."

"Pretty much."

"Man, here I was feeling bad about abandoning Candi, and I left because... man!" Cal shakes his head and runs his fingers through his hair again. "Shit, Declan, I gotta go. I have to go talk to Adara and—"

Declan grabs Cal's arm to stop him. He can only imagine how Adara—Aphrodite—will will react when she finds out, and he wants to put it off as long as possible. "Don't say anything."

"What?"

It takes Declan several minutes to convince Cal it's best for everyone if Athena's death remains as much of a secret as possible for the moment. Cal argues for a bit, but eventually he agrees and goes off anyway, promising not to say anything but still wanting to talk to Aphrodite.

As soon as he's gone, Declan slides off the stool and walks from the club with quick, measured steps. It takes great effort not to run in order to escape the filth, and the moment Declan is around the corner and in the alley again, he vanishes and reappears in his mudroom. He doesn't even take the time to see if Tadd is back before he shucks his clothes and tosses them in the corner, as far away from him as they can get. He wasn't joking about burning them, but he can do that later.

For now, he has a mystery to solve and a husband to find.

TADD is sitting in the kitchen when Declan steps out of the mudroom, completely nude. He smiles as he lets his eyes roam Declan's body, and they're sparkling when he meets Declan's gaze. "Nice outfit."

Declan shudders. "I was at a strip club with Cal, and—"

"You stripped?"

"No!"

Tadd lifts his eyebrows as he leans back in his chair, his eyes pointedly moving over Declan's body once again. "So you went in naked? Declan, I think you're missing the point of strip clubs."

"No!" Declan rolls his eyes. "I undressed once I got back here. That place was slimy." He shudders dramatically, his whole body shaking, and Tadd immediately fixes his gaze on Declan's groin. It

38

stays there as Declan strides forward with slow, deliberate steps. He swings his hips slightly with each movement, making his cock bob in front of him, and rubs it against Tadd as he leans in and wraps his arm around Tadd's shoulder. "I thought," he says in a low voice, "that this wasn't the time."

"It wasn't the place," Tadd growls, as he tangles his fingers in Declan's hair and pulls him in for a deep kiss.

Declan grins evilly when they break apart. "Not the time, either."

"Declan...."

"Nope." Declan backs away. "We have work to do."

"You want me to work when you're standing there naked?" Tadd slides off the stool and stalks slowly toward Declan, who keeps backing up until he hits the wall. "Not possible."

"Then I'll—"

"No, you won't." Tadd takes two large steps to close the distance between them, wraps his arms around Declan's waist, and pulls him close, rubbing their hips together as he leans in and sucks at Declan's collarbone.

Declan gasps, his cock hardening as Tadd's tongue darts along the sensitive skin of his neck, and he thrusts his hips forward. "I won't?" It comes out in a desperate, panting moan that leaves no doubt Tadd is going to get his way.

"No." Tadd slips his hand between their bodies and curls his fingers around Declan's cock. "You won't. You can't parade in here naked, offering this"—he strokes downward, flicking his thumb over the tip of Declan's cock—"and then tell me no."

Declan shivers and tips his head back, giving Tadd better access to the long column of his neck. "Yeah, okay," he breathes as he slides his hands down Tadd's back. He tugs him closer and pulls his shirt free from his pants.

Tadd takes the invitation offered by Declan's exposed neck, sucking and biting his way up to his ear. He swirls his tongue around the shell and nips lightly at the lobe before he pulls back just enough to growl, "Upstairs." It's only a matter of stepping back for a moment, breaking apart long enough for each of them to reappear up in their bedroom, but Tadd tightens his fingers around Declan as he growls the word. He doesn't want to lose contact even for a second.

Declan clearly understands, and he tightens his arms around Tadd, lifts him slightly off the ground. "Okay."

They're in the bedroom in less than a second. It's considerably longer before Tadd thinks about anything besides the taste and feel of Declan beneath him.

HOURS later, they're still curled together, Tadd's head on Declan's chest. Declan traces lazy patterns along Tadd's back with his fingers. "We should do something."

Tadd doesn't move. "We just did."

"No, I mean about Sofia. I had plans for tonight before you distracted me."

"Before I distracted you?" Tadd lifts his head and gives Declan a surprised look. "I seem to recall you're the one who walked into the kitchen completely naked."

"So?"

"So you're the one who distracted me. I had important things to tell you, you know."

"Oh?"

"Yep."

"So are you going to tell me?"

Tadd shrugs and lays his head back down on Declan's shoulder. "Nope."

Declan lightly smacks Tadd's back. "Tadd!"

"Yes, dear?"

"This is serious." He puts on his best stern look, but he feels like it doesn't work very well since he's lying flat on his back, draped in sheets and Tadd and nothing else.

Tadd leans up and kisses him. "I went to Sofia's today."

"Why?" Declan sits up straight, pulling Tadd with him. "What did you do that for?"

"To see what I could find." Tadd scoots around in the bed, arranging the sheets so they're covering him up to his waist, and turns to look straight at Declan. "You're not the only one who can investigate, you know."

"I'm the one who was asked to." A thought occurs to him, leaving him both worried and relieved. "What if the police had been there?"

"I hadn't thought of that." Tadd shifts and looks uncomfortable. "They weren't, though."

"They could have been." It's hard for Declan to get the idea out of his head. There are so many ways that could have gone bad, and though Tadd would have been able to get out of it, he might not have been able to do so with his current mortal identity intact.

"Yeah, well, they weren't." Tadd's tone leaves no room for further argument. "Do you want me to tell you what I found, or do you want to throw a fit?"

Declan opens and closes his mouth a few times before huffing. "Fine. Tell me. What interesting bits of information did you uncover?"

"Well, uh, not much, actually." Tadd rubs at the back of his neck as he looks sheepishly at Declan. "I tried to find any connections she might have to anyone who could kill her. The only one I found was Nikolas Tasso—Perseus."

"That… doesn't seem likely." Declan frowns. "Not with how close they've always been and the things she's done for him. But I guess if Cal's alibi pans out, we'll have to look into him. I don't know where else to start."

"Yeah. They could have had a fight or something." Tadd slides down in the bed. "Let's figure it out in the morning, though, okay?" He tugs at Declan's arm, pulling him down to lie in a reverse of the position they started in.

"We need to talk to Adara. And there's a strip club we need to check out."

"Another one?"

"Cal's alibi is a stripper, believe it or not."

"Oh, I believe it. What's her name? Does he even remember?"

Declan laughs. "Sort of? It's Mindi. Or maybe Mandi or Candi. Some girl with spectacular tits."

"Isn't that sort of a prerequisite for working in a strip club?"

"You would know."

Tadd snorts and rolls his eyes. "Why in Hades would I go to a strip club?"

"You would have loved them back in the day. We both would have."

"Back in the day, we wouldn't have gone to that sort of place. We didn't need to. Or at least," Tadd adds with a mischievous smile, "I didn't need to. I don't know about you."

"Shut up." Declan shoves lightly at Tadd's chest. "I didn't either."

"Of course you didn't, dear." He pats the top of Declan's head. "You go right on thinking that."

Declan rolls his eyes, lifts his head, and presses a gentle kiss to Tadd's lips. Tadd's hand comes up to cup the back of his head, and when they pull apart, they're both grinning.

"We'll talk to Adara in the morning."

"And then the strip club?"

"Yeah." Tadd pushes Declan's head back to his chest. "In the morning."

"Okay." Declan lets his eyes slip closed, and a moment later, Tadd does as well, following him down into sleep.

THE next morning, Declan hangs up the phone and lets his head fall forward onto the breakfast table with a sigh. "Fuck."

"What?" Tadd steps up behind Declan and starts rubbing the back of his neck. "Wouldn't they tell you anything?"

"No, they were happy to help." Declan sighs and leans back to rest his head against Tadd's chest. "The manager wasn't too thrilled about the early hour, but he did tell me they don't have anyone working

42

there named Mindi, Mandi, or Candi. Or anyone who goes by any of those names, as far as he's aware."

"So Cal didn't spend the afternoon with one of them."

"Not at The Red Queen. Unless there's another Red Queen club in town."

"Or the stripper was really named Brandi or Randi or something that doesn't even end with an *i*."

"How do you know Mindi, Mandi, and Candi spell their names with an *i* instead of a *y*?"

Tadd leans down and kisses Declan gently on the lips. "They're strippers, man. Strippers always spell their names with *i*'s instead of *y*'s."

"So Brandi and Randi would spell their names with *i*'s as well?"

"Naturally." Tadd pulls back from Declan.

Declan picks the phone back up with a sigh. "I suppose I should call back and ask about Brandi and Randi too."

"Don't." Tadd pulls the phone from his hand and tucks it in his pocket. "Cal probably got the name completely wrong, if he was with anyone at all. Call later and see if anyone working remembers him."

"Yeah, okay." Declan offers a small smile and rubs at the back of his neck. Tadd immediately takes over, working at the knots in Declan's shoulders with firm fingers that leave Declan boneless and pliant under his touch. When Tadd steps back, Declan rolls his head and squares his shoulders. "So. Sofia's? I know you looked yesterday, but you weren't looking for evidence Cal was there, and neither would the police."

"We should ask around at the museum too."

"Right." Declan stands and stretches up toward the ceiling. "Let's hit her house first, then the museum." He pulls up her address on his phone and stares at the map for a moment before showing Tadd a small park not far from her house. "There? We can walk over and make sure no one else is there."

Tadd nods and vanishes. Declan concentrates as well, willing himself to the park, and appears next to Tadd in a copse of trees that shields them from view of the few people in the area. "Wait here," he says and heads toward Sofia's house at a speed mortal eyes can't track.

He returns after circling the house twice. "There's no cars out front and the house is dark. If the police came, they're gone."

"Let's go then."

Declan concentrates, willing himself to Sofia's house, and appears in the foyer, just inside the front door. The entrance is immaculate; the polished hardwood floor that gives it a slightly softer feel than the dark-gray tiles of Tadd and Declan's home is partially covered by an ornate rug perfectly centered in the foyer, and there's a polished bronze bucket in the corner holding two umbrellas arranged so they're angled exactly the same.

There's nothing there for them to find, though Declan does peer into the closet and run his hands over the coats lined up behind the door before he makes his way down the hall with Tadd, both cautiously stepping along as though someone might hear them.

It's a ridiculous thought, but he still feels strange being in the home of a dead woman. She's hardly the first either have encountered—they both came into contact with dead people of all sorts as Ares and Hermes—but she's the first dead goddess they've encountered, and that feels different.

The kitchen and living area are clean and tidy—too tidy to be used often, and Declan follows Tadd right through them, heading straight for the library that takes up the entire back of the house. This is where Sofia lived when she was at home.

Declan stops in the doorway when they get to the room, staring for a moment as he tries to take everything in once more. The walls are lined with wooden shelves that stretch all the way up to the elevated ceiling and are covered with books. Each side of the room is equipped with two rolling ladders, one going to about where the ceilings of the other first-floor rooms are, and the other going all the way up to the top, where the second-floor ceilings end. Thick leather-bound editions of everything from Homer to Golding fill most of the shelves, but the back left corner is full of encyclopedias and other reference materials, and there are two shelves in the front corner stuffed to the brim with paperbacks. The latest best sellers are wedged in tightly, stacked two deep, but with no less care than the older, more valuable books.

In one of the corners toward the back of the room, there's a desk: a large, heavy wooden one with a wide top that leaves plenty of room to spread out books and still take notes. In front of it and in the other corners, comfortable-looking armchairs are grouped around low tables, all of which have at least one book on them and most of which have more than one.

Walking in is like walking into a museum. Declan moves slowly as he follows Tadd, awed at the wealth of accumulated knowledge and the care with which it was being kept. Tadd heads straight for the desk, opens the top drawer, and pulls out an appointment book, cell phone, and notebook computer. "There might be something in here," he says as he sets them on the desk and pulls out a stack of papers. "I skimmed through them yesterday, but I might have missed something."

Declan takes the stack from him and begins thumbing through as he drops into one of the chairs opposite the desk. It's all invitations to fundraisers and meet-and-greets, and Declan isn't enthusiastic about going through them. "Great. And what are you going to do while I dig through this?"

Tadd shrugs. "Play on her laptop?" Declan narrows his eyes and glares, less than thrilled by the idea, and Tadd's grin widens. "I thought I'd poke around upstairs some. See if I can find anything I missed up there."

"Or you could help me go through these." Declan takes half the papers off the top of the stack and pushes them back to Tadd. "Since you admitted you didn't go through them thoroughly."

Tadd sighs dramatically, but he picks up the papers and starts flipping through them again, this time taking enough time to read every word instead of skimming over them. Declan finds most of his stack boring—lists of names and numbers that mean nothing to him, as well as menus, descriptions of decorations, and lists of donations—but about halfway through his pile, he stops, his eyes widening. "This is the event Lukas went to. The one he said he saw Cal at."

"Give it here."

"No." Declan pulls the papers closer to his chest. "I found it."

"Well, if you want to be the one to read through all the boring papers, be my guest." Tadd leans back in his chair, props his feet up on the desk, and laces his fingers together behind his head. "I'll wait."

Declan arches an eyebrow and points one finger at the pages still in front of Tadd. "Read through those. She printed them out; they have to be important. Otherwise she'd have left them on her computer. Or at work. There might be a clue."

Tadd grumbles but drops his feet to the ground and picks up the papers in front of him. It's not long before he slides one across the desk to Declan. "Did Lukas mention going to more than one fundraiser?"

"No." Declan takes the list and skims over it, raising his eyebrow when he sees Cal's name on the list as well.

They dig through every scrap of paper in the desk; then Tadd sorts through the other rooms while Declan calls the museum and speaks to Sofia's colleagues. They don't leave until after lunchtime, hungry but armed with the knowledge Cal had attended at least three of the museum's fundraisers over the past six months and had become a rather frequent visitor to Sofia's office recently, as well.

ADARA LAMBROS is floating on a raft in her pool when Tadd and Declan arrive at her house and are directed to the back deck by her housekeeper. She's wearing a small pink bikini that leaves very little to the imagination and is holding a half-full martini glass in her right hand despite it still being early afternoon. The angle shows off the little dove tattoo on the inside of her wrist, and when she glances up, Declan and Tadd both wave with their right hands, showing off the spear and kerykeion on their wrists.

"Ares! Hermes!" she coos. "To what do I owe the pleasure?"

"This isn't a pleasure visit, Aphrodite," Declan says, taking a seat on one of the lounge chairs surrounding the pool. Tadd stands behind him, his arms crossed over his chest and a scowl on his face.

"Oh?" Adara paddles over to the side of the pool and performs an amazing feat of acrobatics to get off the raft without letting a single bit of her body touch the water. "You two aren't here to ask me to remove that curse again, are you? I thought you were deliriously happy with each other. Last I heard you were trying to make a mortal life together."

"We succeeded," Tadd tells her shortly. He's not in the mood for her little flirtations. "Now you need to answer a few questions so we can make sure it doesn't fall apart."

Adara looks taken aback as she settles on the lounge chair next to Declan. She stretches out on it fully, crossing her legs at the ankles and leaning back, but she doesn't recline the chair. "What kind of questions?"

"Did Cal come over here Tuesday afternoon?"

"Yes…." Adara leans forward and rests a hand on Declan's arm. "Hermes, honey, I'm happy to help you, but can you please stop Ares from growling at me? It's insanely hot when he does it in bed, but not nearly as attractive when he's trying to be menacing."

Tadd moves forward until his shins are pressed up against the chair Declan is perched on, and leans down, looming over Declan and staking his claim. Adara gave up the right to touch either of them when she cursed them long ago, and he's not letting her take liberties with Declan no matter what the cause.

"It's Declan now. Declan Anagnos," Declan tells her, twisting around so her hand falls off his knee and glancing up at Tadd. "And Tadd Leventis." He leans his shoulder against Tadd's hip, nudging him a little, and Tadd widens his stance so he doesn't fall. He keeps his arms crossed over his chest, but he does let his expression soften a little, smiling slightly as his gaze flickers to Declan.

"Sorry, Declan." Adara puts her hand back on Declan's knee but immediately pulls it off when Tadd hardens his gaze again. She straightens up, curls her legs to one side, and looks at him seriously. "Yes, Cal came over Tuesday afternoon."

Tuesday afternoon isn't specific enough. Athena died at the end of the work day, a little before five, and if they can't track down the stripper Cal claims to have been with that afternoon, Adara is his best chance at an alibi. "What time?" Tadd asks, putting effort into keeping his voice even. They need her to cooperate.

47

Adara tilts her head curiously. "A little after five, I think. Not too long after—" She shakes her head. "Why do you need to know?"

"We're trying to figure out some things that happened Tuesday," Declan soothes. "How did he get here? Did he drive or just show up?"

"He drove, I think." Adara taps her perfectly manicured fingers on the lounge chair and purses her lips. "Yes, that's right. He drove. Parked that big SUV of his right in the middle of the driveway and pissed Egan—Hephaestus—off because that meant there wasn't any room for his truck."

"Hephaestus still lives with you?" Declan's eyebrows slide up his forehead.

"No." Adara says the word so emphatically that Tadd takes a step back and raises his eyebrows. "But that doesn't keep him from thinking he can stop by any time he wants. He *is* my husband, after all."

"But surely he doesn't still have issues—"

Adara cuts Tadd off with a harsh laugh. "Oh, he doesn't have any problems getting women on the side. That doesn't mean he's stopped exercising his marital rights, though. However," she continues, tossing her long red hair back over her shoulders and pulling herself up straighter, "that's not what you're here to discuss. Cal drove himself here."

Declan flashes a sympathetic smile before asking, "And what were you doing when he arrived?"

"Lounging." She hesitates a moment. "I'd planned to be ready for dinner, but when I was about to get out of the pool, I felt this horrible pain. Cal arrived maybe twenty, twenty-five minutes after that. I hadn't gotten out yet."

Tadd nods at the confirmation that Aphrodite had felt the same thing they had, but he lets Declan continue his questions. "And before that?"

"From when?"

"All day." Declan casts a questioning glance at Tadd, and he shrugs. It can't hurt to establish a timeline, and he doesn't want to come back here if it can be helped. Adara has her charms, but she can also be grating and Tadd is easily irritated by her.

"Well, I went into the office in the morning, then out to lunch, and then back here to lie out." She shrugs. "Everything was under control at the office, so there's no reason to go back. I don't need to personally match people with their true loves anymore. We have computers for that."

"Were you here alone?" Tadd looms again, leaning over Declan's shoulder to peer at Adara. "All afternoon?"

"Until Cal showed up, yeah. Why? What are you trying to figure out?"

"Don't worry about it." Declan pats Adara's thigh as he stands. "Thanks, Adara. You've been a big help."

"Are you not going to tell me what I've been helpful with?"

"You'll find out soon enough," Declan tells her as he takes Tadd's hand and leads the way back through Adara's house.

She follows, stomping her feet and cursing as she storms after them. "Tadd! Declan! You can't just show up in my house and demand—"

"Demand what?"

All three of them stop short and slowly turn to see a short man leaning against the counter, a beer in his hand and a beanie covering his long hair. The anvil on the inside of his right wrist flashes as he raises the bottle to his mouth.

"Egan," Adara says, condensation dripping from her voice. "What are you doing here?"

"Stopped by to see you, sweetheart." He hoists the beer bottle in a toast and takes another swig. "Now, you gonna tell me what these two assholes are demanding?"

"Information about Cal," Declan says, putting a hand on Tadd's arm and stopping him from lunging forward and attacking Egan. No one really knows who would win—Tadd is the better fighter, but Egan is much stronger—and Declan clearly doesn't want to find out today. "We just wanted to confirm he was here around four Tuesday."

"He was." Egan takes another swig of his beer. "Fucking douche bag. Kept me from parking my truck in the driveway and wouldn't move it when I asked him to."

"You didn't—"

"I asked!" Egan whirls on Adara, his eyes narrowed and his mouth set in a thin line as he glares at her. "I asked that waste of space three times before you bothered to get out of the damn pool, and when he still wouldn't, I fucking ordered him to." He slams the beer bottle on the counter and grabs another one from the refrigerator. "He didn't listen to me, either, the fucking idiot."

"Thanks, Egan," Declan says hastily, pulling Tadd back toward the front door. Adara huffs as they disappear around the corner, but they're gone before either she or Egan can say anything. The last thing Tadd hears before Declan drops his hand and he wills himself back to their own house is the beginning of a spectacular argument.

"WELL, that was fun." Declan leans forward, rests his hands on the kitchen table, and lets his chin fall to his chest. "I always so enjoy spending time with your ex-flame."

Tadd chuckles dryly as he kisses the back of Declan's neck. "She was never a flame. Just a... distraction."

It's a valid point, but it doesn't make Declan like Aphrodite any better. "An awfully consistent one."

"Who cursed us both." Tadd wraps his arms around Declan's waist and rests his chin on his shoulder. "It was never about anything more than pleasure and getting back at Zeus for forcing her into marrying Hephaestus. You know that. You took her up on it a few times too."

Declan shudders at the memory as he turns in Tadd's arms. "I'm glad we fell in love."

"Me too." Tadd's grin is blinding as he tilts his chin up and pulls Declan's head down so their lips meet. Declan loses himself in the kiss, forgetting about everything he's been dealing with as he explores Tadd's mouth like it's the first time they've ever done this.

"Do you think this was too easy?" Declan asks later, when they're seated side by side on the couch, the papers they collected from Sofia's spread out on the coffee table in front of them, intermingled with

Declan's notes from his conversations with Lukas and Cal. "I didn't think we'd figure it out this soon."

"Me either." Tadd rubs at the back of his neck and twists his head from side to side to loosen the tense muscles in his shoulders. "Everything adds up, but—"

"There's something missing." Declan nods as he absently reaches over to rub at the back of Tadd's neck. Based on Adara's vague recollection of when Cal had arrived, he could have killed Athena and driven to Adara's, particularly if he'd left his car close to her house, but something feels wrong. "It's too easy, almost. Like we're supposed to think it's Cal. I don't know who else it could be, though."

"Yeah." Tadd leans into the touch with a contented sigh, and for a few minutes they sit in silence.

Declan contemplates the mess in front of them as his fingers continue to work at Tadd's shoulders. "I wish I knew what they'd been arguing about."

"What?" Tadd lifts his head, moaning softly as the loosened muscles contract.

"Cal and Sofia." Declan twists on the couch so he's looking straight at Tadd. "Everyone who's connected to them says they were arguing a lot, but what were they arguing about? Lukas mentioned something Cal had overheard on his phone sex line, but he didn't know what, and I can't imagine Sofia called it."

"We could check. Get the recordings if they've kept them."

"Maybe." Declan sighs. "Everything else adds up—he had opportunity, and an argument gives him motive, I guess—but it just…." He trails off with a sigh, slumping back into the couch and staring dejectedly at the papers on the coffee table.

"It just what?"

"I don't know. Seems weird, I guess. I mean, we have enough evidence or whatever, that we could talk to Bront, but I don't know if we should. If he is the killer, we need to, but what if he's not? I'm not sure he is."

"And if it's someone else, we'll tip our hand." Tadd slumps back, too, crossing his arms and scowling at the table. "Fuck."

51

"Yeah." For once, Declan doesn't take it as an invitation. He crosses his arms as well and they sit, slumped next to each other in identical poses, scowling at the coffee table as their brains whirl.

"We could ask Cal," Tadd finally ventures, rolling his head so he's looking at Declan instead of the coffee table but not otherwise moving.

"Just flat-out ask him if he killed her?" Declan has to admit the idea is tempting, but it's also incredibly risky, and he's surprised Tadd suggested it.

"No. Ask him what their arguments were about. If he has nothing to hide, he'll tell us, right? If he doesn't, he has something to hide."

"Maybe." Declan sits up and twists to look at Tadd. "I should go by myself, though. I told him we were fighting. He'll get suspicious if we both turn up."

Tadd's mouth opens and closes a few times before he lets out a soft huff. "Fine. Just... be careful." He takes Declan's hand in his and squeezes tightly as he looks at Declan with an expression that stops all of Declan's protests. "Please."

"I will." Declan says seriously before he leans over and kisses Tadd softly. "I promise." He stands and runs a hand through his hair. "I'm going to go change first; then I'll find him. Order something for dinner?"

"Yeah, okay."

Declan reappears upstairs, strips, and tosses his clothes in the hamper. Naked, he pulls open his closet door, stands in front of his clothes, and frowns. He can change his outfit with a thought if he really wants to, but he likes the feel of the real thing against his skin, and he loves running his hands over the soft fabric in the closet, so he changes the way mortals do if it's possible.

He's debating what to wear when he freezes; his nerve endings alight with pain that comes from nowhere and everywhere at once, fire and ice chasing each other across his body as his senses whirl and his heart thuds in his chest. It's hard to breathe, difficult to think, and impossible to move. He just stands there, ramrod straight as his muscles twitch, and waits for the pain to end.

It does, as suddenly as it began, but this time, instead of taking a minute to reorient himself and wonder what in Hades just happened, he already knows. It's not good. Someone else is dead, and he didn't find the killer in time to stop it.

# EROS

DECLAN reaches out blindly, grabs the first set of clothes his fingers brush against, and pulls them on. His fingers get caught in the fabric a few times, but it's still easier than materializing clothes while reeling from the shock and trying to mentally follow the already faded pain back to its source. When he's dressed, he concentrates and appears in Adara's backyard. Cal is floating facedown in the pool, a bronze dagger jutting out from his back. It's impossible to tell from this far away, but from where Declan is standing, it looks identical to the one that was in Sofia's stomach. Tadd is kneeling by the side of the pool, one hand dipped into the water, the other spread wide on the damp wood of the deck. The pool lights provide the only illumination other than the moon and give Tadd an eerie look while casting the others in shadows. Adara is huddled in a chair near the door to the house, an empty martini glass clutched to her chest and her knees tucked under her as she shies away from every bit of light. Egan and Lukas are standing against the fence on opposite sides of the pool, glaring at each other from the darkness.

It's a peculiar gathering of Olympians, and Declan is the last to arrive.

He walks over to Tadd and kneels down, peering into the pool where Tadd's fingers are trailing through the water. Drops of red liquid are swirling around, churned by the filters, but none of them have touched Tadd's hands.

"What happened?" Declan asks softly as he squeezes Tadd's shoulder. "Did you see anything?"

"He was like this when I got here." Tadd pulls his fingers out of the pool and rises, wiping his hand on his already damp jeans as he stands. "They were all rushing out of the house when I arrived, and Cal was, well." He rubs at the red welt on the right side of his jaw as he casts an angry look across the water at Egan. "You missed the argument."

"It wasn't an argument," Egan jerks away from the fence. "Don't call it that."

Tadd snorts. "What should I call it, then?"

"It was you butting your nose in where you don't belong!" The muscles in Egan's arms bunch up as he limps toward the pool. He's usually good at hiding his disfigurement, especially in this day of custom footwear and ambulatory aids, but when he's angry or moving quickly, it shows. "You show up here, practically before we know anything's happened, and expect us to just tell you everything? Why? Don't you have any respect for grief?"

"You aren't grieving!" Tadd starts around the pool toward Egan. "You hated Cal! You hated everything he stood for! You hated that he existed because he was a constant reminder that your wife doesn't love you!"

"Like you're much better." Egan stands toe to toe with Tadd, frowning up at him and breathing heavily. "He was probably yours, either that or your husband's"—he sneers the word—"and neither of you gave a shit about him. You got all wrapped up in your own problems."

"Because your wife cursed us!" Tadd glares down at Egan. "She obviously didn't want us to know who Cal's father is—if it even is one of us—and she didn't want us around, either. She's not so wonderful I'm going to force myself to put up with her when she doesn't want me around."

"I don't force her to—"

Declan steps forward as Egan draws his fist back. "Stop it!" His heart is thudding in his chest at the idea of Tadd getting hurt fighting with Egan, and his hand trembles a little as he puts it on Tadd's arm and slowly eases him back. As soon as there's space, he squeezes between them and looks at Egan with a pleading expression. "This isn't the time."

"No, it's not." Adara sounds as though she's crying, and her words are slurred. "My son is dead, and you're arguing over stupid things that don't matter! It was thousands of years ago, and he didn't need any of you to be his father! He just needed to be my son." She tips back her martini glass, shaking it as she attempts to get the last drop from the very bottom. "He was my son," she sobs, "and now he's dead!"

Tadd and Egan cast distrustful looks at each other, but they step back and retreat to opposite sides of the pool. Declan walks with Tadd, putting a hand on the small of his back and leaning in close. "You all right?"

"I'm fine." Tadd scoffs as he touches the bruise on his jaw again. "It was a lucky hit. Barely a glancing blow."

Declan touches it as well, his finger ghosting over the inflamed skin. It's hot to the touch and looks painful, but that's not what really concerns him. Tadd will heal just fine, he knows that. "That's not what I meant." He leans in and softly kisses Tadd's lips. "You're awfully quick-tempered right now."

"I'm always quick-tempered, Declan." Tadd smirks as he crosses his arms over his chest. "I'm the god of war, remember? It's kind of a prerequisite."

"I know, but—"

"I'm fine, Declan." Tadd squeezes Declan's hand. "I don't particularly care for anyone here other than you, but I'll behave."

Declan smiles, grateful that Tadd, at least, won't cause him problems. He's sure he'll have enough from the others. "Promise?"

"Yes. I'll stay back here and wait until you need protection so you can sleuth it out. Just don't expect me to shed any tears for Cal, particularly not with them here." He glances quickly at Lukas and Egan before smiling softly at Declan. "Now go."

"Yeah, all right." Declan flashes a fond smile before he pulls away and crosses the deck to talk to Adara. She's clearly distraught, her hands shaking even curled tightly around the glass, and her knees are drawn up to her chest, but Declan wants to talk to her before he talks to Lukas or Egan.

She looks up at him with wide eyes when he sits on the end of her lounge chair. "Why are you here?"

"I'm trying to figure out what happened."

"Why?" She lets out a shaky laugh. "Why do you care what happened to Cal?"

Declan tries to hide his wince. He can't deny he's less upset about Cal's death than he possibly should be, given the history they shared. "Because I don't want it to happen to anyone else."

Adara nods and looks around, her gaze calculating behind her tears. "Who else died?" She blinks at Declan. "That is what happened before. What you were asking me about earlier, right?"

"Yes." Declan resists the urge to sigh and concentrates on keeping his voice gentle. Adara sometimes masquerades as less intelligent than she is, but the sensitivity she's displaying right now is genuine. He knows that from experience. "Sofia—Athena—is dead too. She was killed Tuesday. I want it to stop." Declan leans forward and puts his hand on Adara's knee. "So can you tell me what happened? Please?"

"I don't know. I was inside. We all were." She looks briefly at Egan and Lukas. "I don't know exactly what happened. Cal must have gone outside, I guess, but I didn't look, and then suddenly there was this horrible, horrible pain, and I looked outside and he was—" She breaks off with a sob, waving her hands toward the pool, the empty martini glass wobbling.

Declan takes it from her and sets it on the deck beneath the chair. "So the three of you were inside together?"

"Yes. No. I mean…." Adara shakes her head and sniffs again. "We were all inside, but we weren't all in the same room."

"Adara and I were." Lukas's voice comes from much closer than Declan expects, and he flinches with surprise, though he manages to mostly cover it by twisting to look up at the other man. "Egan was, well, I'm not sure where he was."

He speaks loud enough for everyone to hear despite leaning in close to Declan's ear as though he was going to whisper, and the moment the words leave his mouth, Egan jerks his head and stalks across the deck, his uneven steps thudding hard against the wood.

"What did you just say?"

Lukas turns and looks Egan straight in the eyes. A little bit of his bravado slips at the stony expression on Egan's face, but he doesn't back down. "You weren't in the room with Adara and me, that's all. No need to get all riled up about the truth. Unless," he continues, drawing the word out, "I'm right about you being the one who did this."

Egan grabs Lukas's shirt and slams him into the wall. "I didn't do anything," he growls, hefting Lukas up so his feet are dangling a few inches off the ground. Declan scrambles to his feet, but by the time he reaches Egan, he's dropped Lukas, stepped back, and is scowling as he brushes his hands together. "Stay the fuck away from me."

Lukas shrugs as he smoothes down his rumpled shirt. "It was a suggestion, Hephaestus. You are the only one who was alone this afternoon. Adara and I were talking."

"No, we weren't."

Lukas spins around. "What?"

"You and I," Adara clarifies, sitting up straighter and looking at him with red eyes, "weren't talking. Not when—" She sniffs and swallows hard. "Not when Cal—"

"What do you mean?" Lukas's brow furrows. "Yes, we were. I was trying to convince you that you should—"

"No." Adara cuts him off with a shake of her head. "That was before. You'd left to get me a drink when I felt—felt that."

"So you were alone too?" Egan steps in close to Lukas again. "Maybe you killed him. Slipped out to get Adara a drink and killed Cal instead. Is that how it happened?"

"What? No!" Lukas backs away, his hands held wide. "Why would you think that?"

"Why would you think I would kill him, huh?" Egan keeps walking forward, his steps slow and menacing. "You had just as much opportunity as I did, and you're the one who jumped to accuse me."

"I didn't kill him!"

"Well, neither did I, so don't—"

Declan jumps forward, using his speed to get between Lukas and Egan before Egan's hands connect with Lukas's shirt. "Stop, both of you!"

"Why should we?"

"He accused—"

"You're not helping!" Tadd shoves them both back and pulls Declan from between them. "Neither of you are helping anything, so stop."

"And why do you care?" Adara stands, joining the rough circle and sneering at Tadd. "Why do either of you care? You showed up yesterday asking about Cal, and now he's dead and you're here again. Why? What do you care about Cal being dead?"

"Maybe one of them killed him. They got here awfully fast."

Egan twists to glare at Tadd, his hands again clenching into fists. "Yeah, and Ares beat Hermes. How did that happen?" He takes a step forward, tightening the circle. "Did you kill him?"

"Anyone could have killed him," Declan interjects, trying to stop the argument before it gets out of control again. "It doesn't have to be someone here. Whoever did this could have left."

"Or they could be standing right here." Egan's gaze swings to Declan, and he takes another step forward. "Maybe you killed him and then left and came back so we wouldn't suspect. Is that why he beat you here? You seem awfully curious for someone who doesn't have a stake in this." He draws his fist back.

Declan gulps and prepares to run. "I didn't—"

"Enough!"

Declan squeezes his eyes closed as he slowly turns toward the sound of the voice. He knows what he's going to see—only one being has the power to make his bones tremble like that—but he still hesitates to open his eyes.

Bront and his wife are standing at the far end of the pool. Hera—known now by the name of Mona Doukas—has a sour look on her face as she glares across the water. Her arms are crossed over her designer dress, her hair is swept up in an intricate twist, and as she glances at Bront, she impatiently taps feet sheathed in shoes that probably cost more than Declan pays Rachel each week.

"This squabbling is unacceptable." Bront steps forward, ignoring the water of the pool and striding straight across it. His dress shoes send ripples across the surface and his tie flaps in the breeze, but his suit stays dry. "We're being killed off one by one, and you're fighting like children! This ends now!"

Declan swallows hard and steps forward, Tadd at his side. "I'm sorry," he says once they're standing in front of Bront. "I—we—thought we'd figured it out, but—"

Bront holds up a hand, stopping him. "I know. I expected another murder, but I didn't expect it to happen so soon. That's not why I came."

"Then why did you?" Tadd steps forward, putting himself in position to push between Bront and Declan. He won't be able to do much if Bront is determined, but the gesture isn't about what he can accomplish. It's about what he's willing to try.

"I should have come for Athena," Bront says softly. "I owed her that much, just as I owe Eros that much. You did an admirable job disposing of Sofia's body, Declan, but I'll take care of Cal."

Declan nods. "Thank you. You don't think that...?" He trails off as he gestures back to the others still crowded together close to the wall.

"That I could talk some sense into them?" Bront flashes an amused smile. "I suppose I could. The time for keeping this investigation secret has passed, I think."

Declan tips his head in thanks, more relieved than he dares show. Cal was dead because Declan hadn't been able to ask the right questions, and he doesn't want it to happen again. "Thank you."

Bront returns his nod and goes straight to Adara. "My condolences, Aphrodite. Let me take care of Eros for you."

Adara sniffs and looks at Bront with watery eyes. "Why?"

"I owe him that much."

"Can't you...?"

"Bring him back? No." Bront sounds genuinely remorseful. "Not from this. Only my brother can do that, with my permission. I doubt he will."

"I could ask. If I got him to agree, would you allow it?"

"You can't go to Hades, Adara. You might never return."

"I can—"

"No."

"But—"

"No." The word vibrates through the air, the order behind it clear.

Adara's lower lip trembles as she steps forward and places a gentle hand on Bront's arm. "Please?"

"No." Bront deftly extracts himself from Adara's grip as she stares at him with wide eyes. "I am sorry, but I can't allow this. Cal is dead, and I don't want you to follow him to the Underworld."

"So why are you here, then, if you won't do anything about this?"

"To pay my respects to Cal and to give you instructions."

"Instructions?" Egan glares. "For what?"

"Stopping this. I need you"—Bront looks around at each of them in turn—"all of you, to cooperate with Declan. I've asked him to figure out who is behind this, and he can't do that if you don't cooperate."

"Declan?" Egan rolls his eyes. "So we have to stand here and let him quiz us about where we were and what we did whenever he wants? That's bullshit."

"No, it's not." Bront flexes his fingers, and lightning crackles behind him. "You will cooperate, Hephaestus. All of you will, or you'll face my wrath. Is that understood?"

Adara, Egan, and Lukas stare at Bront with stony expressions for a moment before they grudgingly nod.

"Good. Don't let me hear otherwise." He looks at each of them in turn, his gaze steady and commanding. "I'd best not hear of any trouble while I'm away tonight."

"Away?" Declan steps forward. He'd hoped Bront would stay while he talked to the others so they would understand he was serious. "Where will you be?"

"He's taking me out. Finally." Mona taps one finger along her forearm. "We were already supposed to be at dinner, so don't interrupt us again." She shoots an annoyed look around the deck and then hones in on Bront. "Are you ready?"

"In a minute, dear." Bront waves her off with a complete lack of concern. "You can go ahead if you want. I'll be there soon." He grins as Mona huffs and vanishes; then he turns back to Tadd and Declan. "Let me know if anyone doesn't cooperate. Immediately."

"We will." Declan lies. He'll tell Bront, but he's not going to risk Mona's wrath for anything short of another death. She hasn't lost the temper Hera was so famous for. "And we'll find whoever did this, Bront. I promise."

"I know. Just hurry. Please."

They both nod as Bront vanishes with a dramatic flash of lightning. Another flash immediately follows, striking Cal's body and setting it alight. It burns, the fire unquenched by the water it's floating on, until there's nothing left. As the last of the flames die, Declan squeezes Tadd's hand, steps away, and clears his throat. "So, who wants to go first?"


DECLAN doesn't bother to stop downstairs when they return home a few minutes later. He materializes right in their bedroom, falls flat on the bed, and lets out an overly dramatic moan. "That was horrible."

He's exaggerating, but only a little. The second Cal's body finished burning, everyone vanished, including Adara, leaving Declan and Tadd alone on her deck with a murder to solve and no suspects to talk to. Declan had tried to find them, but though he'd been able to sense the gods and goddesses who hadn't been there, Hephaestus, Helios, and Aphrodite were clearly making an effort to conceal themselves.

Leaving this unfinished feels like a failure, and that combined with the accusations the others had hurled at him and Tadd has put him in a bad mood.

"Oh, yeah, it must have been." Tadd's voice drips with sarcasm as he stretches out on the bed next to Declan, lying on his left side so his bruised cheek isn't touching the pillow. "People were mean to you."

Declan narrows his eyes as he rolls onto his side to face Tadd. "That's not what I'm upset about, and you know it."

Tadd's gaze softens. "Yeah, I know." He offers a small smile as he slides his hand across the quilt and curls his fingers around Declan's. "You'll figure it out, though."

"Before more people die? Or get hurt?"

Tadd opens his mouth, then snaps it shut. "I hope," he says, squeezing Declan's hand. "But I don't know. Whoever is doing this, they know you're investigating now. Whatever they're trying to do, they're going to move faster. There might not be enough time to figure this out before they strike again."

Declan closes his eyes, sucks in a deep breath, and nods. "Then we have to move quickly too." He sits up, pulling his hand free from Tadd's, and slides his phone from his pocket and scowls at it. "Since we can't track people down tonight, what can we do?"

"Try to figure out who had motive." Tadd sits up and pulls his own phone out. "I don't know why Cal was at all the museum events, but historically, he and Sofia didn't exactly move in the same circles. Even if this is from when they were still Athena and Eros, there can't be many people who have grudges against both of them."

"Pissing off one of them would likely endear someone to the other."

"Exactly."

"So, then, what do we do?" Declan pinches the bridge of his nose and tries to remind himself he's a god and therefore doesn't actually get headaches unless he's been injured. It doesn't work, but he forces himself to ignore the dull ache behind his eyes and meet Tadd's gaze.

"We dig." Tadd climbs from the bed and holds his hand out to Declan. "Come on, this will be easier on our computers."

Declan takes Tadd's hand as he stands, and laces their fingers together while they head down to the in-home office they share. "What will be easier on our computers?" he asks as they enter the cozy room in the back of the house.

It's one of his favorite places to work, with bookshelves stuffed to overflowing and two desks positioned with their corners together, forming an L that looks out on the chairs they have set up for reading or visitors. A few weapons are mounted on the walls, though they're strictly decorative—mostly bronze swords and daggers. The functional ones are kept easy to access, a few in every room, and Tadd's collection has its own separate room Declan rarely sets foot in. It's strictly Tadd's domain, just as the collection of old communication devices taking up the other half of their basement is Declan's. The office, however, is shared, just like the rest of the house, and the comfortable-yet-functional décor is as much a mix of their personalities as the imposing desks with pristine surfaces and more drawers and cubbyholes than any person—or god—has the right to need.

Tadd opens his laptop and looks over it with a raised eyebrow. "We need to find anything linking Cal and Sofia and then see if we can connect anyone else to the same things."

"Besides the museum fundraisers?"

"Including the museum fundraisers. Lukas donated. Maybe someone else did too." Tadd leans back in his chair, clasping his hands behind his head and propping his feet up on the desk. "Now get digging. See if any other gods or demigods donated to the museum."

Declan looks over at him with a raised eyebrow, amused by the order. "What are you going to do? You won't find much sitting like that."

"Watch." Tadd flashes a cheeky grin. "You're the spy here, I'm just the bodyguard. I'm going to relax so I'm well rested when it's time to hit people."

"When it's time to hit people?" Declan leans over and shoves Tadd's feet to the floor hard enough he jerks with the impact. "You're not going to hit anyone. Else," he adds, his eyes focusing on Tadd's swollen jaw.

"I'm not?"

"Not tonight, anyway," Declan mutters, "which means you can help me. Do you want to look into Sofia's work at the museum or Cal's phone sex line?"

"Cal's phone sex line?"

"If Lukas was right and Cal was confronting Sofia about something he heard on his line, we need to know what it was and who it was about. I was going to ask him, but I guess we'll have to listen to everything he did."

"I'll, uh, leave that one to you."

"So you'll look into the fundraisers, then?" Declan blinks innocently until Tadd finally pulls his laptop closer.

"Fine," he mutters, "but you're going to owe me for this. Big time."

Declan's voice is dripping with promise as he leans across his desk and looks Tadd straight in the eyes. "I'm sure I can find a way to make it up to you."

Tadd's answering grin is positively sinful.

TADD doesn't wait long to collect. It was late when they started working, long past dinner, which they never ate thanks to whoever killed Cal, and they only work for about an hour and a half before Tadd stands, stretches, and walks behind Declan. "Did you find anything?" he asks as he drapes his arms around Declan and leans his chin on his shoulder.

"Not yet." Declan leans his head back so it's resting against Tadd, and rubs his eyes. "I got the files—that was the easy part—but I haven't found any that feature Sofia yet. There's a lot to go through, though."

"I thought Cal didn't take many calls?"

"He doesn't, but he listens in on a lot and gets the recordings of a lot more sent to him because he needs to hear one specific part of it. You can say what you like about the guy, but he did make sure the people working for him were taken care of. Anything that came across as even remotely off, he listened to himself."

"Huh." Tadd looks at the words scrolling rapidly across Declan's screen. "So what are you doing, then?"

"Transcribing them and searching for any mention of Sofia. My program does the transcription and searching itself and spits out any matches for me to look at more closely." Declan hits a button on the computer, and the words stop moving. "I'm looking at the things it spits out and trying to see if they're a match or not. So far, no luck. Not even anything I want to listen to, just a few people who fantasize about someone named Sofia."

"You sure it's not her they're fantasizing about?"

"Positive." Declan clicks over to another window, double clicks on some text, and a new window pops up with an entire conversation. "This one's blonde, see? And is a lot taller than Athena was. This Raoul likes his girls tall, apparently. And this one"—Declan opens another conversation—"is imagining a specific individual who is about sixty years old and lives in Ohio. There's one where a girl is fantasizing about an actress named Sofia, and another where Sofia is the name of an astronaut, but none of them, whether they're imagining a real person or a fantasy one, are imagining a Sofia who works at a museum."

Tadd mentally reviews the list, hoping but not expecting to come up with some tenuous connection Declan had missed. "Doesn't sound like they're imagining a Sofia who even goes to a museum."

"I know." Declan lets out a frustrated sigh. "It's going to take hours to go through all these calls, even if I narrow the criteria down, and there's no guarantee her name was ever mentioned. If she called Cal, she probably wouldn't have given her real name, and if it was someone calling about her, they might not have."

"So what are you doing, then?"

"Waiting. I'm running searches for her name and the museum and clicking on the ones that look hopeful. I'll cross-reference when the searches are done."

"That's going to take a while, right?"

"Yeah." Declan sighs again, letting his head fall heavily on Tadd's shoulder. "It's going to take hours."

"Good." Tadd grins wickedly and slides his hand down Declan's chest, then circles his nipple with his thumb until it's hard and pert, obvious even through the fabric of Declan's shirt. "We have time."

Declan's breath hitches. "Time for what?"

"For me to collect. You promised you would make this up to me. I think you should start now."

"Yeah, okay." Declan breathes. "Just…." He leans forward, hits a few buttons, and the screen goes blank. "There. Now it'll run all night long without me doing a thing. I'm yours until tomorrow."

"You're always mine," Tadd murmurs as he pulls Declan up for a kiss. It's messy and awkward, with Declan twisted around strangely and still half in his chair, but then he straightens out, kneeling on the desk chair and curling his hands around Tadd's shoulders as he slips his tongue between Tadd's lips. The kiss is frantic and needy, and Tadd is fully hard before he pulls back, panting for oxygen he doesn't really need as he stares into Declan's eyes.

"Upstairs."

"Yeah." Tadd breathes the word into Declan's mouth as he pulls him in for another kiss. This one is slower but no less needy, and he loses himself in the sensations as his heart beats with Declan's and their tongues dance.

This time, when Declan pulls back, he rests his forehead against Tadd's and grins. "Do you think you can stop touching me for a few seconds, or am I going to carry you upstairs?"

Tadd's dick twitches, and he growls as he pushes back from Declan so they're no longer touching. "Go," he says, and then he vanishes.

Declan still beats him to their bed.


THE alarm goes off far too early the next morning. It's on Declan's side of the bed, and for good reason. Tadd has never been a morning person except when it was necessary for surprise attacks on the enemy, and the first time he'd heard Plato's water clock set off its alarm, he'd had to be forcibly stopped from smiting the man. That had actually been the beginning of his relationship with Declan, who had still been Hermes then. Hermes had been the only one able to get to Ares fast enough, and the only thing he'd been able to think of to distract the god of war on a rampage was to provide the sexual release they'd both been denied since Aphrodite had cursed them.

They hadn't fallen in love for centuries, hadn't really even liked each other for years, but they had started taking advantage of the fact that they could still get off with each other even though they couldn't find release with anyone else.

Still, Tadd hates alarm clocks. Declan loves them, claims they're what started their relationship and therefore they're the greatest things ever, but Tadd thinks Declan would love them anyway. He's too much of a morning person not to.

Mostly, Tadd has gotten used to this one, and Declan has gotten good at silencing it quickly and then waking Tadd in more pleasurable ways, but this morning it blares unexpectedly loud and early, and they both jump. Declan smacks at it, hitting it with vigor more characteristic of Tadd, and rolls over to stare at his husband. "Remind me why we're getting up this early again."

Tadd glares at him with one eye. The other is hidden by the pillow. "Because you're evil."

"Me?" Declan puts on his most innocent expression. "Evil? Where would you get that idea?"

"From the fact that you set the alarm for o-dark-thirty in the morning." Tadd lets his open eye fall closed and snuggles closer to Declan, relishing the warmth as he lets his limbs relax.

Declan huffs, though it's all show. "It's not o-dark-thirty."

"Five twenty might as well be." Tadd lifts his head and glares at Declan with both eyes this time. "Why are we up so early, anyway?"

"To talk to Egan before he bolts." Declan pulls Tadd down for a gentle kiss. "You can go back to sleep if you want. There's no need for us both to be up this early."

That gets Tadd's attention. "You want me to sleep while you talk to Egan alone?"

"If you want." Declan shrugs, affecting nonchalance. "We don't both have to go."

"Yes we do." Tadd shoves the covers off and glowers. "If you're going to talk to Egan, I need to be there."

"Why?"

"Because that's my job. Because Bront told me to keep you safe. Because Egan tried to hurt you yesterday and he's going to be in a bad mood." Tadd's face softens. "Because I love you."

The look in Tadd's eyes blows away every one of Declan's arguments. He reaches over, resets the alarm, and pulls Tadd back down to lie on top of him. "All right. We'll go in a few hours."

"Thought we needed to go now." It's a halfhearted protest that completely contradicts the way Tadd is nuzzling into the crook of Declan's neck.

"We'll go later. I need you well rested so you can keep me safe."

"Well, if someone hadn't kept me up until all hours of the morning...."

"I kept you up? I'm pretty sure you were the one pinning me to the bed."

"Semantics. You were definitely keeping me up. In more ways than one."

"Fine." Declan kisses the top of Tadd's head and grins. "We kept each other up. So we'll let each other sleep in this morning."

Tadd's lips twitch into a smile. "I guess I can live with that."

Declan laughs and lets himself fall back asleep.


"ALL right, let's get this over with." Egan crosses his arms and leans back against the wall of his forge, scowling at Tadd and Declan. He's hot and sweaty, despite the early hour, and though he's let the fire die so he can talk, the room is sweltering. Declan and Tadd both started sweating within a minute of entering the dark enclosed area, and Declan tugs at the collar of his shirt as he looks around the room, hoping for a window he can open or a fan to relieve the oppressive heat.

"Do you want to go somewhere more comfortable?" he asks, shoving his hands into his jean pockets and wishing he'd worn something lighter. The dark jeans and the brown Henley he borrowed from Tadd's closet are both casual enough he hopes the others won't feel like he's interrogating them and neat enough they won't think he's not taking this seriously.

"Here's good. Why? Can't you take the heat?"

Declan crosses the room in a flash and stops inches away from Egan. "Just offering." He shrugs and leans against the wall as well. "Thought you might like somewhere to sit."

Tadd makes a soft sound of disbelief from where he's leaning against the frame of the closed door, but he doesn't say anything, just raises an eyebrow and smirks as he lets his eyes roam over Declan's body. Declan lets his eyes roam right back, taking in the shorts and tank top Tadd apparently switched to as soon as Declan's back was turned. It looks a lot more comfortable than what Declan has on, and the way the cotton of the shirt clings to Tadd's muscular chest is distracting.

Declan is about to step away from the wall and show Tadd exactly how much he approves of the new outfit when Egan clears his throat. "I'm not going to stand around and watch the two of you make googly eyes at each other. Eye fuck on your own time."

"Sorry." Declan flashes him an apologetic grin, concentrates long enough to change his clothing into something closer to what Tadd and Egan are wearing, and leans against the wall again, this time resting his left shoulder on it so his back is to Tadd and he's looking at Egan. "Where were you Tuesday?"

"What time?" Egan's eyes narrow. "And why does it matter?"

"Sofia died Tuesday."

"Yeah. And?"

"And she was killed by whoever killed Cal!" Declan pushes himself away from the wall and takes a step closer to Egan, invading his personal space and using his height advantage to loom as menacingly as he can manage. He can't really blame Tadd for snickering behind him—he's taller than Egan and no slouch in the muscle department, but he doesn't spend all day pounding iron either, which means Egan could rip him apart with his bare hands if he wanted to. Declan is relying on Tadd to keep that from happening.

"So you think I killed them both? Is that it?" Egan pushes off the wall and closes the small gap between him and Declan. When they're toe to toe, Declan has to bend his neck at an awkward angle to look at Egan's face, but Egan tilts his head up, making it a little easier as he glares defiantly. "If you want to accuse me, just say it."

"I don't." Declan takes a step back. It's not worth pushing at the moment. "I'm just asking where you were. I'm trying to eliminate people, not accuse everyone I talk to."

"Why the hell would I want to kill Sofia? Hmm?" Egan closes the distance between them again. "What would I get out of her death?"

"I don't know what anyone gets out of her death, Egan." Declan manages to keep his voice calm as he steps back again. This time, he angles his step away from the anvil in the center of the room and toward Tadd. If he's going to be pushed across the forge step by painful step, he wants to be heading for support, not danger. "That's what I'm trying to figure out."

"So you came to start picking on me? Is that it?"

"No!" Declan lets out a heavy sigh. "I'm here because Bront asked me to find out who the killer is. That's all."

"Why did you start here, then?"

"Because Adara is still asleep and Lukas is in meetings all morning."

That deflates Egan a little, and he steps back to lean against the wall again. "Oh." He doesn't look happy, but he grudgingly nods. "All right."

Declan takes a deep breath, focusing on drawing air into his lungs as he wills himself to calm down. "Can you please tell me what you were doing Tuesday a little before five?"

"I was here. Alone. Working on that, actually." He points to a wrought iron gate propped up against the wall. It's beautifully decorative, with swirls and curves perfectly matched on either side of the center pole and each twist in the iron evenly spaced. The top is a delicate curve, but it's the work inside that's breathtaking. This isn't just a gate, it's art.

Declan lets out a low whistle as he looks it over. "Nice," he says, the word slipping out before he thinks about it, but it's a deserved

71

compliment. He's far from a connoisseur of iron work, but even he can tell this is spectacular. "Who's it for?"

"It was for Sofia." Egan limps across the forge to stand next to Declan. "I was supposed to deliver it on Wednesday, but...." He trails off, shaking his head. "So no," he picks up in a rougher voice, "I didn't kill her. Cal either, though I'm not sorry to know he's in the Underworld. I won't miss him."

Tadd saunters over from the doorway and looks down at the gate with a raised eyebrow. He runs one finger along the top, tracing the curve of the cold metal as he casts a curious glance in Egan's direction. "That's a bit harsh."

"No, it's not." Egan growls. "He deserves it. The asshole was always hanging around, reminding me my wife couldn't stay faithful."

"She is the goddess of love," Declan offers hesitantly as his right hand reaches out almost of its own volition and covers Tadd's. Tadd smiles, and the fear that squeezed Declan's chest at the mere idea of Tadd not staying faithful recedes.

"Yeah." Egan snorts. "Love. Not lust or sex or anything else. I understand why Cal was unfaithful, but Adara? She's supposed to love her husband."

Declan blushes, remembering almost-forgotten times centuries ago when he was among the people Aphrodite slept with. She'd been anxious to get revenge on her husband and Zeus for trapping her into a marriage she didn't want, and he'd been promiscuous before she cursed him, but now, looking back on it with perspective granted by a committed, loving relationship that's lasted centuries, it's embarrassing.

"Sorry," Declan offers, patting Egan consolingly on the shoulder.

His hand barely makes contact with flesh before Egan whirls, grabs his hand, and twists it behind him painfully. "I bet you are," Egan growls, pulling Declan down so he's speaking right into Declan's ear. "Coming in here acting all concerned, rubbing what I don't have in my face. Pretending you only care about Cal's death when everyone knows one of you sired him."

"We're not rubbing—"

72

Egan cuts Declan off with a growl, yanking him down further and twisting his arm in a way that's amazingly painful. For a moment, his world narrows to flashes of light and pain, everything eclipsed by the way Egan is bending his arm, trying to force his body to move in ways it doesn't want to. He thinks he's screaming or groaning, but all he can hear is the rush of blood in his ears and the low rumble of Egan's taunts. He can't make out the words and he doesn't want to try. It doesn't matter what Egan is saying, just what he's doing, and Declan needs it to stop right now. If he could get out of Egan's grip, he could flee, move so fast that Egan could never catch him, but Egan is strong, far stronger than Declan could ever hope to be, and there's no way Declan can break free.

He struggles, trying to bend his body in a way that will relieve the pressure on his arm, but every time he tries, Egan twists more, sending shots of pain through Declan's body and leaving him helpless. His arm is about to snap when the pressure suddenly releases, leaving Declan gasping for breath on the floor, his upper body supported by the gate Egan was making for Sofia, as Tadd attacks, sending Egan flying across the room with one shove.

Tadd glances down at Declan, quickly taking in his appearance, and then runs across the forge with a yell. His body slams into Egan's just as Egan gains his feet, and they both tumble into the anvil, knocking the tools surrounding it to the ground with a clatter that grates on Declan's ears.

They fight without finesse or style, throwing punches where they can land them as they wrestle and roll around, trying to pin each other to the ground. They're fairly evenly matched—Egan's superior strength offset by Tadd's superior fighting skills—and it's only a few minutes before they're both bruised and bleeding.

Declan watches with his heart caught in his throat, waiting for an opening that will allow him to speed between them and break up the fight, but even when they pick up tools they've knocked to the ground and the fight turns from a wrestling match into a true battle, they stay too close for him to have any opportunity to get between them. The only time there is ever any distance is when they're both preparing to swing, and Declan isn't sure he's fast enough to get between them then, or that either of them will stop swinging if they see he has. He pulls his feet up beneath him, ready to move as soon as he has the opportunity, but all he can do is watch as they clang the tools together, bashing hammers and tongs with a fury neither of them have unleashed for centuries.

It's dirty and mean, and within a few moments there's no area of the forge undamaged by their fight. Fists and tools fly with equal fervor as grunts and groans are replaced by wordless screams of anger and yelps of pain. It's a battle centuries in the making, with both Tadd and Egan giving it their all, unleashing eons of pent-up anger and hatred, throwing every bit of frustration they possess into the fight.

Tadd gets the upper hand for a moment when he slams Egan into the anvil with enough force to leave him dazed and blinking, but as he's about to throw a knockout punch, Egan regains his senses, flips them around, and knocks Tadd into the anvil hard enough that he blacks out for a moment. As he slumps limply over the hard metal, Declan's heart catches in his throat, but it's not until Egan grabs one of the hammers from the floor and starts pounding it against Tadd as though Tadd is a piece of iron that Declan is able to move.

He flies across the room, using every bit of speed he possesses as he grabs Tadd and flees the forge, not caring that they didn't get the information they needed or that Egan isn't cooperating in their investigation. He'll go back later—alone—and give Egan a piece of his mind, but right now the only thing Declan cares about is the limp body in his arms. Tadd is too still, too unresponsive, and as he flies home as fast as his abilities will carry him, all Declan can think about is how they now know gods can die.

He can't let that happen to Tadd.

TADD opens his eyes as Declan lays him down on their bed. "Uhh," he groans, rolling his head to the side so he can peer at Declan through heavily lidded eyelids. His fingers tighten on the quilt beneath him, and he blinks as he realizes where he is. "How'd I get here?"

"I carried you." Declan tries to keep his tone flat, but it breaks on the last word. He's practically shaking with relief that Tadd woke up so quickly, but he's still bleeding, and Declan can see bruises forming on his arms and shoulders. Tadd is alive and safe, but he's not okay yet.

"Why?" Tadd winces as he shifts on the bed, but his expression is earnest and determined as he stares up at Declan. "You didn't have the answers you needed."

"Egan was trying to kill you!" Declan barely resists the urge to lean in and shake Tadd by the shoulders. "I wasn't going to sit there and let him!"

Tadd pushes himself up, wincing. "Did he hurt you?" He brushes his hands over Declan's chest and shoulders before settling on the purpling bruise on his right forearm. "Have you done anything about this?"

"No!" Declan yanks his arm away from Tadd, cradling it to his chest to protect it from Tadd's questing fingers. "I was too worried about you!" He brushes his thumb gently over a cut on Tadd's cheek. "I'm not the one he hurt, Tadd."

"I'm fine." Tadd bats Declan's hand away and again fixes his gaze on the blossoming bruise on Declan's arm.

"No, you're not!" Declan cups his hands around Tadd's chin and looks him straight in the eyes. "He twisted my arm—and yeah, it hurts—but he was trying to bash your head in with a hammer, so don't tell me you're okay!"

"Declan—"

"No!" Declan shakes his head and leans forward so he's resting his forehead against Tadd's. "He was trying to kill you. I know you're the god of war and you're supposed to get into fights and I'm just a messenger, but Tadd, you can't do that."

"Do what?" Tadd slides his hand up and curls it around the back of Declan's neck as he tilts his head and kisses Declan softly. "I was keeping you safe."

"You have to keep yourself safe too." Declan lets out a slightly hysterical laugh. "I'm not supposed to be the one rescuing you."

Tadd pulls back and gives Declan a serious look. "You shouldn't have. I would have been fine."

Declan's mouth drops open and his eyes widen. "No, you wouldn't! He was—"

"He was using iron and he was mad." Tadd concentrates, and the cut on his cheek heals, leaving no trace of the injury behind. "He wasn't trying to kill me, just to hurt me."

"And that's better?" It is, in a way, because it means Tadd is still around, but Declan can't stand to see Tadd hurt any more than he can stand to think about the idea of Tadd dead, and his voice breaks thinking about it.

"Uh, yeah?" Tadd kisses Declan's forehead. "I'm going to be fine, see?" He concentrates again and heals more of his injuries. He doesn't seem have the energy to take care of them all at once, which is a little worrying, but he's only going to need a few minutes. He is a god, after all, even though his powers are diminished by centuries without proper worship. He was made to survive battles.

"Yeah, but—" Declan breaks off, shaking his head. Even with the visible reminder Tadd will be fine, he's still feeling shaken. "Don't do that again, okay?"

"If anyone else tries to hurt you, I'm going to stop them." That isn't up for negotiation, a fact Tadd makes clear with his steely tone.

Declan responds with a weak laugh. "How about we both run next time, okay?"

"So they'll come after us again?"

"No, just—"

"Declan." Tadd takes Declan by the shoulders and ducks his head a little so he's looking straight into Declan's eyes. "I'll try to, uh, tactically retreat after I've gotten them off you, okay? But I'm not going to just run. That's your strength, not mine."

"I know, but we're best when we combine our strengths."

"Combining them means I use mine too."

"It doesn't mean you let yourself get beat up," Declan says emphatically. "You could have just clocked him a good one and then we could have left. He would have gotten the picture."

76

"Maybe."

"If he hadn't, you could have clocked him again."

"It's not always that simple."

"Humor me, all right?" Declan gives Tadd a watery smile. "Just promise me you won't jump into any more fights like that. Please."

"I'll do my best to avoid them." Tadd rubs his thumb over Declan's lips. "That's all I can promise."

Declan's smile becomes slightly more genuine. "Okay." He nods. "Okay. I can live with that." His expression becomes serious for a moment before he pulls Tadd in for a desperate, passionate kiss. "Thank you," he whispers into Tadd's mouth.

Tadd doesn't pull back to answer. "You're welcome." He slides his tongue into Declan's mouth as he finishes speaking, and for a long moment, neither of them says anything. When they pull apart, Tadd grins. "I love you."

"Love you too," Declan whispers, kissing Tadd again before pulling back and looking him up and down. "Now finish healing yourself so we can go talk to Adara. I don't think she wants to see us looking like this."

Tadd lets his eyes roam up and down Declan's body. Aside from the red mark on his arm, he looks fantastic, muscles bulging from under his tank top and his skin still glistening with sweat. "Oh, I don't know," he teases. "I think she'd love to see us looking like this."

"Yeah, well, I don't want her to." He gives Tadd his best stern look. "Heal and change."

"How about I heal and then you can help me change?"

"Tadd!" Declan's lips twitch into a small smile despite his best efforts to keep them straight.

"Yes, Declan?"

"Come on. We have work to do."

"You're no fun."

Declan climbs off the bed and heads toward the closet. "Yes, well, you love me anyway."

Tadd grins.

FOR once, Adara isn't out by the pool, nor is she dressed impeccably. She looks terrible, something neither Declan nor Tadd has ever been able to say before in the thousands of years they've known her. Today, with her hair a mess and her eyes bloodshot, that's the only word that comes to mind.

"You again," she sniffs when they appear in her living room. "I knew you'd be back."

"We said we would." Declan sits down on the couch next to her, close enough to touch, with his knees angled toward her, and clasps his hands in his lap. "We need to talk to you, to figure out who did this."

"Don't you think I did it?"

"We don't know who did it right now, Adara," Declan says in the calmest tone he can manage. "We're exploring all the possibilities so we can figure it out."

"Right. Of course you are." She tosses back a glass full of rosy liquid and sighs happily. "You'd better hurry up, then. Or maybe you'd rather wait until I start babbling. I might do that when I'm drunk. I can't remember. It's been too long."

"Drunk?" Declan looks over at her with wide eyes. "Adara, is that—?"

Tadd crosses the room with swift steps and pulls the glass from Adara's hands. "Ambrosia," he says, sniffing at it.

"Really?" Declan takes the offered glass from Tadd and wafts it under his nose. His eyes flutter closed involuntarily as he inhales the divine scent. It's been centuries since he's had any, yet he can still taste it on his tongue as he inhales.

Adara snatches the glass back before he can give in to temptation, and cradles it against her chest as she pulls her knees in and peers at him through reddened eyes. "Get your own glass," she says quietly, gesturing toward the wet bar in the corner. "It's over there."

"Tempting, but we're working," Tadd replies, taking a seat in the armchair. Adara isn't exactly a threat to either of them, especially not half-drunk and completely unprepared to face the day. All they'd have

78

to do is step outside and she wouldn't dare follow, not without showering, fixing her hair, and putting on something other than ratty pajamas she had to have dug out of the very back of her closet. No one would believe she's the goddess of love, not today, not looking like this.

"Turning down Ambrosia?" She snorts. "That's a first."

Declan deliberately looks up and down Tadd's now healed body before directing his gaze to Adara's face. "If we drink, we'll miss something, and we might not figure out who killed Cal in time to stop them from killing someone else."

Adara clutches her glass tighter. "Do you really think they will? Kill again, I mean," she adds after taking another sip of the thick rosy liquid.

"Probably." Declan keeps his voice low both so he doesn't irritate the headache Adara has to have and because he doesn't really want to talk about this. "Whoever did this knows we're looking for them. I don't know why Cal and Sofia were killed, but I do know whoever did this won't stop until anyone who might be able to give them away is dead."

Adara swallows hard, downs the rest of her glass, and holds the empty tumbler out to Tadd. He takes it and refills it without a word as she turns to Declan. "I didn't kill him, Declan." She lays a hand on his thigh, the touch only a shadow of the one that had so irritated him the first time they came over here to speak to her about Cal. "You have to believe me."

Declan doesn't bother to pull away. He needs her as calm as possible, and if letting her touch him helps her achieve that, he'll play along. "I'm not saying you killed Cal, Adara. I need you to go over what happened that day, okay?"

"Yeah. All right." Adara takes a sip of the Ambrosia and sets it down on the side table. "I didn't even know Cal was coming. He called while I was talking to Lukas, and—"

"What were you talking to Lukas about?" Tadd slips a coaster under the tumbler and catches Declan's eye. It's not like Adara to set glasses on unprotected wooden furniture—she's all about appearances—but not much that they've seen today is at all like Adara. It's almost frightening.

"Does it matter?"

"Yeah." Declan lays his hand over Adara's and squeezes. "It does. If we're going to corroborate everyone's stories, we need to hear them."

"Yeah, but—"

"Please, Adara." Declan pulls out his best pleading expression, the one that's gotten countless bits of knowledge and thousands of items out of unsuspecting people. It's exactly the sort of lost puppy look Adara can't resist, and she sighs as she reaches over and grabs her glass.

"I was supposed to be alone all day, you know," she says after taking a long swallow from the tumbler and setting it back on the table. Tadd has to move the coaster a little so the glass doesn't topple off it, but at least she aims for it this time. "All you people stopping by, popping in unannounced, it was stressing me out." She lets out a hysterical laugh. "I was worried I was getting wrinkles!"

"You're a goddess," Declan says dumbly. Of all the things he thought Adara might say, that wasn't one of them. "You don't get wrinkles." At least, she wouldn't get ones she couldn't will away, not without some magical intervention. They only have limited control over their physical appearance—hence the reason Egan still limps to this day—but worry lines aren't one of the things they are incapable of fixing.

"I know!" She fumbles for the glass again, takes a long sip, and sets it back on the coaster. The more she drinks, the better her aim gets. "That's why it's so ridiculous! I was going to spend all day relaxing, lying in the pool and drinking martinis or something, and then Lukas called. He said he wanted to talk to me about some business proposition. I told him no, I'd taken the day off, but he swore it would be quick, and I didn't want to worry about him pestering me all day, so I gave in and told him to come over."

"What did he want to talk about?" Declan catches her flailing hand between his and curls his fingers around it as he looks her straight in the eyes.

"He wanted to set up a memorial fund. For—for Sofia. Said we could, you know, donate to the museum or something, fund the, uh, the Greek exhibit she was working on." She shakes her head but makes no move to pull her hand back from between Declan's. "I told him that was a bad idea—I don't even know her officially, and it would attract attention to all of us—but he said it didn't matter because a bunch of other companies would donate too."

Declan frowns. It does seem odd, but Lukas had admitted to knowing Sofia, not just Athena, so maybe it hadn't occurred to him the rest of them didn't. "So he was trying to convince you to donate when Cal died?"

"No. Well, yes. Sort of. But that's not how it started."

"How did it start?" Tadd crosses to the wet bar and pours three glasses of water. He hands one to Declan, sets one next to Adara's glass of Ambrosia, and settles back in the armchair, sipping at the third.

"I wasn't exactly presentable when he called," she says, sounding slightly hysterical again. "Though I guess that shouldn't have mattered. I mean, I looked better than I do now, and it's not like he was any more interested in my charms than the two of you are."

Declan doesn't say anything about whose fault that is, but he does exchange a glance with Tadd. The corners of his mouth twist into a grimace before he directs his attention back to Adara.

"I told him to give me two hours so I could freshen up and prepare myself to deal with people. That was my first mistake." She fumbles on the side table until she finds the Ambrosia and downs the rest of the glass.

"He didn't wait?" Tadd takes the empty glass and replaces it with the one full of water.

"No, he did." Adara makes a face as the water hits her tongue, but she drinks the whole glass before handing it to Tadd as well. "My husband didn't."

"Your husband?" Declan takes a sip of his own water.

"Egan." Adara's tone leaves little doubt she's questioning Declan's intelligence, but he ignores her, and after a pause, she goes on. "He came over maybe, I don't know, an hour, hour and a half, after Lukas called. Just showed up, like always. He wasn't happy when I told him Lukas was coming over, but it's not like he ever is, so I ignored him. Only yesterday, he was really not happy. He and Lukas got into it as soon as Lukas got here."

"They fought."

Tadd isn't asking a question, but Adara answers anyway. "Yeah. Argued, really. I mean, there weren't fists flying or anything, but they were yelling. It's a good thing I don't have close neighbors."

Declan's gaze flickers over to the wet bar. The Ambrosia is sounding better and better, but if he's going to make it through this round with Adara and then talk to Lukas as well, he's going to have to stay sober. Unfortunately. "So how did you end up talking to Lukas, then?"

"Oh, Egan backed off eventually." Adara waves a hand dismissively. "I told him he could either wait his turn or not have one at all. I'm sure you can imagine how well that went over."

"So he was mad, then."

"When isn't he?" Adara totters across the room and pours herself a fresh glass of Ambrosia. "He thinks everything should be handed to him on a platter, thanks to his fucking foot, and he gets pissed at me if I'm not at his beck and call like some old-fashioned housewife! Ugh! If he wanted someone to stay at home to cook and clean and do whatever he wanted, he should have married Hestia!"

Declan takes the drink from her hands as she collapses back on the couch. "You know, Adara, it's a little ironic you have so much trouble in your love life."

"I wouldn't if I wasn't forced to marry that good-for-nothing blacksmith." She crosses her arms over her chest and honest-to-Zeus pouts.

Declan sets the Ambrosia on the far table, where she'll have to crawl across him to reach it, and shakes his head. The situation with Egan and Adara isn't fair to either of them and hadn't been even back when they were simply Hephaestus and Aphrodite, but Declan can't say he regrets it. If Zeus hadn't forced the two of them to marry, Aphrodite never would have cheated on Hephaestus with Ares, Hephaestus never would have tricked them and trapped them in the bed, Helios never would have seen them and had Hermes notify everyone else so they could be mocked and ridiculed, and Aphrodite never would have cursed them. If that hadn't happened, he wouldn't have Tadd, so as much trouble as Zeus's edict all those years ago caused, Declan can't regret it.

Tadd can't either, and the look he shares with Declan while Adara pouts is a mix of exasperation and amusement. "You're lucky I love you," he whispers in Declan's ear as he grabs the drink from the table, takes it back to the bar, and dumps it down the drain with a wince. Adara doesn't even notice, fortunately. The last thing they need at the moment is Adara getting even more upset because they're wasting her valuable Ambrosia.

"What happened after Egan and Lukas stopped arguing?"

"Egan went into the kitchen, probably to get a beer or something, and Lukas came in here with me."

"I thought Lukas was getting you a drink when Cal died."

"He was. So what?"

"So wouldn't he have gone to the kitchen?"

"I guess." Adara slumps further on the couch with her arms still crossed over her chest and the pout firmly entrenched on her lips. "He didn't get it from the bar, so I don't know where else he could have gone. Out, maybe."

"If Lukas went into the kitchen, then Egan wasn't in the kitchen," Tadd murmurs. "They both said they were alone when Cal died."

"Exactly." Declan turns a hard gaze on Adara. "Is there anywhere else Egan would have gone? Anywhere he could have been while Lukas was in the kitchen?"

"He could have been anywhere." Adara sits up with a huff. "He doesn't exactly care about my privacy or personal boundaries. He thinks it's his Zeus-granted right to snoop in all my stuff."

83

"Okay, so, Egan could have been elsewhere in the house, or he could have been outside." Declan is thinking aloud now in the hope that talking out his thoughts will lead to new ideas.

"Lukas might not have gone to the kitchen, either," Tadd points out as he sits back down. "He could have just said he was and gone after Cal. There's really no way to know unless there's a camera or something in there."

"Hardly. Cal was the one with exhibitionist kinks, not me." Adara gets through the sentence without her voice hitching, but it doesn't last. Her hands start shaking and she curls in on herself, drawing her knees back up to her chest and biting her lip to hold back a sob. "He would have loved the idea of a camera in every room. Probably had one."

Declan shudders. He really doesn't want to think about what Cal's kinks were. They were disturbing enough before, but now that Declan is trying to solve his murder, they're just morbid. "When did Cal get here?"

Adara makes a visible effort to pull herself together. "While I was talking to Lukas. He poked his head in, said hi, and headed out to the pool. I didn't even...." She sniffs. "I didn't even say anything to him, I was so uptight and frustrated. I could have... I should have...." She trails off into another sob that leaves Declan and Tadd looking at each other over her shaking shoulders.

Declan awkwardly pats her back. He much prefers delivering messages that let him leave as soon as the bad news is out. "So Cal got here before Lukas left to get you a drink."

"That's why Lukas left. I got irritated with Cal—just for being one more person here when I wanted to be alone—and...." She waves her hand but doesn't lift her head. "He said I needed to calm down."

"I can't imagine why."

The air in the room stills. Adara slowly turns to look at Tadd, rotating her entire upper body and drawing herself up straighter as she moves. "What?"

Her tone sends shivers down Declan's spine. "Adara, he didn't—"

"Yes, he did." She whips around to glare at Declan, her hair flying as her lips pull back into a snarl. "You thought it too. You both

84

think I'm hysterical and stupid and that I need to calm down so I can help you figure this out." Her eyes flash and she puts a mocking lilt on the last three words. "Well, guess what? I can't! I don't know who killed my son! If I did, I wouldn't be sitting here talking to you! I'd be out doing the same thing to them! So I'm sorry I can't give you any answers, but maybe if the two of you were less worried about each other and more worried about what you're supposed to be doing, Cal would still be alive!"

"Adara, we didn't—"

"I don't want to hear it!" She pushes to her feet, her whole body trembling with rage, and points toward the door. "Just leave! I've told you everything I can, so get out there and figure out who did this!"

"But—"

Adara whirls around faster than she has any right to be able to, and her outstretched hand slaps hard against Declan's cheek. He reels back, shocked, his hand covering the reddening mark before he's even fully registered what happened.

"Get. Out." Adara points back at the door again, this time with a steady arm. "Now."

Tadd steps forward, his hands clenched into fists. "Don't do that again." The warning is clear in his voice, but before either he or Adara has the chance to do or say anything else, Declan grabs his arm and pulls.

"Come on. We're done here."

"No, we're not."

"Tadd." Declan tugs again, pulling Tadd farther from Adara. "We're not going to learn anything else right now. Let's go."

"Fine." Tadd turns back to Adara, raising his finger to point in her face as he looks at her with a steely gaze. "I'll let this one slide because of Cal, but don't touch him again."

Adara's gaze narrows. "Don't give me reason to."

"You didn't—"

"Tadd!" Declan moves with all the speed he can muster, squeezing himself between Adara and Tadd before either of them can move. "Let's go. Now." He puts his hands on Tadd's shoulders and slowly walks him away from Adara, glancing over his shoulder as he moves to make sure Adara is letting them walk away.

She stays still, watching them through narrowed eyes until they're almost out of the room. Then she collapses back on the couch, pulls her knees up to her chest, and rests her chin on them as she waits for the room to empty.

At the threshold, Declan turns, meeting Adara's gaze for the first time since pushing Tadd away. "I'm sorry." She nods, and he turns back to Tadd. "Come on."

Tadd nods and leans around Declan. "I am sorry, Adara. We both are."

"I know. Just, please leave. I can't... I need to be alone right now." She buries her face in her arms without waiting to see if they go.



LUKAS is still in the office even though it's a little after five o'clock by the time Declan and Tadd make it to him. They stopped at home first, changed clothes after Declan let Tadd fuss over the rapidly fading red mark on his cheek, and grabbed either a late lunch or an early dinner, depending on how they looked at it. Apparently solving crimes doesn't leave any more time for eating regular meals than being a high-powered business executive does.

Actually, it leaves less. As high-powered business executives, they can schedule lunches on their calendars. As sleuths, they get distracted.

They're full, healed, and alert, ready for another agonizing conversation, but Lukas surprises them, standing when they enter the empty outer office and gesturing for them to come inside. "Declan! Tadd! Good to see you."

"Uh, yeah, you too, Lukas." Declan shakes Lukas's outstretched hand automatically as he tries to wrap his brain around Lukas's greeting. He'd fully expected Lukas to fall somewhere between Egan and Adara in willingness to talk, so the warm greeting is throwing him off track.

It's clearly throwing Tadd off too. He takes Lukas's hand as it's offered, shaking it and nodding. "Lukas."

"You want anything to drink? Coffee? Scotch?"

"We're good. Thanks."

Declan nods in agreement with his husband. "Later, maybe? After we talk." There likely won't be a later—this is the most cordial Tadd and Lukas have been to each other in centuries and Declan isn't about to push it by outstaying their welcome—but it's better than turning Lukas down outright and offending him before they get any information at all.

"Of course." Lukas leads the way over to the same table he and Declan had sat at earlier in the week. He waits until both Declan and Tadd are seated at the table before taking a seat between them, slightly closer to Declan than to Tadd. "What do you want to know?"

Tadd's jaw twitches and his fingers clench in his lap as he realizes the round table will effectively keep him from jumping between Declan and Lukas if the need arises, but he doesn't say anything. They're all being civilized at the moment, so there's no need.

"What happened yesterday?"

"Someone killed Cal."

Declan takes a deep breath while Tadd rolls his eyes. "All day," Declan clarifies. "What did you do from the time you first talked to Adara until we got there?"

"That's a lot of time." Lukas glances between Declan and Tadd with a raised eyebrow. "Are you sure you don't want something to drink while I talk?"

"I'm sure. Just...." Declan sighs and rubs his hand against the back of his neck. "Look, it's been a long day. Can you please tell me?"

Lukas looks at him closely for a moment and then nods. "Yeah, sure." He leans back in his chair before he starts, crossing his legs in front of him, and loosely clasps his hands in his lap as he clears his throat.

The story he tells matches Adara's almost exactly—at first. He confirms what time he called her and verifies Egan was already there when he arrived. He spends about ten minutes telling them about the argument he had with Egan, emphasizing the parts where Egan was loud, belligerent, and close to violence while downplaying his own role in the affair. It's definitely biased, but it's not unexpected, and since it happened before Cal arrived at Adara's, Declan lets it slide.

He gets more specific once Lukas starts talking about his conversation with Adara. "How long were you talking to her before Cal popped in?" he asks as Lukas tries to gloss over the entire encounter.

"I don't know." Lukas shrugs, looking a little tenser than he had when he'd sat down. "I wasn't timing it or anything. Twenty minutes, maybe thirty? It wasn't any longer than that, I'm sure."

"And Adara got upset when Cal said hello?"

"Well." Lukas twists his mouth into a wry grin. "I think she was upset before that, but yeah. It started to show then. It's why I offered to get her a drink. I wanted to let her calm down a little before I tried to pick up our conversation."

Tadd leans across the table to ask the question that's been bothering him all afternoon. "Why didn't you get her something from the bar? It's right there, and that's where she keeps the strong stuff."

"She was into that today, huh?" Lukas shakes his head and then shrugs. "Can't blame her, really, but it's sad, wasting perfectly good Ambrosia on a grief binge."

Declan is halfway out of his chair before anyone else notices he's moving. "Her son was murdered in her backyard. I think she's allowed to get drunk. Even on the good stuff."

"Whoa!" Lukas holds up a hand. "I wasn't... it was a joke, all right?"

"A bad one," Declan mumbles as he sinks back down into his seat. "Now answer the question. Why didn't you get her something from the bar?"

"Because I wanted to give her a chance to cool down, like I said." Lukas shrugs. "She wouldn't have if I was still in the room; she'd have kept ranting and probably gotten pissed at me for touching her precious alcohol. I figured grabbing something from the kitchen would give me a good excuse to get away and her a few minutes to breathe deep and find her inner peace, or whatever she does to calm down these days."

He flashes a smirk that makes Tadd clench his fists. He's not a fan of Adara's, far from it, but even as irritated as he is with her, Lukas's callous attitude toward her grief is rousing the anger he usually works hard to suppress. This whole day has been a trial of keeping his emotions in check, and one more smarmy comment or smug look from Lukas—whom he also doesn't particularly like—is going to drive him fully over the edge.

Declan knows this, and the soft squeeze he gives to Tadd's hand under the table is in complete contrast to the less than amused look he directs Lukas's way. "How long after Cal left the room did you leave?"

"Cal didn't actually come into the room, you know." Lukas's grin fades at the twin flat looks Tadd and Declan give him. "Two, maybe three minutes after he poked his head in the door. It wasn't long. Just enough time to see Adara was upset and make the suggestion, really."

"And was anyone in the kitchen when you got there?"

"Nope. It was completely empty. Though there were a few beer bottles on the counter. Empties. Apparently Egan drinks fast."

This feels more like an interview than a conversation and, though Declan knows that's what he's here for, he misses the easy camaraderie he and Lukas had a few days ago. Getting Lukas to go over the day systematically with Tadd watching instead of teasing the information out of him with a real conversation is painful.

"So then what happened?"

"Cal was killed. I rushed out onto the deck, but it was too late. He was already dead."

"Did you see anything?"

"Just Cal floating in the water." Lukas frowns and shrugs. "There was no one out there, if that's what you were asking, but Adara was right behind me. She saw me walk outside."

Lukas doesn't mention Egan. On one level, Declan can't blame him—Egan isn't his favorite person, either—but it's almost as though he's trying to get Declan to question Egan's motives. He already was, but Lukas's reluctance to bring the other man up has Declan's inner alarm bells ringing, and he narrows his eyes as he leans forward to look straight at Lukas. "And Egan?"

"He saw me too." Lukas shrugs. "He appeared on the deck as I was coming out. Said he'd been upstairs when he felt it, and it was faster not to walk." He rolls his eyes, making his disdain clear.

There's a lot to be said about what Lukas told them, but Declan keeps every one of his comments to himself. "Thanks," he says instead, standing and holding out his hand. "If you remember anything else, let me know, okay?"

Something unidentifiable flashes across Lukas's face, but it's gone before Declan can pinpoint what it is, and he's all smiles as he rises and shakes Declan's hand. He shakes Tadd's too, though not as firmly, and nods his assurances that he'll call if he comes up with anything that will help. "I'm sure I'll see you soon," he promises, patting Declan on the shoulder as he shows them out of his office.

"Thanks, Lukas."

"You're welcome. Happy to help. Now go home and relax." The way he waggles his eyebrows says far more about what he really means than his tone.

Declan rolls his eyes, but Tadd looks pensive as they walk out of the building. "You know," he says in a low, teasing tone as he slides his hand into Declan's, "that's one suggestion of Lukas's I wouldn't mind taking."

"You wouldn't."

"Oh, like you would object."

Declan grins. He absolutely won't.

DECLAN is asleep when his phone rings. He doesn't strictly need to sleep, especially now that he's acting more like his true self than he has in years, but some human habits are nice, and sleeping curled up around Tadd is one of Declan's favorites. There's something remarkably soothing about lying tangled up with his husband, and there's absolutely nothing that warms his heart more than the way Tadd looks when he wakes up, his hair all mussed and his eyes still clouded with sleep. The way he looks at Declan in the morning, like Declan is the answer to everything he dreamed during the night, is Declan's favorite thing in the world, and as far as Declan is concerned, the best part about the curse Aphrodite threw at them all those years ago is he gets to spend the rest of eternity with Tadd looking at him like that every morning.

That doesn't mean he wants Tadd looking at him like that in the middle of the night, especially after the day Tadd had, so he silences the ringer as he carefully extracts himself from under his husband and takes the phone out into the hall. "Hello?" he whispers, keeping his voice low even though there's a door between him and Tadd. It's late enough that it's early again, and if Declan goes too far, he'll wake himself up enough that he can't get back to sleep. If he's too loud, he'll wake Tadd, and then neither of them will get any more rest.

"Declan?" Lukas sounds far too awake for the early hour, but the sun is peeking over the horizon somewhere in the world, so it's entirely possible that he's naturally awake already. It was once his job to pull the sun over the horizon, way back before humans decided it was easier for the earth to go around the sun like all the other planets, and put Helios and Apollo out of a job.

He still remembers that day. Humans had long since stopped believing it was the gods who pulled the sun around the earth, but they still believed they were the all-important center of the universe, and so if Apollo or Helios was bored, they were able to hook up the old chariot and ride across the sky with the sun. Then, seemingly without warning, the world shifted, the universe twisting around itself as it realigned to the beliefs of the majority. When it finally settled again, the sun was no longer a ball that could be towed across the sky but a large, burning star that the earth circled around.

Humans always underestimate the power of belief. That wasn't the first time the earth shifted, nor would it be the last—the universe regularly realigned itself as human "understanding" shifted—but it was one of the more memorable ones. It also might be one of the last the gods of old are around to witness, if Declan can't figure out who is killing them.

He can't let himself dwell on that, though. Instead he slides down the wall to sit on the floor with his knees pulled up to his chest and the phone cradled between his shoulder and his ear. "Yeah."

"Good." The phone crackles as he sighs. "It's Lukas."

"Yeah. I know."

"Right. Sorry."

"It's okay." Declan lets his head fall back against the wall. It makes a dull thunk that immediately has him worried he'll wake Tadd, but the bedroom remains silent and Declan sighs in relief. "What do you want?"

"Is this a bad time?"

"No." Yes. "I was just—" He shakes his head. "I was asleep. Tadd is still sleeping."

"Sorry. I didn't mean to wake you."

"It's fine. Just tell me what you want so I can go back to bed. It's a lot more comfortable curled around Tadd than it is sitting in the hallway."

Lukas's chuckle sounds a little hollow. "You might not think so when I'm done."

"I doubt that."

"It's just—"

"Lukas!" Declan lets out an exasperated sigh. "Just tell me, okay? Whatever it is, stop beating around the bush and tell me, or the next time you piss Tadd off, I won't calm him down."

"Right. Sorry."

The phone goes silent and stays that way long enough that Declan pulls it away from his ear to check the call timer is still turning over the seconds and the call hasn't been disconnected. Declan is about to ask if Lukas is okay when a burst of static crackles in his ear.

"There's something I didn't tell you today."

"Okay...." Declan draws out the word, waiting for Lukas to elaborate. He figured as much from the moment he saw Lukas's name flash across the screen, but there's nothing he can think of related to the case Lukas would be afraid to tell him.

"Tadd got there before you today."

"I know." That's not news.

"Yeah, but, did you think about how?"

"What?"

"Look." Lukas pauses, swallowing so hard that Declan can hear it through the phone. "There wasn't anyone out on the deck when I got outside."

"You said that."

"Right, but what I didn't say was that Tadd stepped onto the deck right after we got out there." He puts a strange emphasis on the last few words.

"Okay." Declan is not awake enough for this. If Lukas doesn't get to the point soon, he's going to have to give in, wake up, and say good-bye to the idea of falling back asleep with Tadd when this phone call is over. "What's your point?"

"That he stepped onto the deck, Declan. He didn't appear there like you did, or Egan did. He was behind the fence, out in the yard, and he walked onto the deck."

"So he appeared in her yard instead of on the deck. Why does that matter?"

"Because it means he could have already been there."

Suddenly, it's crystal clear. Lukas didn't bring this up while they were at the office because Tadd would have jumped down his throat, and Declan would have let him. All thoughts of staying in the cocoon of fuzzy sleepiness and drifting off again as soon as he gets Lukas off the phone vanish, and Declan scrambles to his feet and hurries down the stairs so he doesn't risk waking Tadd as he hisses, "What in Hades are you implying?"

"I'm not implying anything!"

"Don't mess with me, Helios." For centuries, Declan has been the calm one, the rational one, the mellowing influence on Tadd's quick temper. It's led everyone into a false sense of security, let them forget he used to travel around the world, go into the most dangerous places and situations alone, and he always came back alive. Declan isn't a fighter by nature, but when he's threatened, he's more than capable of defending himself. Threatening Tadd is exactly like threatening Declan as far as Declan is concerned. Maybe worse.

"I'm not." Lukas's tone goes from concerned to cold in the blink of an eye. "I'm looking out for you. I know you love the guy, but that's blinding you to the facts. Tadd was there before you were, and he had no reason to be, not unless he knew about it in advance."

Declan's grip around the phone tightens until the plastic casing groans. "Don't you dare say that."

"I'm telling you this as a friend. That's all." His voice softens. "I'm worried about you."

It sounds genuine, and it twists at Declan's heart in a way he didn't think anything could. All of his anger flees faster than even he is capable of moving, and he's left feeling limp and boneless, worn out by the rage and completely hollow now that it's gone. He sinks into a chair at the kitchen table and lets his head fall forward to rest on his arms as his entire body deflates. "He wouldn't do that, Lukas."

"I'm not saying he would. I'm saying you need to think about it. Don't disregard him just because of who he is to you."

"Zeus didn't think—"

"Zeus wants you to solve this. He's going to tell you whatever you need to hear."

The soft, soothing tones of Lukas's voice hurt Declan more than his stammering suggestion or righteous indignation possibly could. The mere idea that Tadd could have done this, that he should even have to consider the man he loves, the man who balances him, the man he wants to spend the rest of eternity with, could possibly be responsible for the tragedies that are turning his world upside down is unfathomable.

And yet, he's thinking about it. He knows why Tadd beat him to Adara's, but, "He was home before me on Tuesday too." It's not something Declan wants to admit, but it's true. It had taken him a few minutes to gather himself together enough to leave the office, and when he'd arrived at home, Tadd was already crouched over Sofia's body, frowning down at the blood spilling out onto the tiles.

This time, Lukas's sigh feels as though it ghosts over Declan's skin as it crackles through the phone. "I was afraid of that. I don't want to say it, but Declan—"

"I can't. Lukas, I can't. I know everyone thinks he's this crazy, violent guy who likes nothing more than inflicting pain, but that's not true. He's... Zeus, there's so many sides to him you don't know. He's my husband, and I love him, and I can't believe he would do something like that. Not even for a second."

"That's why you have to." Lukas's voice is whisper-soft and hurts all the more because of it. "I'm not saying he did—there are valid reasons for him to beat you home and to Adara's, I'm sure—but you can't disregard him because he's your husband. If he's the one doing this...."

"I know." Declan pulls his hand out from under his head and lets it fall against the table. "I just... I can't picture it, you know? I see you being the killer more easily than I see Tadd doing it."

"Me? Really?" Lukas honest-to-Zeus giggles. "Come on, Declan. I mean, Egan I could see, but me? Why would I want to kill anyone?"

"That's my point." Declan lets his lips curl up into a tiny smile. "I was leaning toward Egan too, but...." The smile falls off his face. "I don't know if I can look at Tadd that way."

"I know. I'm sorry. I almost didn't call, but I wasn't sure when I'd get to talk to you without him around, and I don't want anyone else to die. I liked Sofia, and I admit I had my differences with Cal, but that doesn't mean I wanted him dead."

"I know. And, I'm glad you did. Sort of." Declan sucks in a deep breath and lets it out slowly. "Thanks."

"You're welcome. And Declan?"

"Yeah?"

"If you ever need to talk, or whatever, you know you can call me, right? I know even thinking Tadd might be the killer has to be hard, and if you need anything—"

"Yeah, thanks." What Declan really needs is for Lukas to let the subject drop so he can attempt to wrap his mind around it by himself, but he knows his friend means well. "I'll let you know."

"Okay. Just... take care, okay?"

"You too."

Declan hits the End button on his phone with his thumb and lets his arm fall forward onto the table. The phone clatters as it hits the wood, but Declan doesn't hear it. His mind is too busy replaying the conversation he had with Lukas, mixing it together with the conversations he's had with Tadd since Sofia died, and adding in the argument from around the pool yesterday—two days ago, technically, since it's early morning.

Everything tangles together in his brain, words and actions blurring until he's no longer sure who did or said anything, and still, he can't move. Nothing makes sense, and now he's doubting the one person he was counting on to get him through this.

Things can't possibly get any worse.


DECLAN is still sitting at the kitchen table when Tadd shuffles downstairs earlier than he usually does on a Saturday morning. He peers blearily at Declan, rubbing his eyes as he takes in the way Declan is slumped over the table, his forehead resting against the hard surface and his fingers still curled loosely around his phone. Tadd crosses the room with swift strides, all traces of sleepiness vanishing as he takes in the dark circles under Declan's puffy eyes and the way he's curled up as small as he can get while sitting at the table. "Declan? What's wrong?"

"Everything."

Tadd swallows hard and crouches down next to Declan. He curls one hand around the back of Declan's neck, rests the other one on Declan's knee, and leans in so he can better see Declan's face. "What do you mean?"

"I can't—" Declan breaks off, shaking his head as he pulls away from Tadd and stands. His stomach is churning at the mere idea of asking this, but now that Lukas planted the seed, Declan isn't going to be able to think about anything else until he does. He has to know, but he can't ask with Tadd touching him and worrying about him. "I'm fine."

"No, you're not. You didn't come back to bed last night."

"I didn't mean to wake you."

"You didn't. The phone did." Tadd stands as well and takes a step toward Declan. "I kept waiting for you to come back, but you never did. I would have been down here earlier if I hadn't dozed off for an hour or so."

"I'm sorry."

"Don't be." Tadd frowns as Declan steps away from his outstretched hand. "Just tell me what's bothering you."

Declan sucks in a shaky breath and wipes his hands on his pajama pants. He wishes he had pockets to shove his hands into and a shirt to protect him from the sudden cold in the kitchen, but pockets won't help him get the words out and a shirt won't protect him from the cold that's coming from inside him.

"Lukas called," he says after a moment, swallowing hard as soon as he gets the words out.

Tadd's eyes go flat. "What did he have to say?"

"He wanted to make sure I was… aware… of certain things about Thursday." Declan lets out a slightly hysterical laugh. Standing here in their kitchen asking Tadd about this makes it seem like the stupidest thought ever, but he can't stop now. He'll always wonder if he does. "He said you didn't show up on the deck when Cal died. That you walked onto it right after he came outside."

"Yeah. I knew what happened as soon as I felt it, but I wasn't sure if the killer was still there or not. I didn't want to present an easy target, so I went to the yard and tried to look through the fence instead." Tadd tilts his head to the side curiously. "Why?"

"Did you see anything?"

97

"No...." Tadd draws out the word, letting his tone rise at the end to ask why Declan isn't answering his question.

"There was no one there when you got there?"

"Just Cal." Tadd furrows his brow and takes a step closer. "Declan, what are you trying to ask?"

"Already dead?"

"What?"

"Cal. Was he already dead when you saw him?"

"Yeah! I just said—"

"You just said he was the only one you saw. You didn't say he was in the pool or already dead or—"

Tadd's jaw falls open. "You're kidding, right? You're not really asking me if I killed him, are you?"

"Lukas pointed out you don't usually beat me places and you could have been there before they came out and stepped off the deck and hidden, or something."

"And any one of them could have killed him, gone right back inside, and then come back out! Anyone else could have killed him and left!" He steps closer to Declan, his eyes narrowed and his fingers clenched into fists at his sides. "Why in Hades would you think I killed him? I thought you trusted me!"

"I do!" Declan backs into the wall and lets his head fall back against it. "I just... I remembered you beat me home on Tuesday too, and then Lukas was questioning why you got to Adara's before me on Thursday. I know why you beat me there, and I don't think you killed anyone, Tadd, at least not outside of some war you've led, but I had to ask. Lukas said I couldn't let my feelings for you interfere in my investigation."

"Oh, Lukas said, did he? Well, what else did Lukas say? Did he try to convince you that you should turn me in to Bront? Or that you need to be careful or I'll kill you too?"

"No!" Declan steps forward, his hand outstretched toward Tadd. "He said he didn't really think you did it either, but he wanted to make sure I wasn't overlooking things because of my feelings for people! That's all!"

"So, what? The logical reason for me to beat you to the crime scenes is because I'm the killer?" Tadd dodges Declan's arm and steps in close, getting right up in his face and glaring with flashing eyes. "Maybe I beat you because you left and then came back! Maybe you were late because you were busy trying to hide the evidence that you killed them!"

"Tadd!" Declan staggers backward, floundering. "I wouldn't—"

"And neither would I." Tadd's lips curl up into a sneer. "You should know that, but you still had to ask."

"I needed to—"

"To what? To make sure? To soothe Lukas's fears? To make sure Lukas felt safe? Newsflash, Declan, the guy hates me. Always has. Did that occur to you when he was trying to convince you I was the killer, or did you take his word for it and not even think about the history?"

"He wasn't trying to convince me!"

"Then what in Hades was he doing?"

"Trying to help me!"

"And what I've been doing isn't?" Tadd steps back with a sneer. "I guess watching your back and stepping in to save you in a fight isn't nearly as useful as calling and insinuating untrue things about your husband. Clearly, he's the one with your best interests in mind." He snorts as he turns on his heel and heads back toward the stairs. "Why don't you have Lukas help you with the rest of your investigation? I'm going back to bed, since I was up half the night worrying about you."

Declan stares with wide eyes as Tadd stalks out of the room. He's frozen, his fingers still partially curled into fists and his jaw slack. He can't move, can't think, can't process anything besides Tadd's scathing tone and the way he's stalking from the room as though he's going to storm out of Declan's life forever.

It's that thought that gets him moving again. The fear of losing Tadd pierces through his heart, shoving away his shock and dismay and forcing his feet to move. "Tadd!"

"What?" Tadd whirls around, his hand gripping the banister and one foot on the bottom step. His shoulders are drawn back, his eyes wild, and his mouth is set into the scowl that terrified thousands of mortals back in his heyday. He's practically trembling with anger, the power he's capable of unleashing vibrating beneath his skin. This is Ares, god of war, famous for his temper and renowned for showing no mercy. All that's left of Tadd are the navy pajama bottoms hanging low on his hips. Everything else is pure Ares, violence and temper barely restrained as he glares at Declan.

"I'm sorry." Declan keeps his eyes locked with Tadd's as he walks forward. "I trust you. And though Lukas may have a point about not letting my feelings for people get in the way of this investigation, I shouldn't have doubted you."

"But you did." Tadd's voice is steely as he steps down onto the tile floor and stalks across the distance between them. "You had to ask. Not only that, but you were afraid of the answer! You actually thought, even if it was just for a second, that I could have done that. That Lukas was right and I was the killer. You doubted me."

"I know." Declan ducks his head and then forces himself to look up and meet his husband's eyes. Tadd is angry, his true power barely contained as he stares Declan down, but Declan doesn't back away. Even he probably can't move fast enough should Tadd decide to act, but it doesn't matter. He trusts Tadd, despite what he said earlier, and this is the only way he knows to show it. "And I'm sorry."

"You should be." Tadd stares at Declan for another moment before spinning on one heel and stalking back toward the stairs. He doesn't say anything as he pounds up them, his footsteps echoing in the foyer that suddenly feels far too large.

Declan follows, moving lightly on swift feet, and catches up with Tadd at the top of the stairs. "That's it? You're going to walk away after I apologize?"

"What do you want me to do, Declan? Give you a hug and tell you it's all okay? I can't do that. You doubted me."

"Only for a second!" Declan sucks in a deep breath. "I'm sorry. I told Lukas I couldn't think about it, no matter how compelling the evidence was, but he pushed. I shouldn't have asked you, but he brought it up and I don't know who did this. I don't know if it was Egan, or Adara, or Lukas, or someone else entirely, but if he brought it up and I didn't ask and I accused somebody who knew he'd brought it up...." He lets out a hollow laugh, shaking his head as he looks up at the ceiling. "I didn't want it to bite me in the ass."

"Yeah, well, it did." Tadd crosses his arms and stares straight into Declan's eyes. "Next time you need to ask me something so it doesn't come back and bite you, find a better way." He vanishes before Declan has the chance to respond.

# Aphrodite

Tadd flashes from place to place, his whole body trembling with rage as he struggles to think of an outlet for his anger. He wants to throttle Declan, to shake him and shake him until whatever bit of idiocy let him think, even for a second, that Tadd was responsible for Cal and Sofia's deaths falls out, and he wants to pummel Lukas for daring to suggest the idea. He can feel the rage building within him, the primordial desire to hurt and kill growing with each passing second, pushing away the persona of Tadd Leventis and leaving only Ares, god of war, bloodlust, and slaughter.

He flashes through his office and Declan's, through the personal gyms he keeps at home and at work, and through several of Omega Industries' firing ranges and weapons-testing facilities, never staying long enough for mortal eyes or mortal equipment to register. He needs to go somewhere, to burn off this anger before it consumes him, but no place he stops seems right. He needs to destroy things, to rip things apart with his bare hands while he yells and screams his anger to the sky, but there is nothing in any of those places that will let him do that.

Instead, he keeps moving, branching farther afield, stopping in war-torn cities and jungle guerilla camps. There's slaughter in every one of these stopping places, enough that Tadd could join in and not be noticed at all, but it's still not right. These are wars and, as such, are his domain, but what he's feeling is too personal to be satisfied by joining in a large-scale battle. This needs to be about him and no one else, and the tiny spark of Tadd that remains within Ares reminds him he wants to limit the collateral damage. None of the mortals he sees had anything to do with what he's feeling, and even in his anger, the thought of Declan's disapproval sends him on before he finds an excuse to take it out on them.

Eventually, he ends up in the deep jungles of Africa, far from any people he could inadvertently harm. He's still trembling, his fingers clenching and unclenching as he extends his senses, struggling to hold on to that last bit of what separates Tadd from Ares as he makes sure the area is clear.

The second he knows it is, he unleashes the anger he's barely been keeping in check, letting out a scream of primordial rage as he attacks the flora with his bare hands, ripping bushes from the ground and tearing limbs off trees, snapping them like twigs. He hacks at a sapling with a torn-off branch, beating on it like it's a practice dummy and the branch is a sword until the sapling slumps over and he tosses the branch aside to rip it from the ground. It pulls from the dirt with far too much ease, and he throws it as well, yelling out his frustration as it crashes into another tree. He keeps moving, pulling small trees out by their roots and throwing them into larger ones, tearing branches off of larger trees, hurling nuts and fruits into the jungle with all the force he can muster.

Small animals scatter from his wrath, scurrying over tree branches and taking to the air as quickly as they can, chattering and squawking reproachfully as they flee the path of destruction. Tadd ignores them, trusting they'll get out of his way as he tears through the jungle, ripping apart everything he touches as he curses and screams. "Stupid fucking asshole!" He hurls a large boulder at a tree, growling when it sends a shower of leaves and nuts to the ground but fails to dislodge the branch.

"Dammit! Stupid, fucking…." Tadd continues cursing as he throws rocks and branches and kicks at roots and stumps. Even the vegetation seems to be fleeing, getting scarcer as he grabs at it, his hands hitting air more often than not. Each miss irritates him further, and when his fingers barely scrape against a branch he was reaching for, he lets out a loud, long yell that leaves the trees shaking.

When the echoes cease, the area seems completely silent, and it's then Tadd hears it. The bellow slowly filling the void left when Tadd's scream died is low and far away, but challenging. He recognizes the noise, and when he glances over his left shoulder, he can see flashes of black and silver as the beast slowly moves through the jungle.

It's a threat, a real one, something that could do Tadd real harm and let him feel his own blood flowing over his limbs as he tears it apart piece by piece. For a second, he's thrilled, every nerve tingling with anticipation as he envisions chasing after the gorilla. He smiles as he imagines the second he can curl his fingers in the gorilla's fur and actually fight something that wants to hurt him as much as he wants to hurt it. He buzzes with anticipation, imagining taking his anger at Declan out on the poor beast, but then he thinks about telling Declan and he loses all enthusiasm for the prospect.

His stomach knots, twisting with an entirely new feeling, and without even a regretful glance over his shoulder, Tadd vanishes.


DECLAN sighs as he looks around Tadd's empty office. He'd hoped he would find Tadd here so he could finish apologizing and start trying to make things right, but the moment he walked through the front door and got an odd look from the security guard, he knew it wasn't going to happen. Bruce had waved Declan up anyway, probably assuming he was here to fetch something Tadd had left behind, and on the ride up, Declan had tried to convince himself maybe Bruce didn't know Tadd was in, but he'd realized it was futile even before he'd slid his key into the lock and stepped into Tadd's office.

The dim lighting and tidy surfaces are soothing, a stark contrast to the boiling anger Declan had felt from his husband right before he'd disappeared. On the drive over, Declan had hoped the atmosphere would calm Tadd's nerves some, just as he had hoped driving over instead of appearing in Tadd's office or using his speed to get there as quickly as possible would give Tadd a chance to cool down.

Clearly he was wrong on both accounts. When he concentrates, extending his senses and trying to find Tadd, he can feel the shadow of Tadd's presence, but it's too faint for him to have been here long, and all the other shadows of Tadd's position Declan finds are just as faint and fleeting. He could follow them, track down Tadd the old-fashioned way relying on his skills as both spy and messenger, but it only takes a moment to realize that is an extremely bad idea.

Instead, he pulls a piece of paper from the pad on Tadd's desk and writes a short, sweet note he hopes will catch Tadd's attention and persuade him to at least listen to what Declan has to say. He folds it in half, scrawls Tadd's name on the outside, and leaves it propped up like a tent card in the middle of Tadd's otherwise pristine desk.

It's not perfect—Tadd will still have to look at the desk to see it, and he could conceivably be here for some time before he does that—but it's better than if it were on his chair, over his keyboard, or propped up against his computer monitor. At least this way there's a chance reading it will be the first thing Tadd does when he gets here.

And if he goes home first, well, Declan has plans to be there too.

TADD is in the private workout room attached to his office, beating as hard as he can on the punching bag, when Adara walks in, leans against the wall near the door, and crosses her arms over her chest. She watches him for a moment, her eyebrow sliding higher with each punch he throws, and then sighs. "Did the punching bag do something to you, Tadd?"

"What do you want?" Tadd is not in the mood to deal with Adara's needy whining, and his fists clench tighter as he steps away from the bag.

Adara pushes herself off the wall and crosses the room with slow, sultry steps. "Touchy, touchy." She lays a freshly manicured hand on his shoulder. "Who upset you this morning?"

"Don't go there." Tadd jerks away from her touch and throws a hard punch at the bag, rattling its support chains. "Tell me what you want or leave. Now."

"Fine." Adara holds up her hands as she steps back from Tadd. "I need your help."

"And you think coming here and irritating me is going to get it?" Tadd grabs a towel from the bench, wipes it over his face, and dresses himself in more appropriate clothing with a thought. The pajama bottoms he was wearing when he left the house this morning were fine for working out his rage where no one could see him, but he's not going to carry on any sort of conversation with Adara wearing nothing but low-slung pajama bottoms. That's asking for trouble.

A disappointed look flashes across Adara's face as she follows Tadd into the office, but she doesn't say anything until they're both seated in the plush chairs in the corner. "I'm serious, Tadd," she says, staring at Tadd with wide, earnest eyes. "I need your help. Yours and Declan's."

She sounds genuinely worried, an unusual enough occurrence that Tadd forces himself to focus past his lingering anger and pay attention. "With what?"

"Egan." She sits up straight, lifting her head in a regal manner as she looks Tadd in the eyes. It only emphasizes how worn down she looks, giving Tadd a clear view of the dark circles under her eyes. "I think he might be the killer, and I think he might be coming after me next."

"What?" Tadd leans forward, putting himself in Adara's personal space. "Why?"

"Why do I think he's the killer or why do I think he's coming after me next?"

"Both."

Adara gives him a watery smile. "It's the same reason, really. He, uh, came over this morning—uninvited as usual—and got upset with me when I told him I wasn't in the mood for his bullshit."

Tadd winces. He can only imagine how well that went over with Egan. "Ouch."

"Yeah, well." Adara shrugs. "Zeus only knows how I've managed to tolerate him for this long. It wasn't so bad back in the day, when I could keep having affairs to spite him, but then most of my favorite consorts became unavailable." She casts a slightly reproachful glance at Tadd.

He raises his right eyebrow and gives her an incredulous look. "That was your decision, not mine. You chose to curse us, and you chose what you cursed us with. Don't blame me for the fact it kept me out of your bed."

"I blame you for never wanting back in it enough," she says softly, slouching a little in the chair. She looks small now, vulnerable and strangely alluring, but Tadd knows better than to fall for her wiles. "You could have convinced me to lift the curse if you'd asked the right way."

Tadd shakes his head. He's happy with the way things turned out—he wouldn't have ended up with Declan if Adara hadn't cursed them both—but when she says things like that, it's difficult not to be bitter. "Why would I want to? You were the last person I wanted to get involved with again."

"I know." She sighs wistfully and shakes her head. "Sorry." Tadd nods and waits for her to pick up the thread of conversation. It takes a minute, but eventually she sits up, straightens her clothes, and looks him straight in the eyes. "Anyway, Egan got mad when I told him I was too upset about Cal being killed to do anything. He started yelling and screaming and…." She pushes up the flowing sleeve of her shirt to reveal a giant bruise on her arm. "He literally yanked me across the room when I tried to walk away."

"Shit." Tadd gently touches the livid purple bruise, then pulls back when Adara winces. "Why haven't you taken care of that?"

"I wanted to show it to someone." She closes her eyes, focusing her attention inwards for a moment, and the bruise fades away. "I wasn't sure you'd believe me otherwise."

"That wouldn't have been an issue. I still don't understand why you think he's the killer, though."

"Things he said." She twists her lips up into a wry smile. "We argued, only this time he kept telling me how stupid it was for me to be upset about my son being killed. He said Cal deserved it, he was glad it happened, and he hoped whoever did it managed to get away with it. I told him no matter how much Cal irritated him, he didn't deserve to stay in the Underworld for the rest of eternity, but that upset Egan more."

She pauses, sucking in a deep breath, and looks down at her hands. "He said if I didn't stop moaning about it, he'd make me."

107

"And that's why you think he's the killer?" Egan is definitely high on Tadd's list of suspects, but he's not convinced on the basis of an argument with Adara. Except that they fought—which isn't unusual—she's not telling him anything he wasn't already aware of.

"Mostly." She looks back up at him. "He said whoever killed Cal ought to be rewarded, not punished, and when I asked him if he knew who it was, he smirked." She chokes out the last word, gasping for breath and pressing her hand to her lips.

It's a beautiful display of raw emotion. Tadd isn't sure he completely believes it, but Adara is upset and Egan did clearly hurt her some, so he awkwardly pats her shoulder. "I'm going to call Declan, and we'll figure out a place you can stay."

"Can't you call Bront and have him do something about Egan?"

"Adara." Tadd scoots to the edge of the chair and looks her straight in the eyes. "I don't have any proof Egan is the killer, and Bront isn't going to do anything until we do. You know that."

"So, what, I'm supposed to hope you find it before he comes after me?" She stands, pushes past Tadd, and hugs her arms to her chest. "Great. That's helpful."

"No." Tadd carefully takes her by the shoulders and guides her back to the chair. "I'll arrange security for you." He's not sure who, but perhaps he can persuade one of the demigods to stand watch over her for a preview of some of Omega Industries' new weapons. Heroes do love their toys, after all, and it's not as though he expects to need them for long. "Declan and I will focus on Egan, see if we can dig anything up, and I'll let Bront know what we're doing, okay?"

"Yeah." She nods and sniffs as she sits.

"You'll be fine. Just... wait here while I call people, okay?" She's starting to irritate him again, and with the already tenuous hold he has on his temper at the moment, he needs to put a little bit of distance between the two of them, even if it's only stepping across the office to his desk.

Tadd pats his pockets as he crosses the room and bites back a curse when he realizes he left his cell phone sitting on the nightstand at home. Normally it wouldn't be a big deal—he'd pop home, grab it, and be back before anyone knew the difference—but he doesn't want to leave Adara here alone for even a moment. If she's right and Egan is looking for her, he doesn't want to be the one responsible for leaving her vulnerable.

The desk phone and computer will have to do.

He's mentally composing an e-mail in his head, thinking about how he wants to handle talking to Declan right now, since it really isn't the time to discuss their fight, and wondering who he can get to help guard Adara. He doesn't notice the note on his desk until he sits down, reaches for the phone, and knocks it over. It lands facedown, but he doesn't need to see the scrawled word across the front to know it's from Declan. It's something Declan always does when he can't find Tadd, something leftover from his days as a messenger, Tadd supposes. It's always amusing, especially since usually there are several other, faster means of communicating available, but Declan has a particular fondness for notes, and Tadd has to admit he likes them.

He smiles as he flips the folded paper and runs his finger over it. The outside simply states his name in bold block letters, and the paper is too expensive for him to see through, but he can imagine what's inside. His heart softens a little as he thinks about it. They're still going to need to talk later, but knowing Declan left the note lets Tadd push the rest of his anger aside and focus on the issue at hand.

He's midway through sending an e-mail to both Declan and Bront, since neither of them answered his call, when Adara's phone rings, filling the room with Chicago's "You're the Inspiration." As Adara stands and tries to fish it out of her pocket, Tadd stiffens, his spine ramrod straight and his fingers freezing on the keyboard. Every note grates on his nerves like fingers across a chalkboard, and as the song creeps toward the chorus, his jaw starts to twitch in time with the music. He's about to jump up and smash something, preferably the phone, when Adara finally pulls it from her pocket and answers it in a breathy voice that's almost as annoying as the ringtone.

As she talks, Tadd types, his fingers moving frantically across the keyboard. He needs backup on this, and fast.

Adara ends the phone call and perches on the edge of Tadd's desk, leaning over to touch his shoulder when he doesn't immediately turn to look at her. "I'm going into the office."

Tadd looks at her incredulously. "Excuse me?"

"I'm going into the office." Adara crosses her legs toward Tadd and taps the screen of her phone. "There's an emergency."

"You run a matchmaking service, Adara," Tadd says in a flat tone. "What could possibly be so important you have to go in right now?"

"You wouldn't understand."

"No, I wouldn't." He narrows his gaze. "You came here because you thought your life was in danger. Now you're telling me you're going to run off?"

"It's an emergency, Tadd."

"Is it worth your life?" He swivels the chair so he's completely facing her and crosses his arms. "What if Egan shows up?"

"He won't."

"What if he does? Do you want me to keep you safe or not?"

"I want you to do something about Egan! I didn't come here for a babysitter, Tadd! I came here because I want you to stop him before he hurts me or anyone else!" She slides off the desk. "I was trying to help us both. But never mind. I can take care of myself. You keep bumbling along while people die."

"Adara—"

"I said forget it, Tadd. If you decide to do anything about Egan, you know where to find me." With that, she vanishes, leaving Tadd to shake his head at the echoes of her anger.

DECLAN sighs and rubs a hand over his eyes as he stares at the computer screen. Trying to work on the case while waiting for Tadd to calm down seemed like a good idea when he thought of it, but his mind isn't focused on what he's trying to do, and he's not in the mood to be amused by any of the calls to Cal's 1-900 number. His program has identified a few possibilities, but nothing has panned out, and the sheer volume of calls remaining is daunting. For someone who appeared to do nothing but party and sleep around, Cal apparently took his business seriously and listened in on an amazing number of phone calls.

The stuff Tadd was looking at isn't much more interesting, at least not at first, but then Declan finds something odd. Buried deep in the files they pulled off Sofia's computer, he finds a payment from the museum to Egan's company. There's nothing in the records to indicate what it was for, but it gives Egan a connection to the museum that Declan was previously unaware of, and it's enough to raise his suspicions.

He needs to go check it out.

His first instinct is to change clothes and head over to the museum right away. It's a decent drive—about twenty minutes in no traffic—and that will be plenty of time for him to come up with a story that will get him the information he needs. If he goes now, he may have the answer they're looking for before lunch, and then he can concentrate on making things right with Tadd without having to worry about all the distractions.

On the other hand, if he goes now, he has to go alone, and that could lead to all sorts of problems. The last thing he wants right now is to upset Tadd more, and going off alone, especially after Bront specifically told Tadd to keep him safe, is certain to make things worse rather than better. Even if nothing goes wrong and Declan finds the information he needs, Tadd will get hung up on the what-ifs and could-haves and Declan's chances of making things right before the sun goes down will dwindle to nothing.

In the end, it's the fact that he doesn't know where Tadd is or when he'll be back that makes Declan's decision for him. This is literally a matter of life and death, and if going off alone and making things worse between the two of them is what it takes to save someone's life, then Declan will do it.

He compromises by leaving a note for Tadd as well as a message on the cell phone that's still sitting upstairs, telling Tadd exactly where he is and why he went and asking Tadd to meet him at the museum if he gets the message in time. Then Declan changes into work clothes, buttoning his shirt and tying his tie as slowly as possible in the vain hope that Tadd will show up while he's getting ready, and climbs into his car.

The museum is relatively empty this early. It's just after nine on a Saturday morning, barely visiting hours, and not many people managed to get up and out of the house to get through the doors when they first opened. Most of the staff are still going through their opening duties, straightening things and putting items out in anticipation of the larger crowds that will arrive as lunchtime approaches.

Declan ignores patrons and staff both and heads straight to the security desk set off to the side. The guard behind it is surprisingly fit, actually looking as though he could chase someone down. Declan doesn't think he actually does that—most museum thefts probably don't involve smash and grabs during the day, and tackling someone would likely lead to whatever they were stealing getting broken—but it's nice to see the museum is taking at least the appearance of security seriously.

Less than ten minutes after dropping his name and purported purpose in the security guard's ear, Declan is escorted around the side of the museum to the public offices, shown to a comfortable chair, and assured the man he needs to speak with will be with him momentarily. Five minutes later, a middle-aged balding man with a neatly trimmed beard enters the office.

He's wearing a well-cut suit that should look out of place on him but doesn't, and he immediately extends his hand to Declan after he closes the door. "Name's Ian Burke. Nice to meet you."

"Declan Anagnos." Declan takes the extended hand and shakes it firmly. "Sorry to come in so early on a Saturday."

"Don't worry about it," Ian says as he walks around the desk. "We're happy to talk to potential donors any time."

"Any time? Really?" Declan flashes a sly grin. "So I could have come at three in the morning?"

Ian chuckles, shaking his head, and the formal tension in the room drops as they both relax. "Well, almost any time. I do have to draw the line at donors who want to drag me out of my bed in the middle of the night. Unless," he adds, his eyes twinkling, "we're talking really large amounts of money."

Now it's Declan's turn to laugh, and he throws back his head, releasing the tension he's been holding all morning. "Well, Mr. Burke, I would like to make a substantial donation to the museum, but I don't know if it's quite that much money."

Ian leans forward. "How much are we talking, Mr. Anagnos? If you give me a figure, I'll tell you if it's something I'd give up my beauty sleep for."

Declan pulls a business card out of his pocket, writes a figure on the back, and slides it across the desk. It's a larger amount than his usual charitable donations—enough to get the museum's interest—but not so much it will raise many red flags with his financial team or with government auditors. "Well?"

Ian frowns thoughtfully as he nods at the paper. "I'd certainly stay up late or come in early for it."

"But not get up in the middle of the night?"

"Only if this were going to be a recurring donation. I like my sleep. Once I get in bed, it's almost impossible to get me out."

"My husband is the same way." Declan smiles fondly, forcing himself to ignore the pang in his chest as he thinks about Tadd. "Some mornings I wonder if he's going to get out of bed at all."

"He sounds like a man after my own heart." Ian meets Declan's smile with one of his own, holds his gaze for a moment, and then turns all business. "So, then, what do you need from me to make this donation happen, Mr. Anagnos?"

Declan scoots his chair closer to the desk and pulls his phone out of his pocket. He rests his forearms on the desk as he opens up a new e-mail and pulls up the keyboard. "Information."

Ian settles back in his chair and folds his hands in front of him. "On?"

"Museum operations." Declan looks Ian straight in the eyes. "I'd like to know how my money will be spent."

"I can provide—"

"I'm not interested in annual reports or anything I can find myself with a little digging. I want the details, Mr. Burke." Declan waves away the protest before it can leave Ian's mouth. "Just an example is fine."

"I can't—"

Declan glances pointedly at his donation offer. "Come on, Ian—can I call you Ian?—you and I both know there's a lot you can tell me for that amount of money. All I'm asking for is an example of how you put together a new exhibit like the Greek one that's opening soon. Just...." He shrugs. "Tell me where the money to pay for that came from and what it was spent on."

"And that's all you want?"

"Well, no." Declan grins widely and winks. "But that's all I'll ask you for, how's that?"

Ian stares at him for a moment and then lets out a hearty laugh. "I suppose it will do for now, Mr. Anagnos."

"Declan, please."

"All right, Declan." Ian pulls a file from his cabinet drawer and plops it on his desk. It's large enough to thud as it hits, and for a second Declan regrets this line of questioning. The feeling fades as Ian cracks his knuckles, and opens the folder. "Let's see what we've got."

Ian gives up a lot more information than Declan had hoped to get, and by the time Declan leaves, after shaking Ian's hand and patting him on the shoulder, the suspicions that brought him to the museum that morning are even stronger. He can't prove anything yet, but if he's right about what this means, he has something to tie Egan to the deaths of Sofia and Cal.

He barely manages to hold his pace to a jaunty walk as he heads to his car, and he's already cursing the need to drive the car home. He doesn't want to risk arousing suspicion by leaving his car, however, so despite how badly Declan wants to get home to offer what he's learned as an olive branch to Tadd, he's going to have to take the long way.

Traffic is horrible, as it always seems to be when Declan wants to go fast and has to move at a mortal pace, and the notes he took at the museum have drained the battery on his phone, so he can't even call Tadd to share what he found out. By the time he makes it through the door nearly forty minutes later, he's about to burst with excitement. He shrugs off his jacket and loosens his tie as he walks into the house, but before he can even call out to see if Tadd is home, a spark of fire races across his nerve endings, paralyzing him midstride. He gasps, calling for Tadd even though he knows Tadd won't be able to move for the next few seconds either, even if he is home, and tries to focus on the source of the agony.

He needs to know where to go to investigate this latest death.

THE lobby of Adara's office building is empty when Tadd arrives. He appears just inside the door at the same time as Declan and blinks as Declan flashes a tentatively hopeful smile. Tadd returns it with a nod that lightens his heart and moves quickly and silently through the building.

Declan speeds ahead, leaving Tadd behind as he moves toward the back faster than mortal eyes can follow, but even that isn't fast enough. He gasps when he reaches Adara's private office and takes a step back into the hall as he looks over his shoulder at Tadd. "Shit."

Tadd forces himself to move faster, though he knows there's little point now. When he reaches the office in the back eastern corner of the building, he sees Adara already dead, her blood spilling on the carpet, the dagger that killed her still embedded in her chest, and her body cradled in Egan's arms.

Egan glances up just as Tadd steps through the door, and blinks before his expression mutates from grief to rage. "You were supposed to stop this!"

Declan blinks, clearly caught off guard. His mouth opens and closes as he struggles to find the words to respond, and all he can manage is a few stammered syllables, a pathetic answer from the messenger god and the CEO of a communications company.

"Step away from the body, Egan." Tadd has no difficulty finding his words. He's fuming, his fingers clenched into fists and his chest heaving as he sucks in deep breaths that do nothing to calm him.

"Now." He steps in front of Declan, protecting him the way he failed to protect Adara.

"No."

Tadd takes another step forward, his eyes blazing as he glares down at Egan. "Don't make me force you."

Egan barks out a harsh sound that's part laugh and part sob. "You wouldn't."

"Try me." Tadd squares his shoulders as he sizes up the situation, trying to figure out how to best get Egan away from Adara's body without letting him get closer to Declan or risk him getting away. "I will make you, Egan, no matter what it takes."

Egan bristles, his eyes flashing as they meet Tadd's. "You have no right!"

"You have no right!" Tadd barely holds back on the punch he's itching to throw. "How dare you even touch her after what you did?"

"What I did?" Egan gently lowers Adara's body to the floor and stalks over to Tadd. He plants his hands on his hips as he glares up, and the anger in his eyes matches the fire in Tadd's. "I'm not the one who was supposed to keep her safe, though I would have done a much better job."

"She asked me to keep her safe from you!" Tadd takes another step forward, closing the distance so they're standing toe to toe. "She came to me after you threatened her, and she left because she thought she'd be safe here! I tried to stop her, but she said you wouldn't come here. I guess she was wrong."

"I came here to apologize." Egan steps back enough that he can cross his arms over his chest.

"Yeah, some apology." Tadd shakes his head and turns away. "Call Bront, Declan."

Declan slowly pulls his phone from his pocket, but before he activates the touch screen, Egan steps around Tadd and grabs Declan's bicep. "Don't!" Declan tries to jerk away, but Egan doesn't let go. "Listen to me! I didn't kill her. I was out front when she died."

Declan jerks again, futilely trying to free himself. "Let go."

"Listen to me."

Tadd steps forward, grabs Egan, and yanks him away from Declan. "He said to let go. I suggest you listen."

"And what if I don't? What are you going to do?"

Tadd squeezes Egan's arm and pushes himself between Declan and Egan. "I'll make you regret it. If you so much as look at him the wrong way, I'll—"

Declan cuts Tadd off by putting a restraining hand on his chest and leaning in so his lips are right next to his ear. "Tadd," he says, pitching his voice so it won't carry beyond Tadd's ear, "stop. Please." He slides his hand down Tadd's arm and carefully peels his fingers back, forcing him to let Egan go.

"He killed Adara, Declan." Tadd twists around so he's looking straight into Declan's eyes. "He was going to hurt you."

"You don't know that."

"I don't?" Tadd looks incredulously from the body to Declan and back again, then takes Declan's arm and drags him over to the corner of the room. "We found him standing over her body, Declan! What more evidence do you need?"

"He wasn't standing over it," Declan protests as he pulls free of Tadd's grip. "He was cradling her, and he says he didn't do it."

"Well, yeah, of course, let's trust him. I'm sure all murderers readily admit their crimes. I mean, he denied killing Sofia and Cal, but I'm sure he's going to change his mind this time." Tadd rolls his eyes. "He killed her, Declan, and if we don't do something right now, he's going to kill someone else."

"We need more evidence." Declan holds up a hand when Tadd opens his mouth to argue. "Look, I know it looks suspicious. But he wasn't holding the knife when I came in, and he really did look upset."

"That he got caught?"

"No." Declan shakes his head. "He looked upset before he even knew I was in the room, Tadd. I'm not saying he didn't do it. I'm saying we need more evidence. I mean, we were thinking Cal might have been the one to kill Sofia, and then he turned up dead. I'd hate to make the same mistake again. I need more evidence before I focus too much on Egan."

"Fine." Tadd crosses his arms over his chest. "How's this for evidence? Adara came to my office this morning, begging me to keep her safe because she was convinced Egan was the killer and she was going to be the next target. He told her Cal deserved what he got, and I saw the bruise he left on her arm."

"It's circumstantial." Declan sighs. "I found out a few things this morning that make me suspect him, too, but I don't want to jump to any conclusions. We'll keep an eye on him, make sure he doesn't hurt anyone else, and do some digging, okay?"

"Right, and how are we going to do that? There are two of us, Declan, and I'm not leaving you alone to go off investigating again."

Declan flashes a tight smile. "I managed to survive just fine this morning."

"Pure luck," Tadd asserts, ignoring the way his chest clenches at the thought of Declan off investigating on his own. He can't let himself feel that right now, not while they're standing a few feet away from Adara's body and he's still furious. "That doesn't mean you will be next time. You're not going alone."

"Then how do you recommend we handle this? I'm not calling in Bront based on circumstantial evidence. I need to know that Egan is the killer before I say anything."

Tadd rubs at the back of his neck. He's loath to even consider letting Egan go, but Declan is right. None of their evidence says firmly that Egan did it, and if they're wrong, the consequences could be disastrous. "Look. I don't like it, but maybe we can have someone else keep an eye on Egan? Pair people up, maybe?"

Declan laughs. "How do you propose we manage that without putting everyone else in danger? If Egan is the killer, whoever we ask to keep an eye on him is in danger. If he isn't the killer, whoever we pair with the real killer is in danger."

"We'll know who the killer is, then."

"After someone else dies," Declan points out with a sigh. "No. We can't."

"Then we should tell Bront we suspect Egan. He'll hold him while we get more evidence."

"We can't."

"Yes, we can. You don't want to."

"I know. I just—" Declan slumps back against the wall. "I know you're feeling guilty since Adara came to you and now she's dead, but I can't blame the first person we see. That's not fair to anyone."

"I'm not feeling guilty," Tadd protests. When Declan raises one eyebrow and looks at him pointedly, he sighs, his shoulders slumping in defeat. "Okay, fine. I am." Truthfully, he's beating himself up, but he's not going to admit that, not here, not where Egan can see him. Declan might get to know the full extent of his guilt later, but Egan will never know how guilty he's made Tadd feel. "But that doesn't mean that's why I want you to tell Bront. We've been thinking it's him."

"I know. But—"

Declan is cut off by a flash of lighting that fills the room, temporarily blinding and deafening them all. When it clears, Bront is standing in the center of the room, frowning down at Adara's body. Lukas is standing behind him, looking a bit shell-shocked and wide-eyed. Bront acknowledges his presence with a glance before turning his stony gaze onto Declan, Tadd, and Egan. "What in Hades happened here?"

The three of them all start talking at once, telling their own version of the story in response to Bront's question. The result is a babble that fills the room with both complimentary and contradictory sentences, grating on everyone's ears as they all increase their volume, vying to be the one whose story is heard the clearest.

"Silence!" Bront draws himself up to his full height as his command echoes around the room, stunning everyone into compliance at his display of anger. Though it had been typical of him in their heyday, Bront had mellowed over the years as he slowly transformed from Zeus into his current persona, and the sharp reminder of who he really is shocks everyone.

"Now," Bront continues in a calmer voice once everyone has complied with his request. "Declan, tell me what happened here."

Declan shifts nervously under Bront's intense gaze. "I felt someone die, followed it, and found Adara dead. Egan was already here, and Tadd arrived at the same time I did. I didn't see anything else." He throws a warning glance at Tadd. "We were about to talk to Egan when you arrived."

"You'd already started," Egan mutters, crossing his arms and glaring at them from his position on the other side of the room. "You jumped straight to conclusions without even considering I might have other reasons for beating you here."

"Like what?" Tadd draws himself up, holding his body threateningly as he stares at Egan with a narrowed gaze. "Adara was terrified of you. She asked me to protect her from you. So what reason could you possibly have to be here, alone, with her?"

"I already told you, I came to apologize."

"And what, you found her dead?"

"Yes!"

Declan steps forward and maneuvers around Adara's body to get closer to Egan. He looks relaxed, a direct contrast to the tension that's rolling off Tadd in waves, and arches one eyebrow. "Tadd and I only got here a few seconds after she died, Egan, and you were already cradling her body when I found you. How'd you have time?"

"I was already here when she died." Egan crosses his arms over his chest again. "I showed up in the lobby. I knew all the girls would be gone—they leave at noon on Saturdays—but Adara is usually here later, since she's never in before ten." He lets out a soft snort and shakes his head. "Apparently sleeping in is better for her looks."

"That doesn't explain anything, Egan." Tadd takes another step forward and draws himself up so he's looming. His fingers itch to grab a weapon, but he settles for merely flexing them. His eyes never leave Egan, though he's acutely aware of Declan standing behind him and Bront off to one side, watching with a stony expression.

"It explains why I was here. I was heading back to Adara's office when I felt her die. I ran, but by the time I got there, it was too late. She was dead and whoever killed her was gone."

"Convenient." Bront walks to the door of the room and turns to stare at everyone else in turn. "You were here when she died and didn't see anything. You failed to protect her this morning. You couldn't get

120

here fast enough. And you...." He pauses as he stares hard at Lukas. "You don't have any reason to be here."

"I followed you, boss." Lukas shoves his hands in his pockets and shrugs at Bront. "Seemed like the thing to do."

Bront looks at him for a moment before returning his gaze to Declan. "Another one of us is dead and you still don't know who the killer is. Why?"

The expression on Bront's face makes Tadd's blood run cold. It contrasts sharply with the laid-back persona he has adopted, and as his eyes narrow and his lips tighten, Tadd has to fight the instinct to cower and grovel. Zeus may be king of the gods, but Tadd is a powerful entity in his own right, and he's not going to start cowering from Zeus's anger at this point in time.

"I have a strong suspect," Declan says, casting another pointed glance at Tadd, clearly warning him not to say anything, "but I don't have any concrete proof, and I'd like to dig a little further before I say anything."

Bront stares hard at Declan for a moment, but Declan meets his gaze unwaveringly, and Bront eventually nods. "Dig quickly." He slowly looks around, taking in Tadd, Egan, and Lukas as well. "This can't happen again. Is that understood?"

"Of course." Tadd nods as he steps closer to Declan. He doesn't quite put himself between Declan and Bront, but he places himself so he can if it becomes necessary. Declan can flaunt his speed and pretend to be big and bad all he wants, but Tadd isn't going to let him get hurt, not even by Zeus.

"Good." Bront glares at each of them again before he stalks across the room, pulls the dagger from Adara's chest, and tucks it into his jacket pocket. He pauses to brush a stray lock of hair off her face before he straightens, gazes down at her body with an unreadable look in his eyes, and vanishes.

The crack of lightning that replaces him fills the room, throwing everyone backward and eliciting curses all around. When the smoke clears, they're sprawled near the walls and there's nothing left of Adara, not even a singed spot on the carpet.

Tadd climbs to his feet first and pulls Declan up, checking him for injuries with his eyes and his hands. Declan does the same thing, running his palms over Tadd's torso and looking hard into his eyes before nodding and directing his gaze to Lukas and Egan. "Are you two okay?"

Lukas accepts the hand Egan is holding out and nods as he climbs to his feet. "Yeah. You?"

"We're fine," Tadd says in a flat tone as he glares at Lukas, his earlier anger flaring up as Lukas's voice grates against his nerves. The man's presence reminds him of the fight he's still technically having with Declan, and though Adara's death has put most of that on the back burner, he's not going to bypass the opportunity to direct some of his anger at its other rightful source. Bront was right; Lukas doesn't have any reason to be here, and that makes his presence even more irritating.

"Just a little startled," Declan adds, squeezing Tadd's arm as he moves past him toward the other two men. "Egan?"

"Peachy." Egan straightens his shirt and scowls. "My wife's dead, you two incompetent assholes came barreling in here and accused me of killing her, and I got knocked across the room by her funeral pyre. It's exactly how I wanted to start my day. Now if you don't mind, I'm going to go home before the excitement gets to be too much." He vanishes before anyone can say a word, leaving them staring at empty air.

Declan snaps his mouth closed, swallowing the questions he was poised to ask, and turns to Lukas. "Where were you when Adara died? And why did you follow Bront here?"

"You don't think he'd admit it if he was here, do you?" Tadd pushes between Declan and Lukas, positioning his body so Lukas can't get at Declan without first going through him, and crosses his arms over his chest. It's not at all friendly, but Lukas has never been high on Tadd's list of favorite people, and his insinuations last night bumped him straight to the bottom.

Declan lays a hand on Tadd's shoulder and squeezes a lot harder than is strictly necessary. "I'm sure he'll tell us where he was if you give him the chance."

"And you'll just… believe him?" Tadd lets his earlier anger creep back into his tone. If it wouldn't expose his back to Lukas, he would direct the full force of his anger at Declan, but instead he settles for turning sideways and swiveling his glare between the two of them.

"What else would I do?"

"Not take everything everyone says at face value!" Tadd whirls quickly and jabs his finger into Declan's chest. "You're so used to listening to people that you believe everything everyone tells you, even when you know it's wrong! You told me this morning you shouldn't have trusted him"—Tadd flings his hand toward Lukas, almost hitting his cheek—"last night, so why would you now?"

Declan presses his lips into a thin line and sucks in a deep breath. "This is a little different, don't you think? I'm trying to place people, not accuse anyone. I just want to know where—"

"With Bront." Lukas grins sheepishly as both Declan's and Tadd's gazes snap to him. He shoves one hand into his pocket as he rocks back on his heels and rubs at the back of his neck with the other. "I'm sorry about last night," he starts, looking straight into Tadd's eyes. "My brain was working overtime, coming up with crazy ideas, but I shouldn't have said anything to Declan. I was worried. I didn't want, well, this to happen, and I over-thought things." He turns his gaze to Declan. "I really shouldn't be allowed to talk when I'm nervous or worked up or whatever."

"Uh-huh." Tadd arches one eyebrow. "So you thought accusing me of murder was a good distraction?" His tone takes on a harsh edge that makes Lukas back up a step.

"Yeah, I'm sorry. Really. Just…." Lukas holds up his hands in a gesture of surrender. "It was the first thing that popped into my head."

"Right. Well. That makes it better."

"Tadd." Declan steps a little closer. "Stop." He turns his gaze to Lukas. "Why were you with Bront today?" he asks in a hard tone that makes Tadd's heart flutter inside his chest.

Lukas sighs and shakes his head. "A meeting. Hera apparently informed Bront that she needs a new car, immediately, and he wanted to talk to me about producing a one-of-a-kind model for her." He twists his lips up into a wry grin. "I guess I'll have to reschedule."

The tension drains from Declan's shoulders and he shakes his head. "I guess," he says, letting a small smile form on his lips. "Or you could always, ah, forget." He makes finger quotes around the last word, making Lukas roll his eyes and shake his head and Tadd fight to keep the scowl on his face.

"I could," Lukas agrees, drawing the word out, "but I don't think that's the best idea. Bront probably told her about our appointment, and she'll be expecting something."

"And if he didn't, she'll still be expecting something."

"Right." Lukas nods at Declan. "So either way, I'm screwed. I'm better off rescheduling. Soon."

Declan nods his agreement, but the conversation ends there, and an awkward silence fills the room. Tadd waits a few beats to be sure the conversation is over, and then grabs Declan's arms and pushes him away from Lukas. "Great. You've established what Lukas was doing. Let's go."

Declan flounders, not quite ready to leave. There's something about Lukas's story that's rubbing him slightly wrong, and he feels like there's something important here he missed, but it's hard to focus with Tadd's anger filling the room. "We should—"

"There's nothing else here." Tadd keeps pushing Declan back toward the door. "Since you wouldn't let me make any accusations, we have some investigating to do, and not much time to do it in. We need to go. Now."

"Yeah. Okay." Declan flashes an apologetic smile at Lukas, steps back from Tadd, and goes straight to their kitchen. He's standing at the counter when Tadd appears next to him and immediately goes over to stare out the window into the backyard. Declan watches Tadd's fists clench and unclench for a moment before walking up to stand behind him. "You're still mad."

"Yeah." Most of Tadd's anger has been replaced by something closer to irritation and resignation, but it's easier to agree. He doesn't need anything else complicating things at the moment.

124

"I'm sorry."

Tadd sighs as he turns around. "I know," he says, pinching the bridge of his nose and sliding his fingers up to massage away the headache lingering behind his eyes. "That doesn't change anything, though."

Declan nods, swallows hard, and shoves his hands into his pockets. Usually when Tadd gets like this, he'll distract him, either soothing his anger with gentle touches or encouraging him to direct it somewhere that's more enjoyable for both of them. He can't this time, though, because usually it's not Declan Tadd is mad at. "What will?"

"Time." Tadd looks up and meets Declan's gaze. He hates feeling this vulnerable, but he's not ready to put everything that happened this morning behind him yet. "You didn't trust me, Declan, even if it was only for a minute, and that's not something I can just forget about."

"Yeah. I know." Declan reaches out toward Tadd, but stops himself halfway and lets his arm fall back to his side. He sucks in a deep breath, steeling himself, and pushes his hair off his forehead. "Can we, um…?" He shakes his head. "Shit."

Tadd's lips quirk into a grin before he can stop them. "Well, yes," he allows, his smile coming out in full force for a moment. "We can focus on the case, if that's what you were asking."

Declan lets out a sigh of relief. "Yeah. Thanks." He twists his lips up into a small smile. "You want to, uh, go see what the computers have turned up?"

Tadd closes his eyes and centers himself, focusing on relaxing tense muscles and releasing the tight knot of anger in his chest. When he looks up at Declan again, he's able to match Declan's smile and actually mean it. "Yeah. Come on."


"IT'S my fault Adara's dead."

Declan looks up from the program running searches on Cal's recordings. He widened the search, including Egan's and Adara's names in it as well in the hopes he can find something besides their history linking them to either Cal or Sofia, and now he's watching the

125

results scroll across the screen almost faster than he can read. "What do you mean?" he says, furrowing his brow in confusion. "I know you didn't kill her, so how is it your fault?"

Tadd lets out an unamused laugh that makes him sound slightly crazy. "I'm glad you realize that, at least."

"Tadd." Declan sighs. "Please."

"Sorry." Tadd tips his head back and stares up at the ceiling. "She came to me," he says, lowering his gaze so he's looking at Declan again. "She specifically asked me to keep her safe from Egan, and I didn't."

Declan rolls his chair around the corner of their desks and stops it right next to Tadd's. "You did what you could."

"No, I didn't. That's the point. I was pissed off, Declan, mad at you, mad at Lukas, and I didn't want to put up with her bullshit. I told her I needed to arrange protection for her because I couldn't stay with her all day, and she didn't want to wait. She left and I let her go."

"You couldn't have known."

"I should have!" Tadd jerks his arm out from under Declan's hand and slams his fist down on the desk. "She asked me for help!"

Declan waits long enough to be sure Tadd isn't going to hit anything else, and puts his hand back on Tadd's forearm. "You asked her to stay, didn't you?"

"Told her to." Tadd rolls his eyes. "She didn't listen."

"So how is that your fault?"

"I should've—"

"You know how to do your job, Tadd." Declan squeezes Tadd's arm and starts stroking his thumb along the inside of Tadd's wrist. "You couldn't have stayed with her all the time, anyway, especially not if you were going to listen to Bront and keep me safe too. Arranging for help was the right thing to do."

"I could have waited, let her run her errand first."

"And then she would have wanted to run another, and another, and another." Declan lets out a breathy chuckle. "She would have kept you running until you dropped, just because she could, and you would have gone along with it to be nice."

126

Tadd raises one eyebrow. "Nice? Me?"

"Yes." Declan pokes Tadd's shoulder. "I know about the gooey inside under that crusty exterior."

Tadd raises his other eyebrow. "You. Over there. Now." He points back toward Declan's desk with a scowl, but it's mostly faked. Even when Tadd is mad at him, Declan is able to push all the right buttons to calm him down.

Declan slides back around the desk and stops just on the other side of the corner. "Fine, but this doesn't change the fact that I know you're secretly a fluffy marshmallow inside."

"Would you like me to show you how wrong you are?" Tadd narrows his eyes further. "I can."

Declan stills and slowly lifts his gaze to meet Tadd's. "I'm not wrong." His heart is pounding in his chest, and he has to fight to keep his breathing under control. He doesn't want to seem too eager, but he's been itching to touch Tadd. It's killing him that he feels like he can't.

Tadd's blood starts to boil. "Yes, you are," he growls, fisting his hands in his pants to keep from shaking with anger. "I would not have followed her around all day. I—"

"Yes, you would, and we both know it." Declan stands, sending his chair rolling toward the wall as he pushes it away. "If you'd given in and gone with Adara on one errand, you would have spent all day following her around. You'd still be with her."

"And she'd still be alive!" Tadd jumps to his feet and takes a step closer to Declan. "Adara is dead because I didn't go with her!"

"She's dead because some asshole killed her, Tadd!" Declan steps forward, rounding the corner again so he's chest to chest with his husband. "If you want to blame yourself for not going with her, you should blame her for being so stubborn and not listening, and you should blame me for not having caught the killer yet. Hades, blame me for Cal too, while you're at it. I should have figured out who killed Sofia before either Cal or Adara died!"

"You were trying!" Tadd throws his hands out wide as he pushes up into Declan's face.

Declan leans down to meet him. "And so were you! It's no different!"

"Yes, it is!" Tadd moves quickly, grabbing Declan's shirt and shoving him against the desk. The edge digs into Declan's thigh as Tadd manhandles him, laying him out flat across the wide, clear surface. He leans over Declan, his breath hot on Declan's cheek, and growls, "It's my fault."

"No, it's not." Declan keeps his voice quiet and his body still. "It's the killer's fault and no one else's."

"Shut up!" Tadd shakes Declan hard enough to rattle the pens in the cup on the other side of the desk.

Declan looks him straight in the eyes, meeting his gaze calmly as he twists his lips up into a purposely goading smirk. "Make me."

Tadd growls and lunges forward to capture Declan's mouth in a bruising kiss.

It would be easy for Declan to give in, to let Tadd have his way and control this from beginning to end, but that's not what Declan wants at the moment. He wants to get them back on the same page, to eliminate the friction between them, and the only way he's going to do that is to get Tadd to work out all of his aggression now. If there's something he can do to speed that along, he's going to do it.

Especially when it's so much fun.

Declan leans up into the kiss, tangling his fingers in Tadd's hair and holding him close as he slips his tongue into Tadd's mouth. Tadd snarls as he pushes his tongue back past Declan's lips, curling it around Declan's. They battle back and forth, their tongues gliding over and around each other until Tadd growls again, nipping at Declan's bottom lip as he slides his hands up Declan's arms and pins them to the desk above Declan's head. "Don't."

"Don't what?" Declan asks, shifting under Tadd. He lifts his hips, deliberately brushing against Tadd's groin and letting Tadd feel how hard he is. He's aching, his hard cock tenting his dress pants. It almost hurts to have it rub against the silky material of his boxers, and he wants nothing more than to pull it out and let Tadd wrap his hands around it, but instead he lowers his hips back down, twists his head so he can look into Tadd's eyes, and meets Tadd's stare with one of his own. "Don't reciprocate? Do you want me to lie here and take it, Tadd? Let you pin me down and pound all your anger into me?"

Tadd falters for a second, but then his eyes narrow and he leans in closer, pressing his body against Declan's everywhere he can make them touch and putting his lips right against Declan's ear. "Yes."

The word comes out as almost more of a growl than speech, but Declan knows exactly what Tadd means. He waits until Tadd pulls back enough for them to look into each other's eyes, and then lets his lips curl up into a lazy, smug smile. "No."

Before Tadd can do anything, Declan moves, using his speed to twist free from under Tadd and drop to the floor. He lands on his knees, grins, and yanks on Tadd's pants without bothering to unbutton them. The material rips, easily giving in to his immortal strength, and Tadd's cock springs free, bobbing in front of Declan's nose. He leans in and slides his lips all the way to the base in one swift movement.

Tadd's knees buckle at the unexpected sensation. He catches himself on Declan's shoulders, digging in with powerful fingers as Declan grabs his hips, holding him still as he pulls back, licking as he moves.

It's phenomenal. Declan has always had a talented tongue in more ways than one, and he's always enjoyed using it this way. From the first time Declan gave Tadd a blowjob, distracting him from Plato's obnoxious alarm clock, this has been Tadd's favorite of Declan's talents. It's nothing like laying Declan out beneath him and having his way, but the sensations shooting up his nerves and threatening to short-circuit his brain are among the best he's ever felt.

He thrusts hard, fighting against the grip of Declan's hands and the wobbliness of his knees, controlling the pace as Declan continues to suck. His teeth scrape lightly along the swollen skin of Tadd's cock, sending pleasure and pain shooting through his body and leaving him breathless. Tadd thrusts harder, pushing his hips forward so he's fucking Declan's mouth, taking back every little bit of control Declan claimed. He throws his head back, letting his mouth fall open as he moans and his eyes flutter closed so he can focus on the feel of Declan's mouth around his dick.

The world narrows to just this, Declan on his knees, his fingers digging into Tadd's hips and his lips curling around the tip of Tadd's cock. He licks and sucks, humming as he bobs up and down, keeping time with Tadd's thrusts and moving opposite them, pulling back when Tadd does and pushing in so his lips slide down Tadd's cock with a speed he'd have to use his powers to match. He grazes one hand along Tadd's hipbones, brushing fingertips over the sensitive skin before slipping them between Tadd's legs and carefully curling them around Tadd's balls. Tadd gasps, his hips bucking wildly as he lets out a deep moan and starts chanting Declan's name. He digs his fingers hard into Declan's shoulder until Declan stops moving, and then tangles them in Declan's hair and pulls him back.

"No," Tadd growls, dragging Declan up with not-so-gentle pressure in his hair and twisting him around and pressing himself against Declan's back. Declan is still completely dressed, and his pants feel rough against Tadd's cock as he presses into Declan. Tadd fumbles for the waistband as he bends Declan over, and when his fingers curl around both pants and boxers, he yanks, ripping the material with his full strength and tearing it away from Declan's body with ease.

Declan shudders at the sudden blast of cold air, and his cock dips a little bit, but then Tadd rubs his finger along the cleft of Declan's ass, and Declan shudders, his elbows wobbling as he braces himself on the desk. "Hurry," he breathes, pushing back into Tadd and begging for more.

Tadd complies, giving in to Declan's demands easily now that they match his own. He shoves Declan forward, pushes his arms out from under him, and pins him to the desk. His cock presses hard against Declan's ass as Declan curls up over the desk. He's hard and aching, leaking precome onto the mahogany surface, and when Tadd shifts to grab lube from the closest drawer and slides one slick finger inside Declan's body, Declan moans. "Tadd. Now."

"Yes," Tadd breathes, vanishing his shirt as he slides a second finger in. Declan makes his own shirt disappear as he squirms beneath Tadd, shoving back against Tadd's hand as he slides one of his own down the dark wood of the desk and curls it around his cock. He strokes in time with Tadd's scissoring movements, his hand banging against the wood as his ass presses against Tadd's hip.

He's almost at the edge, his hand slick with precome and his cock red and engorged, when Tadd pulls his fingers out, lines himself up, and thrusts in, hard. He shoves Declan down over the desk, pressing his cheek into the smooth surface, and pulls almost all the way out before he adjusts his angle and plunges in again. He thrusts over and over, hitting Declan in his sweet spot every time.

Declan clenches around him, his buttocks squeezing Tadd's cock. His hand grips tight at the edge of the desk, giving him extra leverage, and Tadd pushes hard, slamming forward again. He puts one hand at the base of Declan's spine, holding him to the desk, and curls the other around Declan's cock. He strokes as he thrusts, the movements fast and ragged and yet still falling into a synchronized rhythm as he moves.

It doesn't take long before Declan is whimpering and moaning. "Gonna... Tadd... gonna come."

That's all the warning he's able to give, and then he spurts over Tadd's hand, crying out Tadd's name as his entire body shakes and writhes. He can still feel Tadd inside him, slamming forward and pulling back, and it's the best feeling in the entire universe. It carries him through the aftershocks, and then Tadd pushes forward one last time, leaning over Declan and pressing his lips to the back of Declan's shoulder as he comes.

They lie still for a minute, gasping for breath, their sweat-slicked bodies pressing against the strong polished wood of the desk. Tadd is heavy and warm over Declan, but his weight is comforting, reminding Declan this argument they're having is temporary. He's uncomfortable—sticky and hot and struggling for breath he doesn't really need—but he doesn't ask Tadd to move.

Tadd stays still for a few minutes, his breath ghosting over Declan's neck. When he pulls out, he slides his hand down Declan's back as he stands. "I'm going to shower," he says, stepping away and grabbing his clothes off the floor.

Declan pushes himself up and twists so he's leaning against the desk. "Want me to join you?" He keeps his tone light and hopeful, though he doesn't expect Tadd to agree. Sex is one thing; showering together is probably far more intimate than Tadd wants to get right now, given their earlier conversation.

"No." Tadd manages a strained smile as he looks at Declan. "We have things to figure out. We can't keep getting distracted or someone else might die."

"Right." That's the last thing Declan wants, and it's what he focuses on as he wipes himself down with the bundle of fabric and heads off toward the bathroom.

This job comes first. Then they can work out their issues.


DECLAN comes back downstairs wearing clothing that's much more comfortable than the suit pants Tadd had ripped off him. He can pull off a suit just as easily as jeans and a T-shirt, and looks damn good wearing it, but he prefers a more casual look.

Tadd is already sitting at his desk, wearing a black V-neck shirt and dark jeans. His hair is spiked and still damp from the shower he took in the downstairs bathroom, and he's a lot calmer than he was before he and Declan pulled apart to take separate showers. The coiled anger that sex had only partially dissipated is gone, replaced by Ares's usual tension and a burning need to find the evidence to convict Egan. "So what now?" he asks, shifting his attention from his computer to Declan.

"I'm not sure, actually." Declan gestures to the computer screen with a frown. "I had hoped this would turn up something concrete we could use, but so far all we have is what Adara told you this morning and some circumstantial evidence from the museum. There's nothing we haven't already looked at."

"Evidence from the museum?" Tadd directs a questioning gaze in Declan's direction. "What evidence from the museum? Care to elaborate?"

"Shit!" Declan's eyes widen as he swivels in his chair so he's facing Tadd. "That's right!" He leans forward and looks straight into his husband's eyes. "I found something this morning while you were... out." They both ignore the deliberate pause. "I couldn't do anything with what my computer was finding, so I looked at the stuff you'd pulled up, and I found a payment Egan got from the museum. A big payment."

"Where? And for what?" Tadd has so many windows open on his monitor he doesn't even know where to begin to look, and Declan could have found it in at least three of them. He's been digging in every place he could think to look, including public records that are a pain to access, and he has no idea how Declan could have stumbled across something so easily.

"First window I tried, actually," Declan says sheepishly, lifting one hand to rub at the back of his neck. "And, uh, metalwork." He tightens his fist in the hair at the nape of his neck and grimaces. "I think I know where the murder weapons came from, actually."

Tadd stares at Declan with an intense gaze that would send most other beings running as far and as fast as they could. "And that's circumstantial evidence?" he asks in an incredulous tone as he stands, walks around the corner of the desks, and grabs the arms of Declan's chair. He pulls Declan around so he's in front of Tadd's computer, lets go of the chair, and points at the monitor. "Show me."

Declan obediently turns, pulls up the appropriate window on the screen, and leans back in his chair. "There."

The information is hidden in a list of payments the museum disclosed in response to a probe by a reporter who had been trying to expose fraudulent financial practices. She had given up when she'd discovered her original source wasn't as reliable as she'd first thought, but it was her initial research Declan had referenced when Ian Burke had wondered why he was so curious about every little detail.

Tadd reads it over, leaning down with his hands braced on the desk and his lips pressed into a thin line. "Okay, that's not exactly incriminating."

"Well, no, not by itself," Declan admits easily, tipping his head back a little to look at Tadd. "That's why I went to the museum and talked to the director. I found out exactly why Egan got that payment."

"And?" Tadd twists around, leans back against the desk, and shoves his hands into his pockets.

133

"He created some iron and bronze pieces to go in the new Greek exhibit. Display stands and the like, mostly." Declan waves his hand, dismissing them. "Only, get this: one of the things he created was a display for was a set of six bronze daggers." He taps his finger on the desk, enunciating each of the last three words.

"You sure?"

"Yeah. The director showed me a picture of them when I went over there this morning. They look like the ones the killer used, and if they're really as old as the museum claims they are, they might be able to kill gods."

Tadd closes his eyes and sucks in a deep breath as he struggles to remain calm. There are too many things wrong with that last statement for him to even begin to enumerate them, but if he focuses on any, the fragile peace he and Declan have managed to create will be shattered. Right now, it's especially easy for Declan to irritate him, and even though half the things Declan said would annoy him when they're not fighting as well, he knows he can't push it.

"Let me see," he says instead, slowly opening his eyes to look at Declan.

"Okay." Declan pulls up a search engine on Tadd's computer, types in a few words, and waits. Even though he's armed with the correct name for them, it takes a while for him to find a site with pictures of the daggers—they aren't very well known, even in academic circles—but the moment he finds one, Tadd's breath hitches.

"Fuck." He twists back around and peers closely at the computer screen. The bronze daggers pictured exactly match the ones that have thus far graced Athena's, Eros's, and Aphrodite's bodies. The blades are short, smaller than most daggers, and the handles are just long enough to be gripped comfortably with one hand. Both the blades and the handles are decorated, so they look more like ceremonial daggers than actual fighting weapons, but their looks are deceiving. Tadd remembers the one he pulled from Sofia as well balanced, easy and comfortable to hold. The swirls of wire around the handle and hilt actually make the blades easier to grip rather than more difficult.

The picture on the monitor doesn't do them justice. They're clearly the same daggers, but the image does not reveal the raw power each blade possesses and completely dims the magical sparkle each is imbued with. There is nothing in the picture to indicate these daggers can kill gods. Only a god or demigod who had seen the actual weapons would know.

As far as Tadd is concerned, this clinches Egan's guilt. There's only one problem. "If the museum has the daggers—" he starts, but Declan cuts him off before he can finish the question.

"They don't." Declan pushes his hair back from his face. "They were stolen right before Sofia died."

Tadd turns an incredulous gaze on Declan. "How is this circumstantial evidence? And why wasn't there anything in the news about it?"

"The museum wanted to keep it under wraps." Declan shrugs and leans back in his chair, letting out a frustrated sigh. "Ian Burke was barely willing to tell me about it, but I told him I was worried about publicity if anything were to be stolen, and a maintenance guy overheard us and said something."

"Why wouldn't they say anything?" Tadd furrows his brow as he turns back to the computer monitor. "Wouldn't publicity help them recover the daggers?"

"Not in this case," Declan points out before he sighs again. "Typically, I don't know. They aren't a high-profile item. Maybe they think denying the thief credit will make him less likely to strike again? I have no idea, to be honest."

"Yeah, me neither." Tadd pinches the bridge of his nose and blows out an annoyed breath before pulling the keyboard over and opening up a new window. "Police reports are public record, though, so maybe we can find something there. Did you manage to get the director to tell you who they're insured with? We could maybe get some information from them too."

"No." Declan shakes his head. "I can try to find out, if you want, but I felt like he was going to get suspicious of me if I pushed for more this morning."

Tadd raises an eyebrow and twists his head to look Declan straight in the eyes. "And you didn't like that idea? Go figure." He mutters the last words as he turns back to the computer screen.

"Tadd—"

"If they filed a police report, it should be public record." Tadd doesn't let Declan finish his protest. He knows he's pushing things he'd agreed to drop, but the insult from this morning still stings when he thinks about it, and he let loose the verbal barb without conscious thought. "Let me see if I can pull anything up. If not, maybe you can hack the museum's records."

Declan stares hard at Tadd for a moment, breathing in through his nose and out through his mouth as he attempts to calm himself again. Now isn't the time, and he'll let it go because he knows Tadd couldn't resist the opening he gave, but it still stings. This whole thing sucks, and if Declan gets a chance, he's going to throttle Lukas. Somehow, while trying to be helpful, he made the investigation harder and completely messed up everything between Tadd and Declan.

"I'll, uh, start digging." Declan rolls his chair back around the corner of their desks, deliberately not looking at the wide, clear area they'd made such good use of earlier. "Even if you manage to find the police report, maybe the museum security office has something we can use too." It's a long shot, but that's probably better for everyone. If either the police or the museum had any idea Egan had stolen the daggers, they'd have tried to arrest him, and Declan can't imagine that going well. Assault is probably a minor term for what Egan is likely to do to a police officer who tries to arrest him, and chances are good he wouldn't remember to rein in his immortal strength.

"Good idea." Tadd manages a smile as he positions himself back in front of his computer, getting comfortable in his chair and typing into various search engines. His brow furrows as he concentrates, squinting and leaning in closer to peer at the computer screen despite his perfect vision and the large monitor. "Maybe you'll find something we can take to Bront."

"Maybe." Declan watches as Tadd types. He could spend hours focused on his husband, taking in the flecks of color in his eyes and the freckles that dot his skin, but this isn't the time. Tadd isn't in the mood to be looked at, a position he makes clear with his questioning glances and his tapping fingers, and Declan has work to do.

He can't let himself be distracted right now, and so he reluctantly pulls his gaze away from his husband, minimizes the transcription program that's still going through Cal's records, and opens a new window. The museum security shouldn't be too hard to crack.

"YOU'RE idiots."

Declan looks up from his dinner to find Selene standing in center of the arched doorway to their eating area, one hip cocked with her hand resting on it. She's dressed a lot more informally than the last time she was here, in jeans and a knit blouse with her hair pulled back in a ponytail. She's wearing practical shoes, the kind that are easy to run in, and there's still a silver bracelet around her wrist, but it's easy to imagine her going to an archery range dressed like this and taking out target after target, awing everyone else who is there.

Tadd pauses with his steak halfway to his mouth and quirks his lips. "We are?"

"You're sitting here eating steak when you should be out finding whoever killed Sofia and Adara!" Selene stalks across the room, her bright eyes flashing. She stops at the table, leans on it with her hands in fists, and pushes up on her toes so she can loom over them. Even with them sitting and her stretched up to her full height, she's still barely taller than they are, and with her diminutive size, it's easy to forget who she is and what she can do.

"Cal too," Declan adds calmly as he spears a potato with his fork. He slips it into his mouth and smiles around the utensil, well aware that if Selene had to pick any god to perish, Cal would have been the one. Artemis and Eros have always been at cross purposes, and Selene has shown enough in the brief time Declan has known her that there is no doubt she still feels the same way. The point, however, remains. Cal would not be dead if Declan had been successful in his hunt for the killer.

137

"Yes, him too," Selene says impatiently, rolling her eyes. She doesn't precisely dismiss his death, but it's a near thing, and Declan's hackles rise even though he and Cal were never especially close. "Actually," Selene continues, "Cal's death makes it worse. It gave you more clues, and you still didn't solve this before Adara died."

"And that's what matters, right?" Tadd sets his fork down by his plate, stands, and stalks over to Selene. He looms over her with his hands on his hips and his lips turned down into a frown. "That Adara is dead? That Sofia is dead? If whoever did this had killed Egan or Lukas or one of us next, you wouldn't be here, would you?"

"No, I wouldn't." Selene swivels around to face Tadd and squares off with him, their toes touching. She keeps her fighting stance despite the height difference and tips her head back so she can meet Tadd's glare with her own. "But that's not the point."

"Then what is?" Declan sets down his own utensils and stands next to Tadd. Together they're both so much bigger than she is it's ridiculous, and it would be comical if the situation weren't so dire. "Why does Adara's death matter so much more than any of the others?"

"Because you should have stopped it!" Selene throws up her hands and stalks to the other end of the table, muttering uncomplimentary things about men just loud enough for Declan to hear them. "Sofia's death took us all by surprise, and Cal—" She cuts herself off and shakes her head, clearing what she was about to say out of her mind. "Cal's death was probably unavoidable, especially since Bront pulled me off the case and put you on it. You didn't really have time to do anything before Cal was killed."

The implication she would have if she hadn't been pulled from the case hangs heavily in the air, but Declan ignores it. As she moves, they turn to face her, presenting a united front despite their issues, and Tadd tilts his head a little as he looks at her curiously. "But you think we did before Adara died?" His tone is low and dangerous, sending a shiver down Declan's spine.

Selene ignores it. "Yes," she asserts, again putting her hands on her hips and tipping her nose up toward the ceiling. "You had time and evidence. There's no reason you couldn't have found the killer before Adara died."

"Do you really think that?" Declan asks, his soft tone a sharp contrast to Tadd's angry one. "Do you think we sat around and didn't do anything about Sofia or we didn't try our hardest to figure out who killed Cal? There wasn't evidence, Selene, not anything concrete. All we have is what people have told us, and that's not enough! Everyone's story contradicts everyone else's, and we can't arbitrarily believe anyone!"

"You didn't have a problem last night," Tadd mutters, too low for Selene to hear.

Declan ignores it and keeps his attention focused on Selene. It's the only thing he can do at the moment. "We have leads, Selene, and we're following them up, but you know Bront doesn't want anything short of irrefutable proof, and we haven't been able to get that yet."

"And whose fault is that?"

"Do you think you could have done better?" Tadd fixes Selene with a cold stare and stalks forward with slow, measured steps.

"Of course." To Selene's credit, she doesn't wilt under Tadd's gaze, but matches it with a defiant look of her own. "I wouldn't have barged in there and clumsily let everyone know what I was doing right off the bat, and I definitely wouldn't have demanded answers."

Declan gapes, offended at her cruel description of his methods. "Is that really what you think I did? That I bumbled around and let everyone know I suspected them? Do you really think I'm that stupid?"

"Do you really want me to answer that?" Selene quirks one eyebrow as she peers at him from around Tadd and grins maliciously. "I guarantee you won't like what you hear."

"I never like what I hear from you, sweetheart," Declan drawls, grinning at her with a lazy smile he doesn't feel. "I don't know why this should be any different."

Selene stares at him, spluttering, and throws her hands in the air. "Zeus almighty! How can you possibly be this stupid?"

This time, Tadd raises his eyebrow. "Watch it, honey." The emphasis he puts on the last word makes Declan cringe, and Selene glares up at Tadd, daring him to say more. He does. "If you're not careful, you'll start to give him a complex."

"That wasn't a compliment, you know."

Declan walks up and leans over Tadd's shoulders, ignoring the way Tadd tenses at his touch, and slides his hands around Tadd's waist. "It is if I take it that way. That's the beauty of words; they're very fluid." He smirks at her, squeezes Tadd, and steps back.

Selene clenches and unclenches her fingers a few times, breathing slowly as she stares at both Declan and Tadd. "Fine. Take it however you want. That doesn't change the facts."

"And what are those?" Tadd's voice is cold enough to make the temperature in the room drop a few degrees. He ignores the changed temperature, arches one eyebrow, crosses his arms over his chest, and gives Selene a frosty glare. "Please, enlighten me."

"The facts," Selene says in a steady voice that would have seemed cold if Tadd hadn't spoken first, "are that three gods are now dead, and the two of you have done nothing to bring the killer to justice. You're sitting here, eating dinner like you don't have a care in the world, while three gods are now condemned to eternity in the Underworld with Hades. The facts are that you could have prevented at least one of those three deaths, maybe two of them, but you didn't because you're incompetent and incapable of figuring this out. The facts are that Bront made a mistake when he pulled me off this case and put you on it instead, and that I would have solved it by now. I would have solved it in time to save Adara!"

"Are you sure about that?" Tadd doesn't move, or soften his glare or his tone. "You don't know what the evidence is or what we're doing about it."

"I don't need to."

Tadd growls and lunges, moving quickly enough that Declan has to call on his innate speed to stop him from grabbing Selene by the throat and throttling her. "Stop it!" he yells, pushing between Tadd and Selene and glaring at them both in turn. "Both of you!"

"She—"

"He—"

"I. Don't. Care." Declan says firmly. "Arguing like this isn't going to solve anything. We need to figure out who killed Cal before they do it again."

"It's the same person who killed Adara and Sofia, you know."

"Yeah, well, you seem fixated on them, so I'm going to focus on Cal. It's only fair."

Tadd rolls his eyes and yanks Declan away from Selene. "Great way to stop the argument," he says, sarcasm practically dripping from his words. "That's going to do a lot of good."

"There's nothing we can do right now." They'd stopped because both computers are busy working. The police report Tadd found didn't contain much helpful information, but it did lead them to the insurance company, and while Declan's computer continues to sift through the phone records from Cal's business and the information he pulled from the museum security office before he closed that connection, Tadd's is sorting through the information Declan pulled from the insurance company database. He didn't get much from them—their systems are much more secure than the museum's are thanks to privacy laws—but he has found a few bits of information they might be able to act on. But Tadd and Declan are hoping that when they return, the computers will have found connections they missed.

Of course, that's dependent upon them actually returning to the computers, and if Selene keeps holding them up, that won't happen in time for them to do anything about it tonight. They aren't the police, and they have no official standing in the mortal world beyond the personas they've been living under for the past several years, so they have to make their inquiries during operating hours by asking questions it seems reasonable for Tadd Leventis or Declan Anagnos to be asking. Selene isn't exactly helping their timeline.

"Nothing?" she shrieks, her voice rising several octaves as her eyes widen. "What in Hades do you mean by that?"

"Exactly what it sounds like." Declan fixes her with a stern stare that doesn't even come close to rivaling Tadd's.

Selene takes a deep breath and twists her lips into a hysterical smile. "There's plenty you could be doing. Of course," she continues, the smile dropping from her face, "you would know that if you had any clue how to hunt something."

"I do know how to hunt. And Declan knows what he's doing. Just because we don't do this your way doesn't make it wrong, Selene."

"It makes it less efficient. And taking dinner breaks shouldn't be on the schedule when lives are on the line."

"We're not taking a break!" Declan protests, casting a brief but longing glance at his cooling dinner. He doesn't need to eat it, but he enjoys the way it tastes, and it's never the same reheated.

"Then what are you doing? There's no one else here. You're sitting at your table, eating food you have no need to consume. How is that not taking a break?"

Declan didn't want to tell her this, but the words leave his mouth before he can think about it and stop them. "We're waiting for our computers to analyze data we found. We think we know who killed them, but we need proof we can bring to Bront, and we're working on that. There's nothing we can do while the computers work."

"How about talk to him? Did you think of trying that?" She shakes her head and lets out a scoffing sound. "Of course you didn't. Who is it, anyway?"

"None of your business."

Selene whirls on Tadd with a speed that rivals Declan's. "None of my business? Excuse me? I could be next and you're trying to tell me this is none of my business? I don't think so."

"I do." Tadd crosses his arms over his chest. "If we tell you, you'll mess things up."

"I'll mess things up? Excuse me? I'll mess things up? Who is it that let Adara die because they couldn't find the killer fast enough? Not me."

"Let us do this our way."

"Let me do it mine." Selene steps back, crosses her arms over her chest, and looks hard at each of them in turn. "If you don't want to tell me, fine. I'll figure it out myself, and I bet I find the evidence you need before you do. Computers are all well and good, boys, but nothing beats human contact and a proper hunt." She turns, walks to the doorway she appeared in, and looks back over her shoulder. "Stay out of my way if you know what's good for you. I promise, the best god will win."

She vanishes before Tadd or Declan has a chance to say anything, leaving them glaring with narrowed eyes and clenched teeth at the spot she vacated. "Dammit!" Tadd says, whirling and smashing his fist into the wall. "And damn her!"

Declan can't disagree.

# HEPHAESTUS

AMBROSIA VINEYARDS is much busier than Tadd expected it to be when he and Declan appear in an out-of-the-way corner of the parking lot. It's not quite nine on a Sunday morning, so chances are good that all the cars in the parking lot belong to employees and not guests, but it's still unnerving to see the lot nearly a quarter of the way full when he thought it would be practically empty. Dionysus spends almost all his time here, he knows that, but he didn't expect to find anyone else around.

Tadd immediately steps in front of Declan, scanning the parking lot to make sure there are just cars there and not angry god-killers waiting to jump out at them. He holds Declan back with an extended hand as he peers out, frowning. The parking lot looks empty, but the problem with cars is they provide so many places to hide.

Declan tolerates it for about thirty seconds and then steps forward, shaking his head as he huffs out a breath. "If Egan knows we're onto him and wants to do something about it, he can pop in right behind us, you know. We could be dead before we even knew he was here."

"So keep your back against the wall." Tadd shoots a glare in Declan's direction. Sleep had not made him feel better, and waking up on opposite sides of their large bed instead of tangled together in the middle of it had left him feeling out of sorts even though he was the one who had insisted on it when they lay down. "Then he can't show up behind you."

"And I won't be able to investigate." Declan pushes past Tadd and crosses the parking lot with long strides. He's not using his speed, but he is moving fast enough that Tadd has to run to catch up, muttering under his breath the whole time about how reckless and irresponsible Declan is being. When he catches up, Declan looks over and glares. "I can hear you, you know."

"Yep." Tadd doesn't bother to keep the irritation from his voice. "I meant you to."

Declan stops and turns to look at Tadd with an incredulous gaze. "Do you really want to do this right now? I thought we had agreed to put this behind us and focus on the investigation! I can't focus if you're going to keep acting mad at me!"

"I'm not acting mad at you. I am mad at you," Tadd retorts as he strides up to the entrance to the vineyard's main office building. "And this isn't about what happened yesterday."

"Then what is it about?" Declan catches up with Tadd effortlessly and tugs to make him stop and turn around.

"This is about you letting me do my job." Tadd stares hard at Declan. "I couldn't keep Adara safe. I'm not letting the same thing happen to you."

"Adara didn't listen."

"Exactly!" Tadd spreads his arms wide and steps closer. "You're not listening either! If I tell you to keep your back against the wall, keep your back against the fucking wall!"

"I can't walk around with my back pressed up against a solid surface at all times, Tadd. That's impossible, even for me."

"I'm not asking you to do that."

"Then what are you asking?"

"For you to listen and trust me."

"I do." Declan doesn't hesitate with his answer, and there is no doubt in his voice.

"Really?" Tadd glares defiantly at Declan. He wants to believe that, but the way Declan is acting makes it hard. "Because you have a piss-poor way of showing it."

"What in Hades is that supposed to mean?"

"It means you're not listening to me! I was trying to see if there was any danger in the parking lot, and you waltzed right out before I finished scoping things out! You didn't wait for me to give you the go-ahead, you didn't let me go first, and you're treating everything I tell you like a joke! You have to trust me to do my job, Declan, or you'll end up like Sofia and Cal and Adara. And then I will too," he adds in a softer tone that is nonetheless perfectly clear to Declan's ears.

Declan looks hard at Tadd for a moment and then nods. "Yeah. Okay." He offers up a hesitant smile. "Sorry." Tadd doesn't return the smile, and Declan lets his fall off his face, swallows hard, and gestures to the building behind him. "Shall we, uh, go on in?"

Tadd nods, and together they walk through the door into the lobby of Ambrosia Vineyards.

Dionysus, also known as Denis Varela according to the picture hanging on the wall to one side of the entrance, is behind the tasting bar, a glass of ruby liquid in his hand and his chin resting on his forearm. He looks wasted, which isn't exactly a new state for him, but this seems even worse than usual. Tadd slows as he approaches, wondering what could have caused the god of wine to drink so much he seems to really be feeling the effects.

He looks up as they approach and grins widely. "Hermes! Ares! Long time no see!" He lifts his glass in salute and downs the rest of it in one long swallow.

"Dionysus," Tadd says in a flat tone, stopping at the bar and resting both hands on the polished wood of the surface. "Getting started a bit early, aren't you?"

"Never stopped." He pulls a half-full bottle out from under the counter and pours a generous amount into his glass before filling two more and passing them across the bar. Both Declan and Tadd try to protest, but he insists, and they find themselves sipping a delicious Syrah far earlier in the day than either of them care to imbibe.

"Why did you start?" Declan questions once he's taken enough sips from his glass that Denis has stopped glaring at him. "I know you like to drink, but this is excessive, even for you."

"Didn't you hear?" Denis pours the rest of his glass down his throat and grabs a new bottle. He doesn't bother to fill his glass, just brings it to his lips and takes a swig like it's cheap beer instead of expensive wine. "Aphrodite is dead." He lifts the bottle to his mouth to take another swig.

Tadd stops him before he gets any in his mouth, wrenches the bottle away, and hands it to Declan, ignoring the wine dripping onto the counter as he steps around the bar and grabs Denis by the arms. "We need to talk."

Denis blinks blearily. "We are talking. See?" He gestures vaguely between the two of them, the movement aborted by Tadd's iron grip on his arms.

"In your office," Tadd insists in a harsh tone. "Show me where it is."

"That way." Denis points. Tadd starts to guide him in the indicated direction, casting a glance at Declan to let him know to come along.

Declan does, though he sets the wine down and quickly wipes up the spill first. He catches up to Tadd before they've gotten out of the main room, and slips his arm around Denis's shoulders to take some of the burden. "So, Dionysus—"

"It's Denis," Denis slurs, resting his head on Declan's shoulder and rolling it so he's sort of looking at Declan's face. He stumbles along, only vaguely pointing in the correct direction. He stumbles twice, making Tadd and Declan have to hoist him up and practically carry him.

"All right, Denis, time to sober up," Tadd says once they've reached Denis's office and dumped him on one of the couches in front of the fireplace, which is blazing despite the warm early fall weather.

Denis glares, but Tadd crosses his arms and raises an eyebrow, giving Denis the look that used to terrify armies. It doesn't take long for Denis to close his eyes, shake his head, and sit up. "I hate doing it that way."

"Then maybe you shouldn't have gotten drunk in the first place," Tadd says in a stern tone. "We need to talk, and I want straight answers from you."

"You should have let me stay drunk, then," Denis retorts. "It's easier for me to lie when I'm sober."

147

Tadd pulls back his sleeve to reveal a small knife strapped there. It's not one that will kill a god, even when wielded by Tadd, but it will hurt. "I don't think you'll be lying."

Denis gulps, blinking wide eyes as he gestures for them both to take a seat. "No. I won't."

"Good." Tadd flashes a smile at Denis as he waits for Declan to sit down. Denis doesn't look like he's much of a risk, even now that he's mostly sober, and Tadd knows he isn't the killer, but that doesn't mean he's going to leave Declan vulnerable.

Declan waits for Tadd to take his seat before he leans forward, assessing Denis, and frowns. "How do you know Adara is dead?"

Denis lets out a hollow laugh. "Getting right to the point, huh?" His hand trembles as he looks around, his eyes falling on a bottle of wine sitting on one of the bookcases, but he stays in his seat. He runs his hand over his bald head and sighs. "Egan told me."

"Ah." Tadd swivels in his seat to stare incredulously at Denis. "Why did Egan tell you?"

"He picked up when I called Adara's house." Denis's eyes go back to the bottle of wine as he slumps back. "I, uh, had a party to go to last night. I couldn't reach Cal, so I called Adara to see if she could find him or if she could hook me up with anyone I could take."

"Cal ran a phone sex line," Declan says carefully. "Adara runs a matchmaking business. Neither is an escort service."

"No." Denis leans forward again and looks at Declan as though he's an idiot. "They aren't. But in their line of work, they meet people who are, uh, willing." He runs his hand over his head again and flashes a smile that's far more bravado than anything else. "I can get my own dates, but this was kind of last-minute. I wanted to know if they knew anyone who might be interested."

"Okay," Declan says, in a tone that makes it clear he's trying hard to ignore the defensiveness in Denis's voice. "So you called Adara's house when you couldn't get her at the office?"

"Yeah." Denis's hand comes back over his head and down his face. "Egan answered, told me she was dead." He sucks in a deep breath and shakes his head. "It's a shame too. That woman was smoking."

Tadd narrows his gaze and looks hard at Denis. "You're upset she's dead because she was hot?" Tadd asks, letting his anger creep into his voice. "Really?"

"Well, yeah. Have you seen her?"

"I was her lover," Tadd says flatly. Denis moves to give him a high five, which Tadd ducks away from with a glare. "And she cursed me."

"Oh, right. Yeah. I forgot about that." Denis manages to look sheepish for a few seconds. "Sorry, man. But it worked out, right?"

"Not the point." Declan says, redirecting the conversation. He obviously doesn't want to discuss Tadd's past relationships at the moment, and Tadd can't blame him. "Did Egan say anything else to you when he told you Adara was dead? Anything at all?"

"No. Just that she'd been killed."

"He didn't say anything about who, or where, or how?" Declan asks. "Are you sure?"

"Yeah." Denis leans back on the couch, stretching his arms along the back of it, and crosses his legs. He looks like he's trying to imitate a magazine spread where rich old guys are supposed to look sexy, but he just manages to look ridiculous. Then again, the rich old guys usually do as well.

"He didn't even tell you when?" Tadd shifts in response to Denis's change of position, scooting closer to Declan and looking at Denis with a raised eyebrow. "Really?"

"Really!" Denis lets his head fall back to the couch and sighs dramatically. "Look, guys, I don't know what you're getting at here, but when I called, Egan picked up the phone, told me not to call again because Adara was dead, and hung up. I didn't think it was appropriate to call back. It's not like I've been close to either of them in centuries."

"And then you decided to drink all day." Tadd pinches the bridge of his nose. When Denis told them he'd talked to Egan, Tadd had hoped they'd be able to get some evidence, but those hopes have been thoroughly crushed.

"I am the god of wine. How else should I respond?"

"Right," Tadd says after a moment of stunned silence. Denis has a point, but that doesn't mean it makes sense to Tadd. His instinct is to find out what happened and hurt whoever caused it, not drink himself into a stupor. Although a glass of Ambrosia wouldn't be unwelcome at the moment. "Okay, what about Cal? Or Sofia? Did anyone tell you they're dead?"

"Cal's dead too?" Denis asks in a tone that makes it clear no one told him that. He sits up, looks between Tadd and Declan incredulously until Declan nods. "Really? Shit! I knew I hadn't imagined feeling that again!"

"And Sofia?" Tadd asks, mentally rolling his eyes at Denis's antics. "Did you know about her?"

"Only because Selene stopped by." This time Denis sits up properly, leans forward, and rests his elbows on his knees. "The bitch didn't tell me anything, but I looked in the papers after she left and figured it out. I'm not sure why she stopped by here, though, or why the two of you are here, to be perfectly honest. I don't know anything."

"We're here because you called Cal's phone line multiple times, and we're looking for connections." Declan leans forward as well, mimicking Denis's pose from the chair he'd chosen. "You knew Cal and Adara in this persona. Did you know Sofia?"

"Not really. I mean, I'd met her once. There was this party at the museum, and the girl I was, ah, seeing, wanted me to go with her, so I did. We only stayed for about a half hour, and I talked to Sofia for maybe a minute of that. We weren't exactly best friends. Hades, I think she only acknowledged me because her boss was right there and she didn't want to seem rude."

"Why did you leave so quickly?" Declan asks.

"It was a museum party. Lots of boring suits and extremely subpar wine. They had white zinfandel." He shudders dramatically. "Besides, the girl I was with, she was smoking. I mean, she had to have descended from the nymphs. And when she wanted to whisper sweet nothings in my ear, I wasn't about to say no. I mean, come on. Would you?"

"Yes." Declan says flatly, glaring at Denis for a second before casting a fond gaze at Tadd.

"Yeah, well, you two are odd. I, on the other hand, am a normal, red-blooded male, and I definitely wasn't going to say no to that offer."

"And is that the only time you saw Sofia?" Tadd asks, dragging them back on track with effort. Denis may not pose much of a physical threat to either of them, but he's definitely a danger to the course of the investigation. If Tadd weren't here, he suspects Denis and Declan would spend hours talking about everything other than the murders and the evidence they need to implicate Egan.

"As long as she's been Sofia, anyway." Denis shrugs. "Before that party, it had been centuries since I'd seen her. I figured it would be centuries before I saw her again. We don't usually run in the same circles."

"Thank you." Tadd stands and holds out his hand to Declan without thinking about it. He wants to leave and go on to the next name on their list, and taking Declan's hand is the fastest way to get him out of here.

"You're welcome." Denis stands as well. His lips curl up into a small smile when Declan takes Tadd's outstretched hand, lacing their fingers together and gripping as though he has no intention of letting go. "Sorry I couldn't be of more help."

"It's all right." Declan reaches out with his left hand and pats Denis on the shoulder. "We appreciate you taking the time for us."

"Try and stay sober, all right?" Tadd adds. "I have the feeling it'll be necessary soon."

Denis's gaze goes back to the bottle of wine on his shelf. "That's not ominous or anything." He walks over, pulls the cork out with his teeth, and takes a swig. "I'll take my chances. Something like that, I think I'd rather be drunk."

"Suit yourself."

They walk out of the building together, their fingers still entwined, as Declan refuses to let go when Tadd tries to pull away. When they reach the spot where they arrived, Declan shudders and leans against the edge of the building. "Now I need a drink."

"Yeah." Tadd runs his free hand over the top of his head and sighs. "Denis would probably let us have one… or three."

"No, thank you." Declan shakes his head and gives Tadd a wry smile. "I've drunk with him before. There's no way I can keep pace, and he'll have me so messed up there's no way I'll be able to do anything else today, even if he doesn't bring out the Ambrosia."

"Yeah." Tadd sighs again and pulls a list from his pocket. After Selene left, Declan asked Bront for the mortal identities of the other gods and printed a list of every name the transcription program had identified as calling Cal's phone sex line, and are visiting them one at a time. It isn't the most efficient method, but Selene had pissed them both off, and they hope they can find more information while the computers do their magic. "Home or the next place?"

"Who's next?" Declan leans in close, pressing his torso against Tadd's arm.

Tadd tenses, but manages to resist the urge to pull away. "Demeter. Hermione Demos." He looks back down at the paper. "She runs an agricultural research center, so she'll probably be at home today."

Declan pulls back, staring at Tadd incredulously. "Demeter called Cal's phone sex line? Really?"

Tadd hands the sheet to Declan. "Looks like it. I printed out what the computer gave me."

"I know, but…." Declan looks down at the list. Sure enough, the second name on it is Hermione Demos. It's in the order the computer found them, so she could have only called once, but still. He had not expected to see her name on the list. "Wow."

"Yeah." Tadd leans back against the brick wall. "So where to? Home to double-check this and see what else has come up, or off to see her?"

"Let's go see Demeter." Declan shakes his head as he lets go of Tadd's hand. "Meet you there?"

"Of course." Tadd vanishes.

DEMETER'S house is closer to a traditional cottage than an actual house, but its surroundings more than make up for any lack of opulence in the actual dwelling. It's set on the edge of a large field that's full of almost ready to harvest wheat. A large garden surrounds the building, the flowers blooming fully and the fruits and vegetables ready to be pulled off and brought in at any time. On both sides there are groves, one full of apple trees and the other plum trees. A few small pomegranate shrubs are off to one side of the apple trees, set apart as though they're not exactly welcome there. The walkway up to the house is lined with flowers, and the grass is lush and rich. It's clear the owner cares very much for the land and growing things.

Declan takes Tadd's hand again as they appear on the walkway, and ignores the look he gets as he gently tugs Tadd across the stones. "Come on."

Tadd follows, his fingers curling around Declan's almost of their own volition, and he uses his grip to drag Declan away from the porch and around to the back of the house. Declan looks at him inquisitively and he shrugs, pointing up at the sun. "She's working outside," he says when Declan literally digs his heels in, almost ruining the pristine grass. "Think about it. It's nice out and harvest season. If you were her, where would you be?"

Declan flushes. He was distracted enough by his attempts to pretend everything is normal with Tadd and cataloging every time Tadd reacted poorly to said attempts that he forgot to think about where they might find Hermione. "Oh. Right." He flashes a sheepish grin at his husband as he pushes his hair back from his face. "Sorry."

"Uh-huh." Tadd pulls his hand free from Declan's, sliding one eyebrow up when Declan makes an annoyed sound in protest. "We're here to talk to her. Stop distracting me."

"Yeah, sure, since that's all it is." Declan stalks around the corner of the house, muttering to himself about how stupid people can be, and doesn't wait for Tadd to follow. If Tadd wants to play that game, Declan can play it too.

Hermione is in the back garden on her hands and knees, pulling up weeds, completely lost in her work. She's humming to herself, the tune carrying well enough that Declan has to wonder how he didn't hear it out front, and Declan and Tadd have both managed to carefully cross the garden to her before she looks up as their shadows fall across her face. "Oh!" she exclaims, sitting back on her heels. "Hello!"

"Hi." Declan stuffs his hands in his pockets. He feels unusually tall standing over Hermione where she's kneeling on the ground, but he doesn't want to kneel out of fear he'll squash some plants and start this interview off on the wrong foot. "Can we talk to you for a minute?" Demeter always gives off such a motherly vibe that it's difficult to be anything but respectful to her, which means this discussion is going to be awkward.

Or maybe not. Hermione grins, brushes off her pants, and stands, pulling her gloves from her hands as she leads the way to the deck. "Of course. Let me grab something to drink. Do you want anything?" She waits a beat, completely ignores both their negative answers, and disappears inside. "Have a seat!" she calls over her shoulder just before the door closes.

Tadd sinks into one of the chairs on the deck and lets out a sigh. "That was interesting."

"Yeah." Declan sits in the chair next to him and takes a minute to enjoy the view. The landscape is beautiful out here, all lush greens and browns with splashes of other color that draw the eyes without taking away from the overall beauty. "Do you really think she called Cal's line?" he asks once he can turn his head away from the landscape to look at Tadd. Not that it's a hardship to gaze at his husband either, but he does get to see Tadd almost every day, and the landscape here is new to him.

"I'm not sure I want to ask."

Declan nods his agreement but doesn't say anything. Before he can, Hermione returns, carrying a pitcher of reddish juice and three glasses. She sets them all on the table and smiles. "Homemade pomegranate apple juice," she says as she pours, filling all three glasses up to the brim. "You have to try some."

"Sounds delicious." Declan gets up from his seat and grabs two of the glasses off the table, giving one to Tadd as he sits back down again. He takes a sip, blinks, and takes another. "This is amazing!"

Hermione blushes as Tadd adds his agreement. "Thank you. I made it myself from the trees in the orchard. Tabitha loves it, though why she wants to eat or drink pomegranate anything is beyond me."

Neither Declan nor Tadd comment on that. There are some discussions they've learned to avoid, and the issue of Persephone and the way her time is divided between her mother and Hades is definitely one of them. Instead, Declan takes another sip of his drink, sets the glass down on the wide arm of the deck chair, and leans in. "I'm glad she likes this. It's delicious."

"Thank you." Hermione nods her head in gratitude as she takes her seat. "What was it you wanted to talk about? I'm sure you boys didn't come out just to try my juice."

"It would have been worth the trip," Tadd says, "but no. We're here because Sofia, Cal, and Adara—Athena, Eros, and Aphrodite—are all dead, and we need to know if you know anything about it."

Hermione blanches and sets down her glass as she starts shaking. "Dead?" she asks, pressing one hand to her chest and leaning back in the chair. "Really?"

"You must have felt it," Declan says, leaning forward and patting Hermione's knee. "Everyone else did. It would have felt as if your whole body was on fire for a minute or two. You might have felt overwhelming terror."

"Yeah." Hermione nods. "Now that you mention it, yes. I did. I didn't know what it was, though, and Tabitha wasn't home any of the times it happened, so I didn't realize it had happened to anyone else. I was going to go see Bront after I was done weeding my garden if it happened again." She gives them both a wan smile. "I guess I won't need to do that."

"No." Declan sits back in the chair. "The thing is, we don't know who killed them. I'm trying to find out, and, well, that's why we're here. We hoped you would know something."

"What would I know? I haven't talked to any immortals except Tabitha in years, I think." She takes a sip of her juice and sets the glass back down on the chair arm. "It's been months at least. I haven't left here all summer, and you two are the first gods to come visit."

"We, um." Declan shifts and casts a pleading glance at Tadd. It's ignored, though Tadd does smile slightly, and Declan takes a deep breath. He really hoped to avoid this question. "We know you called Cal's business." He blushes bright red and sinks down low in his chair so he doesn't have to meet Hermione's eyes.

"Is there a problem with that?" Hermione leans forward, ducking her head to meet Declan's gaze. "I wasn't aware there was an issue with me calling him."

"N-no issue." Declan swallows hard and forces himself to sit up straighter. Tadd, the bastard, is letting him take this part of the discussion all by himself. "We didn't expect it, that's all."

Hermione laughs. "Everyone needs some release once in a while. I don't like bringing men around when Tabitha is home, but six months is a long time to stay celibate, even for me. I call Cal's line and get what I need without taking time away from my daughter."

Declan bites back a remark about smothering Tabitha. The girl has been dealing with this for thousands of years, after all, and if she wants something done about her situation with her mother or with Hades, he hasn't heard about it. "Okay. Um." He rubs at the back of his neck as he tries to quickly formulate his thoughts. "You may not know anything, since you only called for... that... but, um, did you ever talk to Cal?"

"No." Hermione shakes her head. "That would be weird. I was thinking about calling Adara the next time Tabitha went back to Hades, but I guess I won't be doing that now." She sighs. "Such a shame. They were both so helpful."

Tadd takes pity on Declan, leans forward, and looks Hermione in the eyes. "And Sofia?"

"Who?" Hermione tilts her head to the side and looks at Declan curiously. "I'm sorry, I don't know who that is."

"That's what Athena was calling herself," Tadd clarifies.

"What about her?"

"Well, you admitted you did business with Cal, and you were thinking about calling Adara. What about Sofia? Did you ever do any business with her? Ever run into her when you visited the museum?"

"No." Hermione shakes her head. "I'm sorry. I didn't. The last time I saw Athena was a long time before she started calling herself Sofia." She takes another sip of her juice and leans back in her chair. "I wish I could help more, but I haven't seen anyone. Tabitha goes out far more than I do."

"Is she here?" Declan looks out over the fields, but he doesn't see anyone else. "Maybe she'll have some ideas." It's a long shot, but if Tabitha is here, it would be stupid to leave without talking to her, even though she didn't appear on the list of gods who had called Devilish Angels.

"Of course." Hermione goes inside and comes back out a moment later carrying another glass. "She'll be down in a minute."

It's closer to five minutes. They fill the time with awkward small talk as Hermione bustles around, straightening the deck, cleaning up nonexistent messes, and constantly checking to make sure both Tadd and Declan have everything they need. It's becoming almost overwhelming when the back door opens again and a slim figure slips out.

"Mother!" Tabitha scolds, taking the pitcher from Hermione's hands and pouring her own glass. "Leave them be."

"There you are, dear." Hermione takes the pitcher back from Tabitha and refills both Declan and Tadd's glasses. "I was about to go back in and find you!"

"I was getting dressed. I was out late last night, remember? And I wasn't exactly expecting any visitors out here."

"Yes, well, I wasn't either, but here they are. So make the best of it."

Tabitha rolls her eyes as she drops into the chair Hermione was previously sitting in. She shakes her head as her mother keeps moving around, but flashes a welcoming smile at Tadd and Declan. "So, what can I do for you?"

Declan gets right to the point. "Do you know anything about Athena, Eros, and Aphrodite dying?"

"Dying?" Tabitha looks shocked and leans forward. Her eyes are wide and her mouth hangs open. "Really? Is that...? Oh shit! That's what I felt this week, isn't it?" She slaps her hand to her forehead and grimaces.

"Yeah." Tadd's tone is dry, but he stops short of true sarcasm. "It was."

"Fuck." Tabitha lets her head fall forward again. "I should have known."

"Why?" Declan tips his head to the side. "How would you know?" He doesn't understand the way most of the other gods and demigods weren't at all curious about any of the deaths, but since he knows Tabitha didn't come to any of the crime scenes, he doesn't find it hard to believe she didn't know. She has no reason to.

Tabitha lifts her head and gives him an incredulous look. "I live in the Underworld six months out of the year. Why wouldn't I know?"

"It isn't exactly common for gods to be killed." Declan leans forward and pats Tabitha's shoulder. He smoothes down her long blonde hair and squeezes her shoulder once more before he pulls back and folds his hands in his lap. "None of us knew until we found Sofia's body."

"I should have," she insists, shaking her head. "I would have if I'd been down there instead of up here."

"It wouldn't have made a difference. You don't get news back and forth, do you?"

Tabitha shakes her head. "No," she says sadly. "That's the thing about being dead; it's separate from the living. There isn't communication back and forth, not really. You used to carry some," she says, looking straight at Declan, "but that was messages for the gods, and since they don't send messages down to Hades much anymore, we don't get any news from up here."

"And you don't get any news from down there while you're here," Declan finishes.

"Exactly." Tabitha gives him a wan smile. "If you'd like, I can see if I can talk to the souls the next time I go down there, but I still have a month up here and then six months down there, so you'd really be better off going yourself."

"Hades is more likely to grant you a boon than me."

"Maybe. But you have the right to see them and the right to leave again right away. I don't."

Declan nods and stands. "I'll think about it. If I need your help dealing with Hades, I'll let you know." He holds his hand out.

Tadd ignores it as he rises, thanking both Hermione and Tabitha before stepping off the deck and threading his way through the garden back around front. He already has the list out of his pocket when Declan catches up to him. "So where now?" he asks, casting a questioning glance at Declan as they head down the path that leads to Hermione's house. "Home, or to see Poseidon?"

"Let's get Poseidon over with," Declan says. "He's hardly ever on shore, so I can't imagine he'll have much information for us. It'll be quick."

"At least there's that," Tadd mutters, but he stuffs the list back in his pocket and vanishes. Declan follows.

POSEIDON'S trolley is out in the middle of the ocean, surrounded by nothing but miles and miles of water. It's a small boat, realistically too small to be out this far if it had been captained by anyone other than the god of the sea, and it rides the swells smoothly, bobbing up and down with the gentle waves of the deep. There's no one else on it when Tadd and Declan arrive, just Poseidon at the captain's wheel, gazing out toward the horizon.

Tadd staggers as he appears on the deck, struggling to find footing on the slippery wood beneath him, but Declan grabs his shoulders and steadies him. "Thanks."

"You're welcome." Declan steps back in response to Tadd's frustrated glare and turns to look at the god of the sea. When there's no response from the helm, he takes a cautious step forward, carefully moving over the bobbing deck, and slowly approaches.

Captain Zale Glaros, as Poseidon is currently known, doesn't appear to have noticed them, but as Declan gets closer, he turns and gives him a gruff look. "It's considered polite to ask for permission before coming aboard someone else's ship."

"It's a little difficult to ask when you're out in the middle of the ocean and completely unreachable," Declan replies with a wry grin, stepping a little closer. "However, permission to come aboard?"

Zale looks over both Tadd and Declan and lets out a deliberately put-upon sigh. "Granted, I suppose. What are the two of you doing out here? This isn't exactly the scene you frequent."

"I didn't know we had a scene," Tadd mutters, shoving his hands into his pockets as he comes up to stand next to Declan. "I thought we just worked."

Declan shoots Tadd a worried glance, but Zale booms out an amused laugh. "That would be your scene, Ares. Or should I call you Tadd now?"

"It's Tadd."

"And Declan, I presume?" Zale directs his gaze to Declan and tilts his head when Declan nods. "Fabulous. Zale Glaros at your service. What can I do for you boys?"

It's not what Declan expected. Zale is almost jovial as he secures the wheel and steps down onto the deck, where he stands grinning at Declan and Tadd. It throws Declan off. He was expecting to come up against the stern god of the sea, and Zale Glaros appears to be anything but. It takes Declan a minute to straighten everything out in his mind, and by the time he does, both Tadd and Zale are looking at him with nearly identical amused looks.

"You call Devilish Angels fairly regularly," he says, figuring that opening with the facts will make it clear this isn't a social call.

"Yeah." Zale leans back against the railing and tucks his hands into his pockets. "And?" He presses his lips together into a thin line that doesn't stop them from curling up at the corners.

"And I need to know when the last time you talked to Cal was," Declan replies, rocking back on his heels and arching his own eyebrow in response.

Zale rubs at the back of his neck and looks up toward the sky. "June, maybe?" he ventures after a minute. "Or maybe it was July. I don't remember precisely when I was last on shore."

"But not since this summer?" Declan's program had sorted by date rather than relevance, and so he'd been hopeful Zale would know something, but that hope is fading fast. "You're sure?"

"Positive." Zale looks Declan straight in the eyes. "I don't go on land much. That's my brother's domain. Mine is the ocean, and I'm perfectly happy to stay here."

"Seems... lonely," Tadd hazards. "Out here all by yourself for centuries. Did you ever try to find companionship on shore? Maybe through Lovely Hearts?"

"No." Zale barks out a laugh, throwing his head back and gripping the rail of the ship to keep himself upright. "I don't need a matchmaking service, especially not one run by Aphrodite. I do just fine on my own." He waggles his eyebrows. "I'm not as alone out here as you think."

Declan tilts his head to one side and furrows his brow. "So why do you call Devilish Angels, then? If you're 'just fine', why call at all?"

Zale gives him an incredulous look. "It's fun."

"Right." Declan draws out the word. Talking to Zale is about as enlightening and entertaining as talking to Cal was, and Declan knows he does not want to take this topic any further. "You didn't happen to run into Hephaestus the last time you were on land, did you? Or stop by the museum?" They're both long shots, but he has to ask. If he doesn't, Zale will be the one with the information he needs.

"The last time I was on shore, I didn't even stay one night. There wasn't time to do anything. Bront wanted to talk, so I swung by, but I try to stay out of my brother's way as much as possible. All of this?" He waves his hand around to indicate their discussion. "That's his business, not mine." His expression stays jovial, but his tone clearly indicates the conversation is over.

"Thanks," Declan says, taking the hint, stepping back, and looking at Tadd. "Home?"

"Home," Tadd echoes, nodding at Zale.

"Meet you there," Declan vanishes, then reappears in the foyer. He heads toward the office as Tadd joins him. "Well," he says, slowing his pace a little to walk next to Tadd, "that was interesting."

161

"That's one word for it," Tadd mutters, rubbing at the back of his neck and sighing as he sinks into his chair. "Not the one I'd pick, but it works, I guess."

Declan looks over as he sits down in his own chair and turns on his monitor. "I don't think I want to know what word you would pick."

"Good. I'm not telling." Tadd lets his hand fall into his lap and swivels his chair so he's looking at Declan. "Find anything?"

"No." Declan scrolls through the list, frowning at it. The only new calls his program has found are from people they already have on their list, and no one has popped up often enough to make him think they have a better chance of having the information he needs than anyone else does. "Nothing. Just repeats of the same callers."

"Great." Tadd lets his head fall forward onto his fisted hand. "So what do we do now?"

"You've got the list."

"Right." Tadd pulls the list from his pocket and frowns at it for a moment. "Do we want to talk to someone we expected to see on this list, or someone we didn't?" There are plenty in both categories, surprisingly enough.

"Someone we didn't," Declan replies without hesitation. He had expected to see Flavian, Kimon, and Arion on the list—Apollo, Morpheus, and Pan were always "take it where they could get it" kind of guys—but the other gods and demigods that had showed up on the list had surprised him, and he can't help but wonder if maybe they had called to talk to Cal rather than to make use of Devilish Angel's services.

"Okay." Tadd's frown deepens. "Mona, Karlyn, or Seth?"

"Not Seth," Declan shudders at the mention of the name Hades uses on his rare trips out of the Underworld. He wants to put off another encounter with Hades as long as he can. Centuries if possible.

"Right." Tadd nods emphatically. "Let's save him for very last."

"Yeah. Which leaves Hera and Hestia, right?"

Tadd glances down at the list again to be sure, and nods. "Yeah. So, queen bitch or meek housewife?"

"Um, housewife?" Declan really isn't in the mood to deal with Hera at the moment, not that he ever is, and talking to Karlyn will hopefully be an easy, calming experience. He hasn't seen her since she stopped going by the name Hestia, but he remembers her as a soothing presence, one that was hardly ever noticed when things got busy but who always made everyone feel welcome. After this morning, he can use some of that welcoming calm, especially since Tadd is still upset with him and he can feel the strain in every word they exchange.

"Hmm." Tadd frowns. "I was thinking we'd want to get Mona over with so she has fewer things to get upset about, but we can talk to Karlyn first. Doesn't really matter."

Tadd has a point. Mona is going to feel slighted already, and talking to Karlyn first will add one more thing to the list. "Good point," he concedes. "If we go to her now, we can tell her we only waited because we didn't want to get her up too early." It's closing in on lunchtime now, so that excuse won't work if they go talk to Karlyn, but they might be able to pull it off if they head to Olympus right now.

"So, Mona, then Karlyn?"

"And then lunch," Declan agrees, standing. He makes it halfway across the room before he's hit with an all-too-familiar feeling and his entire body stiffens in agony. Fire races along his veins, and he arches his back, only barely resisting crying out for help. Tadd is hunched over at his desk, squeezing the wood hard enough to leave marks in it as he breathes into his arm and fights the pain.

As soon as it passes, he vanishes, heading toward the source of the pain without exchanging a word, hoping they can catch Egan in the act.


EGAN'S forge appears to be empty when Declan arrives outside it with Tadd right next to him. Tadd cautiously opens the door, holding a hand up to Declan to stay silent. Declan is half-afraid of what he's going to find inside—Selene, perhaps, having come to confront Egan and invoked his wrath—but what he sees when Tadd opens the door is definitely not it.

The forge is immaculate, only a hammer out of place, its handle on the ground and its head resting against the stack of tools next to the anvil where it was dropped. The head is still rocking back and forth slowly with the momentum of its fall, but the hand that dropped it is all the way on the other side of the anvil, lying palm down on the floor. The body it's attached to is mostly hidden behind the anvil from view, but Declan can see enough of it to know it's not Selene who is lying dead.

It's Egan.

"Fuck," Tadd whispers, pushing the door the rest of the way open and ignoring the screech of the rusted hinges. "We were wrong."

Declan steps into the forge behind Tadd, still hoping there's something else he couldn't see through the crack, and sighs when he takes in the otherwise unoccupied room. "Shit."

"Yeah." Tadd lets out a hollow laugh. "I guess he was telling the truth about Adara. He didn't kill her."

"Do you think he saw who did? Or figured it out? That could be why he was killed." Declan walks around the room and frowns at the still body lying between the forge and the anvil. The flames are still burning hot, so he switches them off, immediately cooling the room, and crouches down next to Egan's body.

Egan is lying facedown on the ground, the dagger that killed him embedded in his back. The remains of a project—still too unformed to tell what it's supposed to become—lie across the anvil, and the only sign of a struggle is the hammer resting awkwardly across the other tools and a small bit of silver sticking out from underneath Egan's body.

Declan reaches around and pulls it out, then frowns as he twists his hand back and forth. The delicate silver linked chains of the bracelet lie across his fingers and dangle a little over either side of his hand. It's small, obviously made for a delicately boned person, and it looks familiar, though at the moment Declan can't remember where he's seen it before.

"He didn't even fight," Tadd remarks, crouching down next to Declan and frowning at the body. It looks like someone appeared behind Egan, stabbed him before he knew they were there, and vanished again before anyone had time to make it to the scene of the crime. The dagger is long enough it should have pierced into his heart, and death would have been instantaneous, not giving him a chance to struggle.

"He was surprised. He had to have been." Declan looks at Tadd with a wry grin. "There aren't many people who could fight him and have a chance to win. You. A few of the heroes, maybe, like Herakles or Perseus, but that's it. No one else would stand a chance." He holds out the bracelet. "Definitely not whoever wore this."

Tadd takes it from Declan, frowning at it as well. "I've seen this before." He stares at the silver links lying across his palm as he mentally rewinds through the past few days, trying to ignore the bad memories and focus on what the people he interacted with were wearing. It's not Adara's or Rachel's, but…. "It's Selene's," he says, looking up at Declan with wide eyes.

Declan looks from Tadd to the bracelet and back again. "Why would it be here?"

"We need to ask Selene."

"Do you think she'll tell us? Really?" Declan looks pointedly at the body on the floor.

"She can't be the killer. There's no way she would kill Sofia and Adara. They're female. She wouldn't kill them even to throw people off track."

"No," Declan agrees easily, "but she would kill Egan if she thought he had killed Sofia and Adara." He crouches back down next to the body, frowning at the angle of the dagger. Selene is shorter than Egan, but she's not so much shorter than he is that the location and angle of the blade is impossible. "Maybe we weren't wrong. Maybe Selene figured out Egan was the killer and took matters into her own hands like she threatened."

Tadd presses his lips into a thin line and stares at the bracelet in his hand. "It's possible," he admits after a minute. "But how do we prove it? Do you think Selene will admit she did this?"

"Maybe?" Declan shrugs. "She might, just so she can brag that she did, but she's not stupid enough to deliberately piss off Bront either." He sighs as he pushes his hair back from his head. "I really don't know. She won't tell us if we ask, though."

"Yeah." Tadd stands, brushing his hands on his pants, and walks around the body, looking down at the ground as he goes. "The bracelet must have fallen off when she stabbed him. Or maybe...." He comes up behind Declan, urges him to stand, and positions him to the side of Egan's body. "If she appeared behind him, stabbing downward, he might have heard her and managed to turn enough to grab her arm." He acts out the stabbing motion from behind Declan, and Declan swivels as he moves, grabbing his arm as Tadd's hand comes into contact with his back. "She had the bracelet on her right wrist the day Sofia died, but if she was wearing it on her other wrist, it's possible Egan saw her."

"Which means he would be able to tell us." Declan lets his head fall forward and squeezes his eyes shut. He does not want to do this. "Fuck." He blows out a heavy sigh and slides his hand into his pocket to pull out his cell phone. "I guess I should call Bront, since he's not here."

"Yeah...." Tadd looks around. "Does this seem weird to you? Every other murder, people have showed up at the scene, usually before we got there. This time, there's no one."

Declan freezes with his fingers hovering over the surface of his phone, and looks up at Tadd with wide eyes. "Shit. I didn't even think of that, but you're right. If Selene didn't do this, she should be here, especially after the lecture she gave us last night. And Bront should definitely be here."

"And Lukas, for that matter," Declan adds. "He's managed to turn up at every scene."

"Who has?" Bront's booming voice startles Declan and Tadd, and they swivel as one to look at the king of the gods. He looks worn down this time, weary rather than angry, and he sighs deeply as he kneels next to Egan and pulls the dagger from his back. "Do you know who did this?"

Declan takes Tadd's hand, curling his fingers around the bracelet, and shakes his head. "Not yet." He meets Bront's gaze steadily, though his hand is trembling where it's curled around Tadd's.

"Not yet?" Bront slips the dagger into his coat pocket and stands again. His face is a mask of anger that reminds Declan of the days when he slung lightning bolts at anyone who irritated him, but it doesn't appear to be directed at Declan. Yet. "And how do you plan to figure it out?"

"I'm going to Hades." He still doesn't want to go again, but there's no other choice now. He realized that the moment Tadd pointed out Egan could have seen Selene just before he died. The only chance he has to prevent more deaths is to convince Hades to let him talk to the dead gods.

"What?" Tadd steps forward, grabbing Declan by the shoulder and spinning him around. "We decided we weren't going there unless it was the last resort!"

"It is the last resort, Tadd, but you're not going. I am." Declan turns back to Bront. "Make him stay here, please."

"No." Tadd squeezes Declan's arm tightly. "You're not going down there without me. It's too dangerous."

"It's too dangerous for you to go." Declan lets his gaze swivel between Tadd and Bront and ends with his eyes focused on Tadd's. "I have safe passage granted in and out. You don't. If you go down there, Hades doesn't have to let you leave."

Tadd casts an imploring look at Bront. "You don't have *safe* passage. Hades will let you leave. He won't do anything to make it safe." He huffs, runs his hand through his hair, and lets out a deep breath. "Whoever did this, they have to know we'll find them soon. A trip to the Underworld would be a perfect opportunity for them to ambush you. If they don't, there are a lot of people down there who won't look too kindly on you, even if it's just because you get to leave. It's too dangerous."

"It's more dangerous for you." Every bit of Declan's being rebels against bringing Tadd into the Underworld with him. The path in isn't pleasant, but it's getting out that really worries him. After Hades's

167

oblique threats earlier, he can't risk that Hades will trap Tadd down there.

"I can take care of myself."

"And I can't?"

"Not the way you might need to," Tadd growls, stepping close and glaring into Declan's eyes before turning to Bront. "Tell him he has to take me. Please."

Declan casts an imploring glance at Bront, but before he can muster any further argument, Bront holds up a hand. "I agree with Tadd." He leans in close to Declan, his bright blue eyes piercing deep into Declan's soul. "I told him to take care of you when this started, Declan. I'm not changing my mind."

"But—"

"Don't. My decision is final." Bront steps back. "Be careful, and come back with answers." He flashes away without giving either Declan or Tadd a chance to answer, and a moment later a bolt of lightning illuminates the room, blinding its occupants and incinerating Egan's body.

"Well," Tadd says, flashing a strained grin. "Let's go visit Hades."

"NO." HADES leans to the side, putting his elbow on the arm of the bone throne and resting his chin on his fist. His legs are crossed, his left ankle resting on his right knee, and he looks far more like a bored playboy lounging in a chair than the god of the Underworld at the head of his audience chamber. It's a disconcerting contrast, especially when he narrows his gaze and stares hard at Declan. "You can't talk to them. I told you that already." The soft vowels roll easily off his tongue, emphasizing they're in a completely different world now.

"Why not? You never gave me a satisfactory answer." Declan steps forward, closing the distance between himself and the throne, ignoring Tadd's soft hiss and the hand on his shoulder. "They are down here, aren't they?"

"Of course." Hades shifts so he's leaning back in the throne and affects a bored expression.

"So then what's the problem?" Tadd steps up next to Declan, standing so he can easily move between Declan and Hades if the need arises. "If they're here, let us talk to them."

"No." Hades presses the tips of his fingers together as he looks at them smugly. "I don't think I will."

Declan casts an exasperated glance at Tadd. The trip down here had been just as he had remembered, free from the extra challenges and obstacles he had secretly feared they would face. The easy journey had given him hope, and he had entered Hades's audience chamber confident his request would be approved and they would have the answers they needed before the hour was out.

He had not expected Hades to refuse to cooperate.

"You have to," Declan says, directing his wide-eyed gaze back to Hades. "Zeus—"

"I don't care what my brother wants me to do. He does not rule down here. I do, thanks to his treachery, and I will not let him tell me how to run my domain."

"He's not trying to tell you how to rule it," Declan protests. "He wants us to talk to them. We're not trying to break them free or usurp your authority or anything. All I want is for them to tell me who killed them."

"Why do you care? Whoever it is didn't kill you."

"Because they'll kill again." Declan takes another step forward, again putting himself in front of Tadd. "I don't want that to happen. You shouldn't either."

"Why should I care if gods die or not? I rather like the idea. It gets a bit dreary down here, and I need new entertainment."

"Death isn't entertainment."

"It is for me." Hades says haughtily. "Now, give me one good reason I should consider letting you talk to your friends."

Declan has a whole list of reasons he needs to find the killer before someone else dies, but none of them will appeal to Hades, so he

169

discards them all in favor of looking Hades straight in the eyes and saying one word. "Persephone."

Hades stiffens. "What about her?"

"You don't want her to die, do you?"

"Of course I do. Then she'd be with me all the time, instead of with her mother six months a year."

"As a spirit. Right now she comes to you as a living, breathing woman. If she's killed, her shade will be trapped with the other gods, and you'll get to torment her instead of love her." Declan takes another step forward, shadowed by Tadd. "If you love her, you want her to be happy, and she is. She wouldn't be as a shade, though. You know that."

Hades's expression hardens, but he doesn't look away. "How do you know she's happy?"

"We saw her," Tadd says, stepping slightly in front of Declan. "This morning. We went to visit her mother, and she was there, so we talked to her too. She offered to try to help us talk to Athena, Eros, and Aphrodite, but she can't come down here for another month, and it'll be too late then."

Hades's expression hardens further. "Get out." He points toward the door of the audience chamber and glares at both of them. "Now."

"We can't." Declan sighs and lets his expression turn pleading. "We have to talk to them."

"No, you don't."

"But—"

"Did you really think that telling me you got to visit with my wife when I can't see her was going to persuade me to your side? The two of you are getting on my last nerves. Don't push me."

Tadd takes Declan's arm and starts to head out of the audience chamber, but Declan resists. "No." He turns, wrenching his arm free from Tadd's grasp, and looks straight at Hades. "Please, let me talk to one of them. It will only take a minute, and then—"

"Declan!" Tadd grabs his arm again and tugs harder this time.

"I suggest you listen to your lover boy there."

Tadd drops Declan's arm and turns to glare at Hades, bristling at the term. "I'm not his lover boy."

"No, you're not, are you? Not right now, anyway." Hades curls his lips up into a sly smile. "I heard the two of you were fighting. Some friends of yours mentioned it when I sent them to Tartarus. I didn't think I'd get the chance to see it for myself, though. I have to say, it's not as spectacular as I thought it would be. You must be calming down in your old age, Ares."

"I'll show you calm." Tadd surges forward, his arms outstretched as he reaches for Hades's neck, and only Declan's superior speed lets him get between the two of them.

"Don't!" he yells, straining against Tadd. "This isn't the time."

"Yes it is." Tadd pushes forward, shoving Declan to the side with little effort. Declan stumbles, staggering a few steps before his feet catch up with his upper body, and Hades laughs.

"That's more like it," he says, stepping out of the way as Tadd surges toward the throne again. "I'll leave the two of you to it. Have a safe trip home, and don't forget to say hi to Charon on the way out." He waits until they're both looking at him, wiggles his fingers in a little wave, and vanishes.

Tadd whirls, looking around the room with wide eyes. It's empty except for him and Declan, and he curses under his breath as he looks around. "Dammit."

"Yeah." Declan pinches the bridge of his nose and sighs. "So what now? He said they were in Tartarus—"

"No." Tadd shakes his head before Declan has the chance to finish the thought. "We are not trying to bust into Tartarus. I'd like to be able to leave, thank you."

"So, what, we just go? We made the trip all the way down here, Tadd. Now you think we should leave without getting any information? Do you really want to tell Bront we still don't know who is killing everyone?"

Tadd sighs and rubs at the bridge of his nose. "No, I don't, but I don't know what else to do, Declan. Hades won't help us, we can't just waltz into Tartarus, and I don't particularly want to stay here, do you?"

"No, but we need to do something. We can't go back to Bront empty-handed."

"What then, Declan?" Tadd spreads his arms wide and takes a step forward. "If you have an idea, tell me! But otherwise we're leaving."

Declan doesn't have the chance to think of any ideas. He's about to tell Tadd to calm down and give him a minute when the ornate doors to the audience chamber swing open, revealing the huddling masses of souls waiting for their chance at an audience with Hades. The line stretches for miles: gaunt, gray shades shuffling forward an inch at a time. The ones near the front are dressed in clothing reminiscent of the glory days of the Greek gods, and when they see Hades isn't in his chamber, an angry rumble goes through the crowd.

The air in the room grows oppressive as the news of Hades's absence makes its way back through the lines of waiting shades. The discontented rumblings become louder, escalating from mutters into yells, and then one shade raises his arms, points at Declan and Tadd, and yells, "They have Hades! Get them!"

The crowd surges forward, filling the audience chamber as Declan and Tadd watch in horrified fascination. They're near the back of the room, close to the throne and not far from the small side door they entered through, but the crowd gets closer with every second, and the audience chamber is half-full before Tadd shakes himself out of his shocked stupor and grab Declan's arm. "Let's go."

"Yeah." Declan shakes his head as he runs, clearing it from the fog that had filled his brain. He glances back over his shoulder and puts on a new burst of speed, dragging Tadd behind him as he desperately tries to stay in front of the angry mob. It would be easy if they could just vanish, but Hades doesn't want anyone popping in and out of his realm and has eliminated their ability to do that here, the same way Zeus has in his casino. They have to run and the shades are almost able to match Tadd's speed.

The room is two-thirds of the way full by the time they reach the door, and the shades are only feet away when they surge through it and yank it shut behind them. There's no lock, no real way to secure the door besides holding on to the handle and pulling against the shades, but fortunately, they seem unable to open the door, no matter how hard they try. They stop pulling quickly, resorting to wailing and banging, and slowly, Tadd relaxes his grip and lets go. The door stays shut, and they both breathe a sigh of relief.

"That was close." Declan sucks in a deep breath and lets it out in a heavy sigh as he leans over, resting his hands on his knees and breathing deeply, like a runner catching his breath after a race. He's not winded from running—he can do that all day at much faster speeds— but his heart is thudding in his ears and his adrenaline is racing from the excitement.

"Too close," Tadd agrees, leaning back against the wall next to the door and focusing on returning his breathing and heart rate to normal. "We need to go. Now."

Declan doesn't argue. He still wants to find something to tell Bront before they leave here, but Hades definitely won't help them now, and the shades in the audience chamber seem far more bent on releasing their anger than talking. Even if they could find the entrance to Tartarus, they'd have to battle through shades angered by the sight of living beings to get there, and that would be the easy part. Tartarus is where souls go to be tormented for eternity. No one leaves, ever.

"Yeah," he agrees, standing up and shaking out his shoulders. "This way."

Declan leads the way around the Asphodel Meadows to the Acheron, and pauses on the dock that juts out into the river of sorrows. The fog is heavy across the river, but the lamentations of the paupers and the friendless dead on the far side, trapped forever in Erebus because they lack the coin to pay Charon's fee, carry easily, filling the air with a mournful sound.

Tadd steps a little closer to Declan as the fog parts, revealing a boat moving slowly. It's derelict and old, made of weather-worn wood that creaks as it glides across the misty water. At the helm is a gaunt figure with light hair, dressed in modern clothing that's incongruous with the boat and the setting. His expression is downright creepy as he watches the shades depart, a shockingly small number of them staggering off and looking around with dazed expressions as he looks on.

When they're gone, he turns his gaze to Declan. "Hermes."

"Charon."

"It's Hector now. Hector Carras. At least, it is when I get to take shore leave." He lets out a hollow chuckle as Declan tries to imagine Charon doing anything but ferrying souls across the Acheron. "It's not very often, but sometimes the boss likes to cause trouble, you know? And it's not like most of the poor souls over there are ever getting across. People seem to have forgotten about leaving gold coins with their dead." He grins, looking maniacal, and shakes his head. "A few of them have tried to pay me with paper and nickel."

Declan twists his lips wryly. The Underworld hadn't changed when the belief of humans shifted the Earth and the sun because of all the souls in it that believed in the way it was. Souls who truly believed in the afterlife of modern religions—good or bad—simply appeared in whatever section of the Underworld matched their belief. People without a strong belief ended up in Erebus. Someday, perhaps, the Underworld would change, too, but until then, Charon would have to learn to adapt. Declan hoped he could. "That is the accepted currency these days. Gold hasn't been the standard for years. You're more likely to get gold jewelry than gold coins."

"I've noticed." Charon makes a wry sound. "I've taken a few that look like coins—they're not worth as much, but at least I know they're the real thing, and I kind of feel sorry for the saps, standing there forever. It's not their fault their friends are idiots."

"Getting soft in your old age, man." Declan pats Charon on the shoulder companionably. "Back in the day you never would have let anyone cross without the correct fare."

"Yeah, well." Charon shoves his hands in his pockets. "What else am I going to do? If I don't have anyone to ferry across, the boss'll let me go. Downsizing is the big word topside, isn't it? I don't want him to get any ideas."

"No, you don't." Declan shakes his head and shudders dramatically.

Charon grins. "Anyway, I'm sure you didn't come down here to chat with me. Need a ride across?"

"If you don't mind."

"It's what I'm here for. You'd better hope Cerberus remembers you, though. He's been feisty lately with all the people trying to get back out once they discover they're stuck here."

Declan laughs and moves toward the boat, Tadd right behind him. He steps on and holds out his hand to guide Tadd on board, but Charon slams his pole down over the gap, nearly hitting Declan's hand. "Just you."

"He's with me."

"Does the boss know about that?" Charon pulls a phone from his pocket and taps at the screen. "You have safe passage in and out, guaranteed. You don't get to take passengers."

"Yes, Hades knows. And Tadd's not a passenger. He's alive. He's my husband. You know, Ares?"

"Doesn't matter." Charon frowns at the phone and sticks it back into his pocket. "He's not on the list, and no one told me he's allowed to go. I'll take you across, but he has to stay here."

"I'm telling you," Declan growls, shoving the poll aside and stepping back onto the dock. He's not going to risk staying on the boat and letting Charon take off without Tadd on board. "Now let him on."

"Sorry. It's worth my job if I do, and this isn't much, but it's all I know. He doesn't get to leave."

"He's not dead."

"He will be once he wanders into Tartarus or the Asphodel Meadows." Charon's grin turns evil. "Zeus, given who he is, he may be torn to bits by the shades waiting to be judged or the souls in the Elysian Fields. He's responsible for a lot of people being down here, you know."

"It's his job." Declan steps forward, but he's stopped by Tadd's hand on his shoulder.

"Declan." Tadd nods in Charon's direction. "Let me." He steps into Declan's spot and lets his lips curl up into a grin that matches Charon's. "It's a good thing I'm not in any of those places, then, isn't it?"

Charon's face falls and he gives Tadd an unamused look. "You will be. I'm not taking you across."

"Oh, I think you will." Tadd pulls a dagger out from where he had tucked it into his pants and holds it up so Charon can see. He tilts it back and forth, letting the fog curl around it. "Do you know what this is?"

Charon shakes his head no, but Declan looks at it with wide eyes as he realizes what Tadd had brought. "Is that...?"

"The dagger that killed Athena." Tadd looks over his shoulder at Declan. "Do you think it would work on Charon as well? I know he's not strictly a god, but that would make him easier to kill, right?"

"Right." Declan forces a grin, reminding himself that Tadd is playing a role and they need to do this to get across the Acheron. Charon is right about what will happen to Tadd if he encounters a lot of the souls down here—the incident in Hades's audience chamber proved that, and those weren't warriors who had died fighting battles in Ares's name.

"That's what I thought." Tadd winks at Declan as he turns back to Charon.

Declan can't deny there is a part of him that is enjoying the way Tadd is tormenting Charon, and he knows Tadd will use the dagger on Charon if that's what it takes to get on the boat, but he really just wants Charon to let them cross. He just wants to scare Charon into helping them.

Fortunately, he doesn't have to take it any further. Charon gulps, looks from Tadd to the dagger and back to Tadd again, and gestures shakily to the boat. "Welcome aboard."

Tadd lets his grin relax into a more genuine one. "Thank you." He lets Declan board first, the dagger held ready the whole time in case Charon changes his mind, and then gets on himself. Once he's safely aboard, he tucks the dagger back into his pants and lets Charon climb back on the boat and take his position at the helm.

They glide across in silence. Charon keeps sending angry glances in Tadd's direction, but Tadd keeps his hand near the protruding dagger hilt and his fingers loose and ready, and Charon stays at the front of the boat, grudgingly poling them across the water. In less time than Declan remembers it taking, the boat is knocking against the dock on the far shore, and Charon is standing in his position at the side of the boat, ready to defend it from anyone trying to board without the proper payment.

Tadd and Declan squeeze through the tiny gap Charon makes between his body and the boat railing to let them disembark and start to push through the crowd. It's nearly impossible to move, fighting against the flow of the crowd, but for the first few feet, that's all they have to fight against. The shades nearest the boat are too concerned with trying their currency or attempting to climb aboard without Charon's permission to worry about who is pushing next to them. Their only concern is other shades fighting for their spot. They don't care about live people heading away from the boat.

Farther out, the crowd thins, divided into two types of souls—the ones who have waited on this shore for so long they've given up and the ones who have been here for so short a period of time they haven't adapted to where they are and haven't grasped that they need to get on the boat if they don't want to be stuck here for eternity. Mostly, the new arrivals are in clumps, gathered together to listen wide-eyed to the stories passed amongst them, not quite ready to believe but not able to actively disbelieve either. The old souls are more solitary, wandering between the shore of the Acheron and the boundary of the Underworld, steering clear of Cerberus and doing their best to dodge the harpies.

Moving is easier once the crowd is gone, and Declan picks up the pace, pulling Tadd along as quickly as he can, doing his best to dodge both the small groups and the solitary travelers. He's successful until they round a boulder and nearly smack into a bearded old man wearing a leather kilt. Declan pulls back quickly, backing Tadd up as well, but he's not fast enough, and the man's eyes narrow.

"I know you."

Declan pushes Tadd behind him. The man was obviously a soldier, and though Tadd's clothing is definitely different from what he would have been wearing when the soldier saw him last and his hairstyle has been modernized significantly, his face is still the same as it was thousands of years ago, and it's entirely possible the man really does know who he is. "You must be mistaken."

"No." The man tilts forward like a drunkard with too much alcohol in him and rests his hand heavily on Declan's shoulder. "I know you both," he whispers as he bares his teeth in a maniacal grin. "You're gods."

Tadd steps forward and pulls the man's hand off Declan's shoulder. "Go back to the shore, old man."

"Why? So I can wait there for eternity, watching as it gets more and more crowded because no one knows about the ferryman anymore? I was killed in battle, and the enemy buried me without any coin, deliberately leaving me to rot here on the shore, but I have to listen to these pups whine because their friends didn't know." He squares his shoulders and positions himself between the two boulders marking the path out of the Underworld, blocking the way. "I'm not going down there."

"I don't blame you," Declan says in his most soothing voice as he clasps the man on the shoulder. He takes care to keep the touch lighter than the one the man had on him, and he forces sympathy and understanding into his voice. "But you might want to get off the trail. If you're lucky and let them wander, maybe Cerberus will get them." He's hoping that by focusing the soldier's attention on the other shades he seems to hate so much he can distract him from the fact that he and Tadd are leaving as well and that, as gods, they are likely to make it past the three-headed dog guarding the gates to the Underworld.

It doesn't work. The soldier shakes his head and fixes an angry stare on Tadd. "Nice try, but I'm not letting him leave without a reckoning." He points at Tadd with his chin, his face set in an angry mask.

"A reckoning? For what?" Tadd tilts his head to the side, pretending to be clueless, and slides his hand along his body toward the dagger handle.

"For the way I died." The soldier clenches his fingers into fists and spreads his legs into a fighting stance. "You killed me."

Tadd pushes in front of Declan, shielding him from the angry shade. "Then it was an honorable death." He nods his head in recognition of the man's sacrifice.

The shade isn't listening. He clenches his fists tighter and brings them up in front of his chin, holding them at the ready. "If it weren't for you," he snarls, "I would have died at home and been given a proper burial. You are the reason I'm stuck here!"

He sends his right fist flying straight for Tadd's head. Tadd steps forward and catches it with one hand while grabbing the man's arm with his other. "Don't." The man's left hand flies around, heading for Tadd's ear, and Tadd moves again.

The scuffle is short and violent and ends with the shade gasping for breath he no longer needs as he lies limply on the ground. Tadd stands over him, his hands still clenched, and looks down. "Only the heroes have a chance of victory when fighting the gods, and you're no hero."

"Tadd." Declan carefully steps over the man and places a hand on Tadd's shoulder, squeezing as he walks by. "Come on. We need to keep moving." The scuffle, though short, attracted attention, and more shades are wandering away from the shore of the river and heading up the path toward them. They mostly look confused and curious, but Declan can see anger burning on a few of their faces, and they don't have time for that right now. With Hades unwilling to let them talk to the shades of the slain gods, they have to find actual evidence, and they're running out of time before the killer strikes again.

Tadd hesitates for a moment, glaring down at the beaten soldier and gritting his teeth as he tries to rein in his anger, then turns to follow Declan through the boulders and along the path leading from the Acheron to the Styx. He moves up next to Declan as soon as the path allows, unwilling to let Declan take the lead but also unwilling to let him fall behind.

Erebus, as the area is called, is a desolate wasteland, intended to make the recently dead want to cross the river to find out their fates. It's gray and misty, with boulders and turns that make the paths difficult to follow, and the wailing of the dead souls mingles with the screams of the harpies and the growls of Cerberus to provide an ominous soundtrack.

The mob behind them is growing, led now by the shade of the soldier Tadd took down, and their cries fill the air as the soldier eggs his compatriots on, inciting them to anger. Declan picks up the pace, cursing under his breath and glancing around repeatedly, looking for the harpies he can hear flying nearer. "Come on."

Tadd draws the dagger and holds it ready as they hurry along through the increasingly hostile terrain. The shades are as encumbered by the boulders and twisting paths as they are, but exiting the Underworld isn't easy, even for gods, and if the harpies attack, the friendless dead will catch up.

The cries of the harpies grow louder as the terrain gets rougher. They're close enough to the exit that they can hear the scrape of Cerberus's chain against the rock and the click of his toenails as he paces back and forth in front of the exit when the first harpy attacks. She screams something unintelligible as she swoops in, swiping with her claws as she flies by, and only Declan's speed lets him knock Tadd to the ground fast enough that they both avoid injury.

Tadd rolls them over, pinning Declan to the ground beneath him. It leaves his back exposed, but he'd rather that than Declan's, and he doesn't plan to stay like this for long. "When we get up, run."

Declan juts out his chin. "Not if you're staying."

"I have to hold them off."

"And I have to get you out of here. The only way Cerberus might let you by is if you're with me. I'm not leaving without you." Declan would cross his arms if they weren't pinned between him and Tadd. Instead, he sets his jaw and narrows his gaze so Tadd knows he's serious. "I can hold my own against harpies."

Tadd isn't eager to test that assertion, but he isn't given a choice. The harpy swoops back in, screeching loudly, and this time she's quickly followed by two of her sisters. Tadd barely has time to roll off Declan and jump to his feet before large black claws are thrusting at his face, aiming for his eyes as the hideous winged woman shrieks curses at him.

He ducks and swipes blindly with the dagger, missing completely but managing to dodge the sharp claws. He brings the dagger back up again, shifts into a fighting stance, and backs up three steps as he holds it at the ready and watches the hovering woman grin at him. Her naked body is thin to the point it looks emaciated, but other than the clawed feet that came so close to cutting Tadd and the wings holding her in the air, her shape is humanoid. Her breasts sag horribly, looking like wrinkled, misshapen lumps on her chest, and her face is so grotesque that it's difficult to look at. Long hair falls around her shoulders and down her back, but even that is so tangled it's hardly recognizable.

Another harpy comes in from his left, yelling in her harsh voice as she reaches out for him. Her hands don't have claws, but her nails are long and thick enough they're almost as bad, and when Tadd turns to deal with the new threat, the first harpy swoops in again, making him spin rapid-fire, slashing with the dagger as quickly as he can to keep the deadly women away from him.

Declan jumps to his feet as the third harpy swoops in. They're not coming for him—they won't attack him after what happened the one time they tried to violate his safe passage—but he's not going to sit idly by and watch them attack Tadd either. He doesn't have a weapon, but the ground is littered with loose rocks, and he grabs those as he rises and hurls them quickly at the harpies. "Leave him alone!"

The harpies whirl at the onslaught, giving Tadd the opportunity to slice the dagger across one of their hamstrings. She hisses, pulling her legs up close to her body, and whirls on Tadd, but Tadd slashes again, this time hitting her forearm. The cuts are red and nasty, standing out strongly against her grayish skin, and when Tadd strikes a third time, she flies away, shrieking loudly. The other two hiss and snarl, swooping again toward Tadd, but then follow their sister, flying off quickly into the distance.

Declan drops the remaining rocks he was holding and runs over to Tadd. "Are you okay?"

"Fine." Tadd wipes the dagger off on the ground, leaving harpy blood on the dirt, and finishes the job on the hem of his undershirt before tucking the dagger back into its sheath. "They didn't get me."

"Good." Declan grabs Tadd's wrist and pulls. "Come on. We don't want to be here when they come back."

The trail gets harder the closer they get to the end of the Underworld. The boulders become bigger and the path steeper and more winding. Coming from the other direction, it's an easy series of switchbacks that make travelers want to know what's on the other side, but heading out, it's steep and foreboding, discouraging the shades congregated by the river from even trying to escape.

Cerberus himself is chained on the banks of the river Styx, just before the path leads to the surface. Dead souls appear beyond him and never see him unless they try to escape, but the living who want to enter Hades's realm have to walk by him to get in, which he almost always allows, and again to get out, which he never does. Only Declan, Tabitha, and Hades can walk by without inciting his anger, and his three heads mean sneaking by him is impossible.

That doesn't stop Tadd from trying.

Before they approach the dog, Declan stops and looks Tadd straight in the eyes. "You have to let me stay closer to Cerberus."

Everything in Tadd's being rebels against the thought. He's the warrior; he should be the one closer to the threat. Only this time, the threat is to him alone. Declan should be able to walk by without any problems, and would be if Tadd wasn't with him. "Do you think it will help?"

"No." Declan shakes his head. "But it can't hurt. And maybe he'll be hesitant to bite you if he'll risk getting me too." He knows that's not true, but it's a nice thought, and he'll delude himself into thinking it's possible for as long as he can. It makes him feel a little bit better about the situation.

Tadd pulls the dagger back out, holds it ready in his hands, and nods. "All right." He lets Declan step in front of him, fighting down the urge to push his way forward. "Let's go."

Declan casts an amused glance at the dagger as he starts up the trail. He knows it won't do much good against a giant three-headed dog determined to rip Tadd to pieces, but at least he won't be going into this defenseless.

182

Cerberus is lying down with his back to the gates and all six of his eyes closed when Tadd and Declan approach, but the moment they come into the range of the thick iron chain that encircles the spot where his three necks join his torso, he jumps to his feet, snarling with all three heads. It's an awful, magnificent sight. Standing, Cerberus is about four times as tall as Declan. Drool drips from all three of his mouths, and his lips are curled back to reveal wickedly sharp teeth. His paws are as thick as Tadd's knees and sport nails that look as wicked as a harpy's. His fur is thick and black, comparatively short over most of his body but sticking up in tufts in front of each of his pointy ears.

"Damn," Tadd whispers, tightening his grip on the dagger.

Declan nods and motions for Tadd to stop. They stand completely still as Cerberus lowers his middle head, sniffing with enough force to send gravel rolling back down the path and lift Declan's hair back from his face. He spends a minute snuffling all over Declan, huffs, and pulls back, lowering all three of his heads in the signal that means Declan is free to pass.

Declan lets out a deep sigh of relief and motions for Tadd not to say anything. There's a chance Cerberus won't realize he only sniffed one of two people trying to get past him. He's not stupid enough to think the dog's instructions include letting him take anyone else out of the Underworld with him—otherwise he would have been called upon to free trapped souls—and he's not certain the fact that he's alive, or the fact that he's the god of war, is enough to get him through. After what Hades said, those things might work against him rather than for him, though he doubts the dog knows enough to do more than differentiate between the three people allowed to leave and everyone else.

They get halfway to the entrance when Cerberus sniffs again and his rightmost head snaps up and twists around so he's looking straight at Tadd and Declan. His leftmost head twists and comes at them from the back, and the middle head leans down, pressing in close enough to Declan he can feel the moisture on his nose. He tries to keep himself between Tadd and the dog, but they're being watched and sniffed at from three angles, and he can only cover one of them. It doesn't take long before Cerberus lowers his right head and starts sniffing at Tadd.

The dog's eye is close to Tadd's right hand, and it would be easy to swing the dagger and take out Cerberus's eye and possibly penetrate into his brain. It wouldn't be as easy to take out the rest of the animal—three heads means three brains, and Tadd knows he'd have to kill all of them to kill Cerberus—and if he were to succeed, he knows Hades would find some way to make his life horribly difficult. It's not worth it, especially while there's still a slim chance the dog will let them walk out.

Cerberus huffs as he pulls back from Tadd, and for a second, Declan thinks they're going to be allowed to leave unhindered. He takes a step forward as the dog draws back, and breathes out a sigh of relief that's cut short as Cerberus scrambles onto the path in front of them and barks loudly with two of his heads. He lowers the third down in front of Tadd and Declan, baring his teeth and letting out a menacing growl that sends chills down Declan's spine.

"What now?" Tadd hisses, taking a step back to try to avoid the dog's foul breath. It penetrates the air, filling it with a foul odor that would surely leave any mortal unconscious.

"I don't—"

"Problem, boys?" Hades steps out from behind the towering boulder Cerberus's chain is attached to and flashes a smug grin in their direction.

"Call off your dog, Hades," Declan grits out through clenched teeth as he glares. It takes a lot more to get him angry than it does to rile Tadd up, but Hades has managed it, and Declan isn't going to hold back if Hades doesn't give him what he wants. "You wanted us gone, so let us leave."

"No. I wanted you out of my audience chamber and to stop asking me for favors I have no reason to grant. I'm perfectly happy to keep you in the Underworld." He pats Cerberus on one of his noses and rocks back on his heels. "Though I suppose I can't stop you from leaving if you really wanted to, Declan. Cerberus here will let you by."

"Tell him to let Tadd by too."

"No." Hades tucks his hands into his pockets. "I don't think so. I like the idea of letting the shades know who he is. Could be fun! Sport like I haven't seen in years." His grin widens as he looks at Tadd. "I'm going to enjoy watching this."

"No, you won't." Tadd tightens his grip on the dagger. Cerberus's middle head is still between him and Hades, but that won't stop him from trying to drive the bronze weapon straight through Hades's eyes.

Declan steps closer to Tadd, carefully putting himself between Tadd and Cerberus's snarling head. "You let other people leave, sometimes, even dead people, when someone else comes for them. Why can't I take Tadd with me?"

Hades scoffs. "Not many."

"But some. Even one sets a precedent, Hades, you know that. Now give me one good reason I can't take Tadd with me, or let us both leave. Now."

"Love." Hades scratches behind Cerberus's ear as he looks between Declan and Tadd. "The people who got to leave had someone who loved them so much they were willing to do anything, even brave me, to be reunited. And even then it wasn't easy. The two of you... you couldn't even get along for the ten minutes we were talking earlier. You're only together because of a curse." He shakes his head. "That's not love."

Declan bristles, but Tadd slips the dagger back into its sheath and shakes his head. "Is that really what you think? That because I was upset with him, I don't love him? That because a curse and the need for pleasure brought us together, we haven't fallen in love? Really?"

Hades looks nonplussed, but he manages to keep his tone level. "Of course."

"That's sad." Tadd steps forward and curls his fingers around Declan's. "And not at all true. A fight doesn't mean we've stopped loving each other." He squeezes Declan's hand before he lets go, steps closer to Hades, and smiles. It's not a friendly look but one that's incited terror in armed men. "And you would be amazed at what we'll do for each other. There might be a lot of souls down here who don't like me, Hades, but I guarantee none of them like you. I think I could persuade them to see my point of view."

185

Declan represses a shudder at the frost in Tadd's tone. He can feel his husband's anger building to dangerous levels, but this time, he's not going to stop Tadd if he wants to unleash Ares. He feels the same way, and as he steps forward with one final offer he has to make so he can tell Bront they did genuinely try, he hopes Hades refuses and Tadd has reason to let go.

"Let Tadd leave with me, Hades, and I'll help you."

Hades's gaze swings to Declan. "With what? There's nothing you can do here that I can't."

"Except come and go as I please." Declan looks Hades straight in the eyes. "I know you haven't talked to Persephone since she left. I'll carry a message to her, and I'll work on developing something that will communicate between the surface and the Underworld without the need for messengers, but only if you let Tadd leave with me."

"Carry a message and I'll let him go when you bring a reply."

"No." Declan draws himself up to his full height so he's towering over Hades. "I'm not taking anything to Tabitha unless Tadd comes with me. I won't leave without him."

Hades laughs, the sound dry and unamused. "Is that supposed to be a threat? If I keep him, I get two living gods instead of one. Double the fun."

"Double the trouble," Tadd counters. "People like him. He'll win them to our side, and I'll teach them how to rise up against you. By the time Tabitha returns, you won't be ruling here anymore, and she'll have no reason to stay."

Hades glares hard at him for a minute and kicks at a stone lying on the ground. "Dammit!" He holds up his hand, concentrating on the air above it until a rolled, wax-sealed piece of parchment paper appears in it, and he holds it out to Declan. "Here. Take this and go. Both of you." He walks backward, sliding his hand down Cerberus's neck, and curls his fingers around the edge of his giant collar. "Come on, boy." He tugs once at the collar, whistles, and walks back to the boulder where the chain is fastened.

Cerberus slinks away, heading toward his master with agonizing slowness and growling at Tadd with every step he takes. When he's far enough away the path is clear, Declan takes Tadd's hand, laces their fingers together, tucks the parchment into his pocket, and starts back up the trail. "Thank you," he says, flashing a grin at Hades that's met with an angry glare. "Be seeing you."

"Oh, I hope so," Hades replies, letting his lips curl up into a smile.


TADD slams his fist into the wall the moment he appears in their house. It leaves yet another hole in the plaster he'll have to get patched, but after their discussion with Hades, his blood is boiling, and their detour on the way home to deliver his message to Tabitha didn't help at all. She was grateful for the message and promised to contact Declan when she had read it and had one to return, but she was soft and polite, and the manners that seemed charming when they had talked to her earlier had grated on his nerves this evening.

Declan steps back, his eyes wide. "Tadd?" He clearly hadn't been expecting that. "What's wrong?"

"I'm pissed. What do you think?" Tadd sucks in a deep breath, struggling to calm himself. It's not Declan's fault he's upset; Declan did everything he could to mitigate the situation, and he kept their visit with Tabitha as brief as possible. Neither fact does anything to soothe Tadd's anger, though. "I'm going to go work out."

"Yeah, okay." Declan flashes a smile. "I'm going to go to the office and see if any new leads have come up in those searches. I think we're going to have to go see Selene, though, and try to persuade her to talk."

"Right." Tadd nods. "After I take care of this." He doesn't wait for Declan's response, just heads straight for the gym and immediately starts pummeling a punching bag. It's not as satisfying as hurting someone would be, but he can pretend it has Hades's face on it, and that gives him enough satisfaction to start calming down.

After a few minutes of rhythmic pounding, Tadd's thoughts wander away from his anger. They haven't learned anything new since Egan died, but there's something about this whole situation that's bugging him. It's possible Selene switched her bracelet to the other wrist, and he can definitely believe she would have killed Egan if she thought he'd killed everyone else, but he's surprised she hasn't come along to taunt them and rub in the fact she solved the mystery before they did. That is very unlike her, and it makes him wonder if maybe....

He doesn't finish the thought before he rushes into the office. "We were wrong." He hurries around to Declan's desk and stands next to Declan's chair as he takes the mouse and scrolls through the list of transcribed calls on the computer screen. "Look—"

A picture frame falls and hits the ground. Tadd jerks and swirls around, gasping as his eyes meet the flashing bronze blade of a descending dagger.

# HELIOS

DECLAN moves without thinking, relying on his innate speed as he steps to the side, knocking Tadd out of the way, and swings his arm up to deflect the blow. The dagger nicks him, and he cries out and cradles his arm to his chest as he struggles to focus through the burning agony and dodge the next swing.

Tadd surges to his feet, growls at Declan, and barrels in. He dodges the dagger with skill honed by centuries of war and immediately begins grappling with the intruder, forcing him back toward the wall and squeezing his wrist until he has no choice but to drop the dagger.

The dagger hits the wall before landing on the carpet with a dull thud. Declan swoops in and grabs it as Tadd continues to wrestle with the intruder. He barely has time to get out of the way as Tadd pushes the man to the floor, lands on top of him, and tries to push his arms above his head. The man fights back, rolling over and taking Tadd with him, his legs locked around Tadd's as they tumble over each other until they hit Declan's desk.

For a second, it looks like Tadd is going to win despite the dirty trick, but then the intruder slams Tadd's head against the desk drawers, stunning him, and pulls the sixth missing dagger from his jacket pocket. "Don't move."

Declan can't sit by, not while Tadd is lying on the floor, his eyes unfocused, with a crazed god pinning him down and holding a dagger to his throat, but there's nothing he can do, not without risking Tadd. Even with his speed, Declan can't be sure he would get to the dagger before Tadd's throat is cut, and though he knows how to use the dagger he's holding, it's been centuries since he fought with it. He'd be trusting his and Tadd's lives to rusty skills and a throbbing arm, and he can't.

Instead, he slowly lowers the dagger to the floor and stands again, holding his hands up in surrender as though he's a mortal being held at gunpoint. "Don't do this," he pleads, his eyes never leaving the dagger pressed against Tadd's throat.

"I have to." Lukas looks from Declan to the dagger in his hand and shakes his head sadly. "It's a shame, really. I liked stabbing, and to get the two of you like that would have added a certain symmetry, but I suppose my final kills can be different."

"Final kills?" Tadd barely moves his jaw, but a small trickle of blood still runs back his throat to his ear. "Why would we be the last?"

"Don't you know?" Lukas laughs bitterly, making the dagger shake and widening the tiny cut on the side of Tadd's throat. "Are you really that stupid?"

"Pretend I am and explain it to me," Tadd snarls. He catches Declan's eye to let him know he's about to move. "I'm curious."

Lukas shakes his head. "No. Nice try, but no. I'm not some movie villain who monologues when he's about to win. I'm just going to kill you." He glances over and grins at Declan. "And then I'm going to kill you."

Declan winks briefly at Tadd to let him know he's ready for whatever happens, and smirks at Lukas. "You'd have to catch me first."

"You can't run forever."

"I can run long enough." He sets his jaw, staring hard at Lukas and doing his best to pretend he wouldn't be completely unable to move, much less run anywhere, if Tadd were dead. "I can outrun you."

"But your lover will still be dead." Lukas presses the dagger harder against Tadd's throat, making him gasp in pain. The trickle of blood running down his throat swells to a steady stream as the cut in his neck widens, and Lukas smirks as he looks down at Tadd. "I'm going to enjoy this."

Tadd squeezes his eyes shut, gasps in as much as he's able with a dagger pressed hard against his windpipe, and moves, pulling his legs up to knee Lukas in the back at the same time he swings his arms, knocking Lukas's arms away from his throat and sending the dagger spinning across the room. Declan lunges for it and grabs it as Tadd rolls over, pinning Lukas to the floor by sitting on his legs and gripping his wrists tightly as he presses them down.

"Call Bront," he says, glancing at Declan long enough to make sure he heard. "And tell him to hurry." He looks down at Lukas and smiles grimly. "You're not killing anyone else."

"We'll see." Lukas flashes a smarmy smile as he wriggles around, testing the limits of Tadd's grip. "You haven't won yet."

"Yes, we have." Declan picks up the phone and crosses the office, speaking quietly into it when Bront picks up. He keeps the conversation brief, holding back his argument when Bront surprises him, and returns quickly to Tadd's side. Lukas looks small and vulnerable pinned to the floor, and it brings out an uncharacteristic rage in Declan. He puts one foot on Lukas's neck, pressing hard enough to let Lukas know he's serious, and arches one eyebrow. "Bront knows you're the killer."

"So?" Even pinned to the ground by both Declan and Tadd, Lukas still manages to look smarmy. "He's not here to do anything about it, is he?"

"He doesn't need to be. We're taking you to him." He presses a little harder on Lukas's neck with his foot. "Everyone will be there."

"Can't wait." Lukas shifts a little, tucking his chin into Declan's foot and straining against Tadd's grip on his wrists. "How're you going to get me there?"

"Easy." Declan shifts his weight onto his forward foot, making it impossible for Lukas to move without crushing his neck, and Tadd lunges, releasing Lukas's wrist and hurling his fist toward Lukas's face with one swift movement. The blow lands square on Lukas's temple, leaving him looking dazed, and the follow-up punch has his eyes rolling back in his head as his muscles go slack.

Declan stares down at Lukas's limp body for a moment, nodding when it stays that way, and steps back, holding a hand out to Tadd. "I'm not carrying him all the way to Olympus."

Tadd laughs as he takes Declan's hand and lets Declan pull him to his feet. "I thought we'd drive. We'll tie him to something so he can't vanish on us, and dump him in the car."

"Yeah, that could work. Bront is summoning everyone else. He wants to have a trial right away." Declan shakes his head. He understands why Bront wants all the gods and demigods present to witness Lukas being brought to justice—they need to see the threat to them has been eliminated and realize that even now, there are some things that will not be tolerated—but Declan can't help but be a little annoyed he and Tadd are expected to transport Lukas themselves. Bront could at least have sent Pegasus or a griffon.

Instead, he's leaving Tadd and Declan to improvise, and it's not working well. Declan doesn't see anything in the office he could possibly use to tie Lukas up, which means one of them is going to have to leave. He doesn't like the idea of leaving Tadd alone with Lukas after the fight they had, but he doesn't see any other option. There's no way Tadd will let him stay behind, not even with Lukas unconscious. "I'll go find some rope. You watch him. And do something about these. Please." He brushes his fingers over the shallow cuts on Tadd's neck, ignoring the blood that stains them when he pulls away.

"You too."

Declan focuses his attention on his own wound. They're tiny and shallow enough they wouldn't merit the effort it takes to heal them if they'd been made with a different weapon, but the daggers Lukas stole were designed to kill gods. The cuts burn with a fire that hovers on the edge of his awareness, and he wants them gone.

Now.

It should be a matter of a moment's thought, a brief second of concentration to restore his body to the way it's supposed to be, but as Declan thinks about the skin knitting back together, he's hit with a sharp punch of pain that leaves him gasping for breath and fighting the urge to stagger backward. A fresh trickle of blood rolls down his arm, and when he touches the wound, the fire there intensifies until it's claiming all of his attention instead of hovering at the edge of it.

Declan stops and crouches down next to Tadd. "Don't try to heal this," he says, putting his hand on the back of Tadd's neck and brushing his thumb along the narrow cut there. "It doesn't work."

"Fuck." Tadd sucks in a deep breath.

192

"Yeah," Declan agrees. Neither of them is in any danger from their wounds, but Declan hates the sight of blood on Tadd's neck reminding him of how close Lukas was to success, and it's disconcerting to have to keep them until they heal on their own.

Assuming they do.

Declan pushes that thought away—it's not going to help anything now—and gives Tadd a wan smile. This is not how they were supposed to solve this case. It was supposed to happen through teamwork and deduction, and they should have exposed Lukas in time to save someone's life. Instead they realized too late and ended up fighting for their own. It sucks, and now that Declan knows who the killer is, he feels like it was so obvious he should have known before Cal died. Instead, he let Adara and Egan die too, and almost lost Tadd.

"I'll be right back," he tells Tadd once he has his thoughts back in order. He doesn't wait for Tadd's answer, just leaves, dashing away from the house as quickly as he can move.

They don't own any rope that Declan is aware of, so instead of wasting time searching, he zips down to the store, moving faster than mortal eyes can see as he grabs zip ties and bandages off the shelves and leaves cash in their places. Chances are good that the cash will make it into people's pockets instead of the store's registers, and it's doubtful it will ever be associated with the missing product, but Declan doesn't have time to wait in line. He needs to get home. The token effort will have to do.

Lukas is still unconscious when Declan returns, and Tadd is still standing over him, both daggers now clenched in his hands. He looks ready to slice Lukas up right then, but he grins boyishly when Declan stops in front of him, the hardened warrior melting away into the besotted executive. "That was fast."

It's almost the teasing tone Tadd would have used before their fight, and when Declan looks into his eyes, he sees the joke for the olive branch it is, and smiles. "I try. Don't want to keep you waiting, you know."

"Of course not." Tadd matches Declan's smile, though he doesn't look away from Lukas for long. Lukas hasn't stirred yet, but Tadd is honestly surprised he hasn't, and he's not going to take any chances.

Lukas is a god, same as they are, and no blow to the head is going to keep him out for long. "Tie him to your briefcase," he says, pointing at it with his chin as he shifts the daggers in his grip. "If you still have that proposal in it, it should be heavy enough to keep him with us."

Declan hesitates. He's itching to pull out the bandages and cover the cuts on Tadd's neck, but Tadd is right. They need to take care of Lukas first, while he's still unconscious and can't cause any more trouble. "Sure." He drops the bag he snagged from the store onto the floor after pulling out the plastic zip ties and thick plastic cord he'd taken. They're stronger than rope, and easier to secure, and it only takes him a few minutes to fashion crude cuffs to secure Lukas's hands behind his back before he wraps him with the cord, which he loops through the handle and around the briefcase to ensure Lukas can't get away from it.

"We're going to have to carry him to the car," Tadd says as he looks at Declan's handiwork. "There's no way he'll be able to walk like that."

It's true, but that was Declan's intention. "I don't think he would walk with us even if I left his legs untied. This way it'll be easier to carry him."

"Good point." Tadd sets the knives down on the desk and glances at the bag lying on the floor. "What else did you get? I don't think we need anything else to get him to Bront."

"Not to get him to Bront." Declan twists his lips into a half smile as he grabs the bag and moves closer to Tadd. "To take care of us." He sets the bag on the desk next to the daggers and brushes his fingers over the cuts on Tadd's neck once more. Tadd pulls back, biting down on a hiss, but Declan slides his other hand down Tadd's arm, curls his fingers comfortingly around Tadd's wrist, and pulls him back in. "Hold still."

Tadd scowls and shoves his free hand into his pocket. "Why?"

"So I can take care of it." Declan takes a box of butterfly bandages out of the bag and pulls one free. "People will talk if you don't cover those up somehow, and this might help it heal faster."

Tadd looks from the bandages to Declan and back again. "Is it really that bad?"

"Yeah." Declan looks from his arm to Tadd's neck. The cut on his arm is bad enough he's going to put a bandage or two over it as well. He could probably get away with leaving it uncovered—he's noticed mortals don't tend to worry as much about covering up scratches on their arms as nicks on their necks—but he'll take care of it, even if it's just to make Tadd do the same. He holds out his arm so Tadd can see the scratch there, and looks his husband straight in the eyes. "There are four cuts. And they're all worse than this."

Tadd frowns down at the cut and frowns. "Okay." He takes the bandage from Declan's hand. "You first."

Declan shakes his head and smiles softly. It's ridiculous, really, but no less than he expected. Tadd could have lost a limb and he would insist Declan be taken care of first. Since they're talking about what amounts to insignificant cuts despite their location on Tadd's neck, Declan acquiesces easily and tilts his arm to give Tadd the best angle. "All right."

The box gives clear instructions on the best way to apply the butterfly bandages, and after reading them thoroughly, Tadd carefully lays the sterile strips across the cut on Declan's arm, pulling the skin together and mostly covering the wound. He covers it up with a plain bandage from the last box remaining in the bag and beams at Declan when the cut is completely obscured from view by the protective covering. "There."

"Thanks." Declan looks down at the bandages for a moment before pulling another set of butterfly strips from the box and stepping closer to Tadd. "Now it's your turn."

Tadd's wounds are a little harder to treat. The blood has smeared enough that Declan has to clean it off before he can get anything to stick, and then it's still awkward stretching the soft, sensitive skin of Tadd's neck. The angle is wrong, and as Tadd's Adam's apple bobs up and down, Declan's mind travels down paths it shouldn't be taking.

When he's done, he straightens so he's looking down at Tadd instead of up at his neck, cups Tadd's chin, and pulls him in for a kiss. It's soft and gentle, their tongues lazily curling around each other. Tadd tangles his fingers in Declan's hair, pulling Declan closer, but the kiss remains gentle, soothing them both after their rough day. There's passion in it, and lust, but it's mostly love and caring, reassuring each other they are okay and offering a final branch of forgiveness over their earlier arguments.

It's exactly what they both need right now, crazed killers and impatient leaders aside, so of course it's when Lukas starts to stir, thumping loudly on the other side of the desk. Declan pulls back with a reluctant sigh, tugging on Tadd's bottom lip, and flashes a small smile as he slides his hand down Tadd's arm and laces their fingers together. "Duty calls."

Tadd's answering smile is slightly strained. "We'll pick this up later," he promises in a low voice as he steps slightly in front of Declan, letting his hand slip behind him so he can keep it wrapped around Declan's.

"Promise?" Declan falls into step behind Tadd, humoring his need to protect even though Lukas is immobilized. It's a small price to pay for the peace of mind Tadd will get from staying in front, and Declan is happy to give it to him.

Tadd looks over his shoulder, smiling wickedly. "Of course."

"Spare me." Lukas thumps again, trying to sit up despite the bonds securing him and the briefcase secured to his chest. "Please."

"Having trouble there, Lukas?" Tadd drops Declan's hand and crouches down next to Lukas. He lets his grin turn evil as he tugs on the cord wrapped tightly around Lukas and re-centers the briefcase over his chest, pinning him to the floor. "Better?"

"Fuck you." Lukas jerks again and the briefcase falls to the floor with a dull thud, pulling Lukas to the side a little as it catches on the cords securing it to him. "What in Hades did you put in that, anyway? Bricks?"

Declan smiles down at Lukas as he stops behind Tadd and rests his hands casually on Tadd's shoulders. "Wouldn't you like to know?"

"Not that badly." Lukas scowls up at both Declan and Tadd. "Now let me go."

196

"No." Declan squeezes Tadd's shoulders and steps back. "Not a chance in Hades."

Tadd interprets Declan's squeeze as intended and lets his smile widen as he looks at Lukas appraisingly. There's bruising still showing on Lukas's right temple and his jaw is a little swollen, but most of his injuries from their fight have healed. It might take another two or three punches to knock him out again, but if he hits just right, Tadd may be able to do it in one.

He tilts his head back and looks up at Declan. "Anything else you want to say?"

"No. Do your worst. I don't want him babbling and fighting all the way to Olympus."

The punch Tadd throws is hardly his worst, given the awkward angle and the fact that it's difficult for him to pummel someone who has no chance to defend himself, even when they've pissed him off as much as Lukas has, but it gets the job done, knocking Lukas out cold before he can do more than widen his eyes at Declan's words. Tadd throws another one for good measure, to be certain Lukas will stay unconscious until they get him loaded into the car, and then brushes his hands on his jeans and pushes himself to his feet.

Declan steps up behind Tadd, wraps his arms around Tadd's waist, and leans his chin on his shoulder as he peers down at Lukas. "Nice."

"Hardly." Tadd twists a little in Declan's arms, turning enough to see his face and place a quick, chaste peck to Declan's lips as he pulls free. "But it works. We should get him to the car before it wears off, though."

"Yeah." Declan sighs, eyeing Lukas's body. "How you want to do this?"

Lukas is significantly shorter than both Declan and Tadd, but tied up the way he is, with the briefcase weighing him down so there's no way he can disappear, it's not going to be easy for either of them to carry him. Eventually, they settle for Declan taking his feet while Tadd hooks his hands under his arms, and they carry him between them, doing their best to balance the briefcase on his chest.

It falls to hang beneath him before they get out of the office, but since it's still securely attached, they don't bother to stop to fix it. They don't stop at all until they get to the garage, where loading Lukas into the car is yet another exercise in patience and problem solving. It's a lot harder to get a tied-up, limp body into the backseat of a car than the movies make it look, and by the time they get Lukas in, they're both bundles of nerves, half expecting Bront to call them at any moment, demanding to know what's taking them so long.

Declan dashes back inside and grabs the two daggers from the desk. He puts one of them on the front seat and hands the other to Tadd. "You want to ride back here with him?"

"Yeah." *Want* isn't exactly the right word, but Tadd isn't going to take the chance Lukas will wake up while they're traveling and cause further problems. He's tied securely, but that doesn't mean he won't cause some sort of problem, and Tadd does want to get to Olympus so they can get Lukas off their hands.

He's ready for this to be over.

"Okay." Declan climbs into the front seat while Tadd climbs into the backseat next to Lukas, holding the dagger ready in case Lukas stirs. "Let's go, then," Declan says as starts the car. He looks at Tadd via the rearview mirror as he pulls out, and when he puts the car into gear, he finally lets himself wonder if this is a good idea after all.

It's too late to do anything differently now.

THE traffic outside Olympus Casino is ridiculous. The sun has set, and as it descended, the gamblers came out, anxious to lose their money to Bront and the other casino owners. A few of them are dressed in what they think are appropriate clothes—modern interpretations of ancient Greek clothing that makes Declan's skin crawl—but most of them are wearing comfortable clothes and shoes, ready to spend hours sitting or standing in one spot. The cars out front move as quickly as the valets can manage, dropping off new arrivals that fill in the spaces left by hotel patrons leaving for the evening to try their luck at other casinos.

The street is horribly crowded, cars arranged bumper to bumper at every light and only crawling a few feet each time it changes. They're pressed close together, all of them lost in their own worlds and ignoring the other drivers as much as they possibly can, but Declan is still nervous as he carefully navigates the streets, attempting to use the GPS and his innate sense of direction to find the road that leads to the back of Olympus Casino. As he steers the car around the numerous obstacles that keep popping up, Tadd maneuvers Lukas around, pushing him so he's lying flat on the seat and no one in the passing cars can see him. The last thing either of them wants is to attract attention that would lead to questions about why they have a man trussed up in the backseat of their car.

That would let Lukas get away, which could easily mean another death before he is caught again.

It's a nerve-wracking trip fraught with near-misses and people cursing out the window when Declan manages to turn faster and get into the good locations before other drivers, but eventually Declan locates the correct road and swings the car down it, throwing Tadd and Lukas to the side with the speed of the turn.

"Dammit, Declan!" Tadd pushes himself back up and pushes Lukas off him. "Slow down!"

The look Declan gives him through the rearview mirror is amused. "Sure, Tadd, I'll work on that. As soon as we're done with this."

"Oh, fuck you." Tadd finishes shuffling around and arranges himself so he's mostly comfortable again, with the dagger held ready in case Declan's antics jarred Lukas awake. It won't be long before he stirs. It won't be long before they need to get him out of the car either, but Tadd isn't counting on the two events coinciding. He figures Lukas will wake up before they get there, just in time to cause problems in the car and when they try to drag him into the casino.

Amazingly, he's wrong. Declan parks the car in the lot in the back and climbs out without Lukas stirring. He's still unconscious when Declan pulls open the back door and starts dragging Lukas out, and he remains unconscious while Tadd climbs out of the car and takes

Lukas's feet so they can carry him inside. Even Bront's spectacular arrival outside the casino doesn't rouse him.

He doesn't wake up until after Bront takes them on an elevator in the back corner of the building and presses his thumb against a seemingly empty area of the wall, revealing a hidden screen. As Bront traces over the illuminated area with his fingers, Lukas's eyes snap open and he jumps into awareness, thrashing around so badly that Tadd and Declan are forced to drop him.

He hits the floor with a thud as the elevator starts heading up. "You assholes!"

"We're not the ones who killed people, Lukas." Tadd walks up toward Lukas's head and puts one foot on his shoulder. "I think that makes you the asshole."

Lukas lets out an annoyed sound as he tries to shift away from the pressure of Tadd's foot. "Prove it."

"That's why you're here," Bront says. Lightning crackles along the walls of the elevator before arching up to the top and meeting in the middle of the ceiling. "To figure this out."

"I didn't—"

"Don't." Bront clenches his fingers, and tiny crackling bolts shoot between the tips. "I don't want to hear anything until we get upstairs. I don't appreciate being lied to."

His gaze swivels to Declan and Tadd as he steps back toward the wall, letting them know his comment wasn't directed solely toward Lukas. Declan swallows hard, fighting to ignore the fear that clenches in his stomach. He didn't lie, knows he didn't lie, and that Tadd didn't either, but with the way Bront is looking at them all, he can't help but be a little nervous. It's that syndrome he's heard Rachel talk about, where she gets nervous every time she sees a police officer, despite not ever doing so much as stealing a candy bar.

He hates it.

The elevator returns to normal silence as Bront directs his gaze back to the panel he opened and stares at it with his hands clasped behind his back as though it's the most exciting thing in the entire universe. It's surreal after that display, but the calm doesn't last long.

As soon as it's clear Tadd isn't moving, Lukas squirms and twists, struggling against the cord binding him, and glares up at Tadd and Declan. "Are you going to untie me any time soon?"

Tadd opens his mouth to tell Lukas there's no chance in Hades he'll be untied before they reach their destination, but Bront cuts him off before he can utter so much as a syllable.

"Let him up."

"Are you sure?" Declan pushes off the wall he's leaning against and steps closer to Bront. "He killed—"

"We're not discussing it now. Let him up." Bront doesn't look at any of them, just keeps his gaze fixed on the panel, frowning at it.

"But—"

"This isn't open for discussion, Ares. Let him up."

Muttering unflattering things under his breath, Tadd pulls the dagger from his pocket and uses it to slice the cords wrapped around Lukas, cut the briefcase off, and frees his legs. He leaves Lukas's hand secured behind his back, but hauls him up and sets him roughly on his feet, barely giving him time to catch his balance before letting go. "There."

"My hands?"

"What about them?" Tadd looks flatly at Lukas. "You don't honestly think I'm going to cut them free to, do you?"

"Bront said to let me go."

"He said to let you up." Tadd moves closer to Lukas, forcing him to back into the elevator wall, and lets his eyes rake up and down Lukas's body. "You are up."

"He meant—"

"Drop it!"

The elevator coasts to a halt and the doors slide open, revealing a large oval-shaped room filled with every god, goddess, and demigod that survived into this century. Many of them are people Declan has talked to recently, like Demeter and Dionysus, but others are ones he hasn't thought about in years. He scans the room, his eyes wide as he takes in the scene before him.

Pan is perched in one narrow end, sitting backward on a chair with pipes in his hand. His wavy blond hair is falling into his face as he bobs his head in time with the music he's playing, but he doesn't push it back, just lets it fall forward as he focuses on the music. Morpheus is sitting on the floor behind him, leaning against the wall, his head tilted back to reveal his long throat and his legs crossed in front of him. Hestia is sitting on a blanket near the fireplace recessed into one wall. It's soft and clean, but as she watches the room, she brushes away imaginary dirt with one hand.

Hades is in the narrow curve opposite Pan and Morpheus, Persephone standing by his side, casting glances between him and her mother. In the middle of the room, already perched on the throne reserved for him, is Poseidon, looking cleaner and dryer than when Declan and Tadd talked to him earlier but still appearing scruffy and irritable. None of the other gods approach either of them.

The heroes are all gathered together away from the circle of thrones in the middle of the room. The two far ends are claimed, so they're gathered closer to the fireplace than anything else, but keeping a respectful distance from Hestia. They look at her more fondly than they look at some of the other gods and goddesses, but ultimately, they're young men who were never allowed to grow up, and their mere presence often spells disaster. The world outgrew its need for that kind of hero, but the young men selected to live forever thanks to that perfect combination of blood and deeds did not outgrow their need for the world.

Tadd's eyes widen as he takes it all in. He remembers what this court used to look like back when it was located on the real Mount Olympus. "It looks the same," he whispers, grabbing Lukas roughly by the arm and yanking him away from the wall.

"It is the same." Bront steps out of the elevator, smiling softly and winking before he turns around to frown out at the room.

Declan gets it first. "Shit." He steps up next to Bront, leaving Tadd to handle getting Lukas out of the elevator. "Do they know?"

"No."

Now that he's aware, it's obvious to Declan they're not in the top level of Olympus Casino. This room doesn't just look like the area where they used to hold trials centuries ago, it *is* the room where they used to hold trials centuries ago. They're home, on Mount Olympus, in a place Declan never thought he'd see again. "How? I thought...." He trails off, shaking his head as he struggles to figure out how to ask.

"That we couldn't come here?" Bront shrugs. "We can, we just shouldn't."

"But it's all still here, right? Our temples, and Tadd's armory, and—"

"It's here. But you can't go see it."

"Why not?"

"For the same reason I tell everyone we can't come here anymore. If they knew they were actually on Mount Olympus, they'd never want to leave, and then we'd all die. We're gods, Declan. We need to be worshiped in order to survive, and we won't get that here."

"I'm not worshiped down there." Declan twists his lips up into a smirk and nudges Bront with his elbow. "Unless you count Tadd worshiping my body." He waggles his eyebrows as Bront steps away, shaking his head and rolling his eyes.

"No." Bront shudders dramatically. "That doesn't count."

"Then what does?" Tadd drags Lukas out of the elevator and shoves him forward, letting him fall to his knees as he staggers. "I overheard. Lukas did, too." He looks around. "It's easy to tell if you know what you're looking for."

"That's intentional." Bront shoves his hands in his pockets, rocks back on his heels, and frowns. "There isn't any other place like this anywhere. It hurts sometimes, knowing the days of this glory are gone, but we can't get them back. We aren't worshiped here."

"But we are down there." Tadd doesn't make it a question. "At least," he says slowly, his breath hitching as full understanding hits him, "Ares isn't. But Tadd is."

"Exactly." Bront beams. "It's not the kind of worship we got used to, but everyone knows your company, your name. They may not sacrifice animals to you anymore, but they think about you, and that's what you really need."

"So we can't come back because then they'll forget."

"And we'll die." Tadd nods and pats his pocket, making sure the daggers are still there before he moves forward and grabs Lukas by the back of his shirt. "Can't have that."

"No." Bront pulls his hands out of his pockets and draws himself up to his full height. He's gathering enough power standing there that he manages to look imposing even though he's shorter than both Declan and Tadd, and as he strides forward, people start to notice his presence. "We can't."

The room quiets as Bront walks through, everyone focusing on him and ignoring Declan, Tadd, and Lukas as they move to their places. The major gods take their seats on the thrones arranged in a circle, the lesser gods stand next to them or sit on the daises at their feet, and the demigods hover behind them, their hands jammed into pockets or crossed over their chests and their jeans and suits looking completely out of place in the ancient room.

Tadd shoves Lukas into the middle of the circle before heading to his throne. Declan follows, takes a seat on the next one, and stretches his hand across the gap between them to take Tadd's hand. The seat used to belong to Aphrodite, and for a minute, Declan feels strange about taking it even though they unofficially traded centuries ago. It was fine when she also slipped into his old chair, but looking across the circle at the empty seat feels wrong.

The moment their hands touch, Lukas rolls his eyes. "Oh, look. The lovebirds are causing problems. Again. Go sit in the right seat, Hermes. This is messed up enough without you confusing people."

Tadd doesn't let Declan pull away. "Stay," he says, curling his fingers around Declan's and squeezing. "This is your seat. Not over there."

An argument could really be made either way, but before Declan can bring it up, Pan blows a trill on his pipes, catching everyone's attention, and stands. "What I want to know," he says, tossing his head to get his hair out of his eyes, "is why Helios here is tied up. And why he hasn't done anything about it." He plays another trill and the zip ties Declan had used to secure Lukas's hands behind his back come open, leaving Lukas completely free.

Lukas grins as they fall to the floor. "You, my friend, are a good man." He clasps Pan on the shoulder and squeezes. "If you ever need a car, let me know. I'll hook you up."

The room erupts into chaos, gods and demigods scrambling to get closer or farther away. There's yelling, wailing, and a few displays of power, but Pan ignores it and steps closer to Lukas. "I'd need a bus, really. The Arion Xylander Band wouldn't fit in one car. But if you figure something out, let me know. I'd definitely be interested." He flashes a smile at Lukas as he steps away, lifting his pipes to his lips and playing a soft song as he vanishes back into the riled-up crowd.

Declan and Tadd stand up together, their hands still joined, and survey the room from their thrones. It's complete chaos, with gods off their thrones, demigods brandishing swords, and no one listening to anyone else. Morpheus is running around the room, touching the demigods and making them drop to the floor, sound asleep, while Demeter and Hestia are huddled near the hearth, watching the chaos through wide eyes. They're not afraid, that much is obvious from the way they look out over the crowd, but it's clear they want nothing to do with the chaos. It goes completely against their peaceful and ordered nature.

Tadd drops Declan's hand and steps into the crowd. Declan follows, prompted by the sight of Lukas moving slowly toward the door where the elevator used to be. He catches up to Tadd in two swift steps and gets his attention with a hand on his shoulder. "Can you clear a path?" He could go around the outside of the room to intercept Lukas that way moving at full speed, but no matter which direction he moves, he's going to have to get through a teeming mass of gods and demigods, none of whom are likely to cooperate without an explanation he doesn't have time to give.

Tadd hesitates for a second, looking at Declan askance, but when Declan points at Lukas with his chin, he nods. "Yeah. Stay close."

As if Declan would do anything else.

The crowd parts easily. Half the people there have no idea what is going on, but they all saw Tadd and Declan arrive with Bront, and most of them clearly don't want to interfere in what is obviously a serious matter. The few gods who do are easily quelled by Tadd's scowl, and

205

they end up crossing the room much faster than Declan thought they would.

Tadd slips his hand into his pocket, curling his finger around the dagger as he strides forward. He doesn't draw it yet—he doesn't want to accidentally hit anyone with it as he moves through the crowd—but he doesn't want to fumble with it when they get to Lukas. They fought too hard to get him here to let him go now.

They're almost there when Lukas reaches the doors and pulls one open. He could easily pull them open a crack and slip through without anyone but Tadd and Declan knowing where he went, but instead he yanks hard and opens one of them all the way to reveal the dusty, aged splendor of the rest of Mount Olympus.

For a moment, everyone freezes, their eyes widening as they take in their former home. The temples and gardens are still intact, dirty and overgrown but flourishing. The streets look a little rough from centuries of abandonment, but the water in the fountains still sparkles brilliantly, and in the brief silence, while everyone stares, the melodious chirp of birds can be heard. It's entrancing, beautiful, and tugs on the heartstrings of every person in the room. Even Tadd steps closer to the comfort of his former home. Declan falls into step next to him, taking his hand again as they move toward the doors, and for a moment, he's caught up in the thought of spending eternity here with Tadd.

It's a wonderful thought that almost makes him forget about Lukas. He's too wrapped up in each other and the memories of what it was like to live here, basking in the glory of his worshipers.

Then the doors slam shut, the thud of their closing echoing through the room and shocking everyone into stillness once again. Lukas lets out a curse that breaks the silence, the obscenities echoing almost as loudly as the thud of the door, and then the air is filled with the sounds of his rage as he pulls on the handles with all his strength.

"Enough!" A bolt of lightning shoots upward, hits the marble ceiling in the exact center, and splinters into six individual bolts that race along the curve of the ceiling to the floor. "Everyone to your places!" Bront's hands are both crackling with the lightning bolts he has clenched tight in his fists, and the gods and demigods move toward their spots without a word of protest. Declan heads back to his spot as well, Tadd at his side, but before he gets far, Bront gives them a command they are powerless to resist. "Bring him back to the center. And guard him this time."

Lukas attempts to avoid them, dashing around as though he hopes to find another way out of the sealed room, but Declan is faster and intercepts him as soon as he figures out the pattern to his movements. "Give it up, Lukas," he says as he grabs Lukas's arm to hold him still. "You can't get away."

If they were forced to rely on mortal strength, Declan would easily win, but Helios is fairly well matched with Hermes in terms of supernatural strength, and Declan uses his superior height and bulk to pin Lukas to the wall until Tadd arrives and easily secures Lukas with an iron grip on his biceps. "Come on."

Tadd doesn't bother being gentle. He drags Lukas along, both hands wrapped around one of Lukas's arms, and only worries about getting him completely upright when they've stopped in the center of the circle and are facing Bront. Lukas tries to yank his arm free as soon as they stop, but Tadd digs his fingers in and refuses to let go. "Don't even think about it."

"Where am I going to go?" Lukas tugs again. "Come on, man, let me have a little dignity."

"You don't deserve it." Tadd lets go with one hand so he can pull out the dagger again and holds it ready as additional insurance in case Lukas tries to flee. "You've already run once. Why should I believe you won't run again?"

"Let him go," Bront commands before Lukas can answer. "But stay close so he doesn't run."

Tadd drops Lukas's arm and steps back. He keeps the dagger in his hand, held so that with one swing he could easily hurt or kill Lukas. "Don't try anything stupid."

"I would never."

Declan rolls his eyes. The idea doesn't even merit a response, but the urge is there, and the only thing that keeps him from replying sarcastically is Bront's stern gaze. Instead he takes position next to Lukas, ready to grab him if he runs.

The silence that descends over the gathered crowd when Bront stands up and tells them why they've been called together is absolute. No one moves a muscle as Bront details the charges against Lukas, and when Declan steps forward to recount what he and Tadd found, his soft footfalls sound almost deafeningly loud.

Declan starts at the end. "About an hour ago, Lukas—Helios—showed up at our house and tried to kill us." He pulls the second dagger out of his pocket and holds it up while gesturing to the one Tadd is holding. "He attacked us with these—two of the six daggers stolen from a local museum that possess the power to kill gods."

"How do you know?"

"How did he steal them?"

"Where are the others?"

"Safe." Declan holds up a hand and waits for silence. "Bront—" He shakes his head and corrects himself. "Zeus has three of them. The other is safely locked up in Ares's armory." He walks closer to Bront, leaving Tadd and Lukas standing in the middle of the circle, and turns so his back is to Bront and he can look at everyone else. "I know they can kill gods because I saw them sticking out of Athena, Eros, Aphrodite, and Hephaestus."

"That doesn't mean it's what killed them." Selene stands and gives Declan an amused look. "Maybe they were stabbed later and something else killed them. I could kill you and then stick an arrow in you. It would only look like you were shot."

Declan bites back the urge to respond sarcastically and instead holds up his arm and pulls the bandage off. Tadd winces, and Declan wishes he didn't have to do this, but it's better for him to show off the wound on his arm than the ones on Tadd's neck. "I was cut by one of them, and I can't heal it." He makes sure everyone can see the red line held together by the butterfly bandages, and then presses the covering bandage back down and lowers his arm. "Trust me, they can kill a god."

Selene's smiles evilly. "Are you sure you're not just incompetent?"

"I can't heal them either, Artemis." Tadd lifts his chin so the bandages on his throat are visible. "But if you don't believe us, I'm sure Declan would be happy to cut you, and you can try for yourself."

Her smile fades as she realizes she lost this round, and she slowly sits down again. "No. I believe you."

"Good." Declan holds the dagger up again. "As I was saying, an hour ago Helios attacked Ares and me with these daggers. He was trying to kill us so we couldn't accuse him of killing Athena, Eros, Aphrodite, and Hephaestus and share the evidence with you."

"You don't have any evidence, because I didn't do it." Lukas takes a step forward, stopping when Bront raises a lightning bolt and Tadd tightens his grip on the dagger. "You're accusing me because you're too besotted to accuse him." He points at Tadd before taking another step forward and addressing the circle. "I told him he needed to look at his husband, and I thought he was going to, but when I came over tonight to give him more evidence, I was attacked without provocation. He sided with Ares."

"You didn't come over to do anything but kill us, and all your accusations were designed to do was distract him."

"Prove it." Lukas spreads his arms wide as he turns to face Tadd. "Prove to them that you didn't do this and I did. Show me this plethora of evidence." He raises one eyebrow and makes a show of looking around. "Well? Where is it? I don't see it. Could it be that there isn't any? That you're trying to accuse me to save your own ass?"

Tadd lunges, moving more quickly than anyone but Declan is capable of, and ends up with Lukas pulled back against him, pinned with one arm across his chest and the dagger to his throat. "Shut up. Now. Or you won't have a chance to stand trial."

Lukas's answering laugh is low and hollow. "Nice temper, Ares. Which one of us just acted like a killer?"

"I've never denied what I am. I'm the god of war, Helios. I'm supposed to be a killer. And yet you're the one who sneaks around, murdering your fellow gods."

"You can't prove that."

"Yes, we can." Declan touches Tadd gently on the shoulder. "Let him go. We know he's guilty. Don't kill him before we prove it to everyone else."

"Good luck with that." Lukas shakes his shoulders as Tadd steps away, and turns to address Bront. "I don't think this is a very fair trial, Zeus. I've been assaulted in the middle of this assembly, and yet I'm the one being accused of murder. Hardly seems logical."

"It is when you think about the fact that you were the one who knew Sofia well enough to know in advance about the daggers in the museum exhibit," Declan counters. "I imagine she came to you, concerned about them being included, maybe even let you see them, and you jumped at the opportunity to take them. That's why she died, isn't it? Because she figured out you were the one who stole them and she wanted to confront you about it."

"I knew Sofia, but I'm not the one who stole the daggers." Lukas draws himself up to his full height. "And even if I had, why would I want them? Why would I kill Eros, or Aphrodite, or Hephaestus? Cal was my friend."

Declan lets out a soft snort. "He was also the only person who could easily dispute the information you gave me about Sofia calling Devilish Angels. He died before I got a chance to talk to him about that. That's motive right there."

Lukas rolls his eyes. "Puh-leese. That's ridiculous. And even if it were right, what was my motive for killing Adara and Egan?" He pinches his lips and taps his chin, pretending to think for a moment. "Oh, right, there isn't one. Because I didn't do it."

"Shut up." Tadd steps closer to Lukas, brandishing the dagger once more. "You'll get your turn to talk."

Declan smiles his thanks at Tadd and turns to face the assembled crowd again. "He is good at the innocent act. He had me fooled, even though he showed up at every crime scene, even the first, before anyone knew what that sensation we all felt was." He lets out a hollow laugh. "He even got me to question Tadd for a little while. It almost derailed my investigation."

The murmuring in the crowd swells, but Declan ignores it and pushes on, explaining how Lukas had deceived them, leading them to think it was Cal, then Egan, who was the killer. He talks about how they had even momentarily suspected Egan had killed Sofia, Cal, and Adara, and Selene had found out and killed him.

Everyone looks to Selene for her response to that, but she disappoints and simply rolls her eyes. "I would have shot him, not stabbed him. But I knew he didn't do it. I'm not surprised you thought he did, though."

"I didn't see you trying to blame Lukas," Declan shoots back. He can't help but feel immensely pleased by the fact that despite Selene's claims that he and Tadd were bumbling around messing everything up, they were the ones to solve the mystery. Granted, it happened about two seconds before Lukas tried to kill them, but they did figure it out. And they survived to tell Bront about it.

"I would have. But please, do go on telling us how you figured it out. It's vastly entertaining."

"Thanks," Declan says dryly before he picks up the narrative with their trip to the Underworld, which elicits a smug smirk from Hades in his place at the foot of the circle. Declan doesn't leave out how Hades refused to let him speak to any of the dead gods, but he does leave out how Hades had tried to trap Tadd in the Underworld. He hasn't forgiven Hades, but he does understand where Hades was coming from, and that part of their trip isn't relevant to the current discussion.

He finishes by telling the audience that after they returned home, they realized what hadn't been adding up. They had, on Lukas's suggestion, been looking for mentions of Sofia on Cal's phone line, but none of them had panned out. She hadn't called, and she didn't associate with the kind of people who would call. Lukas, on the other hand, did, and the search on his name had pulled up a very interesting call two nights before Sofia had died—the same night the daggers had been stolen.

"It seems," Declan says, pacing across the circle in front of Bront's throne with his hands clasped behind his back, "that Lukas got all worked up over stealing the daggers. So worked up, in fact, he was hoping one of Cal's employees could help him with his little problem." He pauses and smirks right at Lukas. "It didn't work, did it?"

Lukas snarls and charges toward Declan, only to be stopped short by Tadd grabbing his arm and tugging backward. He lands on the floor when Tadd lets go and steps back, leaving Lukas to sprawl in an undignified heap in the middle of the room. "I wasn't worked up because I stole the daggers. I was trying to see if Aphrodite's curse had worn off yet."

"Right." Declan turns to Bront. "We would have called you as soon as we got the search results, but Lukas showed up just as I was showing them to Tadd, and then we were too busy fighting for our lives."

Lukas snorts, but Bront holds up a hand, stopping him before he says anything. "Is that all?"

Declan resists the urge to look down and shuffle under Bront's intense glare. He's all Zeus now, his whole body sizzling with power that's incongruous with his casual, modern clothes, and the undercurrent of command in his voice is enough to send shivers down Declan's spine. "Yes. The records of his calls are on my computer at home if you need to see them, and we have records of Lukas's donations to the museum and some of his correspondence with Sofia too."

"Thank you." Bront turns his gaze to Lukas, tilting his head to the side slightly as he stares with unblinking blue eyes. "Do you have a response?"

"Of course I do!" Lukas sputters. "Are you just going to believe him?" Lukas turns around, looking at each of the assembled gods and goddesses in turn. "He's a bumbling idiot looking for a scapegoat because he can't stand the thought that his husband might be the real killer here! And you're going to take what he says at face value?"

"And what should we take at face value, Helios?" Artemis steps down off her throne. "Your word? Why should I believe you any more than I believe them? Hermes, at least, was a reliable messenger in our heyday. I don't like him, but I do trust him a little. I don't trust you at all. So why should I believe you?"

"Why should you believe them? It's their word against mine, and you know neither of them would ever say anything against the other." Lukas rolls his eyes. "This whole trial is a farce. There's no real evidence, and yet you're ready to blame me because those two said I attacked them."

"Did you?" Zeus leans forward, rests his chin on his fist, and raises one eyebrow. "Or do you expect me to believe they made that up too? Maybe they attacked each other."

"They do have the daggers." Lukas crosses his arms over his chest. "I came to talk to Declan, and I ended up pinned to the floor by Tadd."

"You mean you came to kill me. 'Stab' and 'talk' are not synonyms in any language."

This time, it's Tadd who calms Declan down, taking his hand and squeezing it in a silent message to be patient. It's not something either of them is good at, Tadd less so than Declan, but he's enjoying Lukas's stumbling attempts at defending himself too much to want this to end yet.

"I mean talk." Lukas smirks. "And you can't prove otherwise. It's my word against yours, after all, and since your husband ended up pinning me to the floor, I think we all know whose side you're going to be on, no matter what really happened."

"I don't have to lie to defend Tadd." Declan sucks in a deep breath, squeezes Tadd's hand, and steps toward Bront. "There is another way to determine this. If you don't believe me," he continues, turning back to face the circle, "maybe you'll believe the gods he killed. Hades can bring them here, and they can tell us what happened."

"I'm not letting them out of Tartarus. I already told you that." Hades leans back in his chair, his legs crossed and his hands hanging over the sides of the throne. "They're where they belong, and I won't set them free."

"I'm not asking you to set them free," Declan protests. "You can take them back when we're done. Just let me talk to them."

"Well, when you put it that way...." Hades taps his finger on his chin. "No. Definitely not." He smirks at Declan. "I'm not sure why you think I'd want to stop anyone from killing you lot. It's about time some of you are trapped down there with me, and if you're dead when it happens, even better. It's good business."

Zeus stands. "Bring them up, brother."

"Or what? You'll banish me to spend eternity down in the Underworld? You've already done that." Hades stands and stares across the circle at Zeus. Poseidon stands as well, taking his place at Zeus's side as the two gods who rule the realms of the living face off against the one who rules the realm of the dead. Hades doesn't back down. "It's my realm, thanks to your trickery, and I decide who can leave."

They stare at each other for a moment before Zeus turns and flings his hand at the hearth in the far wall. A lightning bolt hits the back wall with a sharp crack and fire springs up, filling the opening with blue flames that don't produce any heat. "Call them there," he commands as he turns back to Hades. "They'll stay in your control, in the Underworld."

"In your flames? I don't think so." Hades twists his lips into an unamused smile. "They wouldn't be under my control then."

The flames die. "Then bring them here, Hades."

There's a tone of command in Zeus's voice no one in the room would dare disobey, not even Hades. "Fine. Have it your way."

HADES reappears a few minutes later with four shades at his side. The dead gods are pale and translucent, looking very much like the modern movie version of ghosts. They're dressed as they were when they died, though their clothing lacks the distinctive bloodstained holes it had the last time Tadd saw them. They look good, except for the fact that they're clearly dead, and as Tadd looks at them, he feels a pang of regret he and Declan weren't able to figure out Lukas was the killer sooner. If he had, maybe there would only be one or two shades in front of him instead of four.

"What happened? How did we get here?" Athena's voice sounds soft and far away, so unlike the strong, commanding tone Tadd remembers that he feels another pang of guilt.

"I brought you here. Don't get used to it." Hades settles back in his throne and gestures toward Declan. "This idiot was trying to figure out who killed you, but it seems he can't spin a very convincing argument. Our deposed sun god doesn't like being accused of murder."

"Why not?" Egan's voice is also a shadow of what it used to be, but he still manages to look menacing when he crosses his arms over his chest and glowers. "He deserves it."

"You were stabbed in the back," Lukas counters. "How would you know?"

"How do you know he was stabbed in the back?" Tadd counters, smirking at Lukas. They have him now, though Lukas hasn't admitted it yet and probably won't for a while. "That's the only crime scene we didn't run into you at. The only way you could know is if you were the one who stabbed him."

"There aren't many people in this room who could have successfully stabbed Hephaestus if he saw them coming." Lukas meets Tadd's stare evenly. "You, Perseus, Herakles...." He taps his chin. "Maybe a few of the other demigods. But that's it. It's a safe assumption. So," he continues, turning back to Egan, "how do you know who stabbed you? I saw your forge. There wasn't a fight there, so you were obviously taken by surprise."

"The thing about polished steel, Helios, is it reflects things." Egan narrows his eyes further and glares hard enough that Lukas takes a step backward. "I couldn't turn fast enough, but I saw you."

"I did too." Adara moves to stand next to Egan. She doesn't exactly walk. Her legs move, but when Declan looks closely, he can see they don't touch the ground, and she moves too smoothly to be actually walking.

"So did I." Cal comes forward as well and crosses his arms over his chest. He manages to look comical rather than threatening, but he glowers almost as well as Egan does. "Water is reflective too, you know."

215

"And I knew who I was running from." Sofia seems to have gathered her bearings as she comes to join the others. "I knew you were the one who stole those daggers, Helios." She looks up and directs her attention to Bront. "I saw him at a museum fundraiser the day we got the daggers in. I knew what they were, and I was going to tell you, but I couldn't decide if I should tell you right away or wait to see what else showed up in the collection. Lukas convinced me to wait, and then, when they went missing, I called him to see if he had any ideas what could have happened." She shakes her head. "Stupidest thing I've ever done."

Adara slings her arm around Sofia's shoulder and pulls her close. "We all do stupid things every now and then."

"She doesn't." Egan juts his chin out. "She's the goddess of wisdom. She's not supposed to be stupid."

"Egan!" Adara pulls away from Sofia and glares at him with both hands on her hips. "You don't have to—"

"No." Sofia pats Adara's shoulder. "He's right. The first time I do something stupid I manage to get all of us killed. I just... I thought Lukas would be as worried about the daggers being loose as I was. Then he showed up at my house brandishing one and I couldn't run fast enough."

"See?" Egan looks pointedly at Adara. "I was right."

"For once. Don't get used to it."

"Maybe you should get used to it. I'm right more often than you think, Adara."

"No, you think you're right more often than you are."

"Silence!" Zeus's roar echoes around the room, stunning everyone to stillness. Lightning flashes behind him as his body expands, growing until his head is almost touching the ceiling. "Helios," he booms, his voice filling the entire chamber, "you have been found guilty of murder. Do you have anything to say for yourself?"

Lukas smirks as he rocks back on his heels. "Nah. Not really. You wouldn't listen anyway."

"You're not even going to tell us why we died?" Adara crosses her arms and stomps her foot, though it doesn't make a noise. "You stabbed me, you asshole, and now I'm stuck down in Tartarus with these idiots and the worst humanity had to offer. I deserve an explanation."

"We all do." Egan glides forward so he's right in Lukas's face. He doesn't try to touch him, but he leans in, glaring straight into Lukas's eyes, and snarls. "Why did you kill us?"

Lukas stares back at him, and for a moment, it seems as though he's going to keep denying everything. Then he shakes his head and lets out a soft snort of a laugh. "As if the two of you don't know."

"We don't." Egan leans in closer. "So why don't you tell us?"

"Because she"—Lukas flings his arm out, letting it pass through Egan's ghostly form before pointing at Adara—"cursed me."

Tadd steps forward. "She cursed us too."

"Yeah. The same curse she put on me: that the only way we could get off or fall in love is with each other. And then the two of you discovered you're deliriously happy together and her stupid curse doesn't matter, which means the only one hurt by it is me! The guy who hardly did anything!"

"You started it!" Adara slides forward so she's next to Egan and leans into Lukas's face. "You're the one who alerted everyone!"

"I alerted Hermes! He told everyone else! And it wouldn't have mattered if you hadn't been cheating on your husband with Ares!"

"I didn't want to be married to him! He didn't love me! He wanted to own me!" She casts a sidelong glance at Egan. "Still does!"

"You cheated on me in my bed!"

"It was my bed too! And if you hadn't rigged it so it trapped us there, none of this would have happened!"

Tadd shudders as he remembers the iron bands that had unexpectedly sprung up that day, trapping him in bed with Aphrodite. The humiliation of being stuck there, naked, had been bad enough, but then Helios had looked down from his position in the sky and seen them, and he'd told Hermes, and soon all the gods in Mount Olympus

217

had come down to jeer at them. His blood had boiled for days, and then Aphrodite had made it worse by cursing him along with Hermes and Helios.

That had been the end of his good relations with Aphrodite.

"She cursed all of us, Lukas."

"But she's the one who did something wrong." He whirls around to glare at Tadd. "You and her, not me."

"You were as wrong as I was." Declan tries to calm Lukas with a hand on his shoulder, only to have it thrown off in disdain.

"And which one of us is still suffering? Huh?" Lukas pushes up on his toes as he shoves himself in Declan's face. "Not you. Not Ares. Not Aphrodite or Hephaestus. Me! I'm the one who did the least, and I'm the one who's still suffering from her twisted curse!"

"So this was all about revenge, then?"

"Yes!" Lukas whirls on Tadd, leaning in close so their noses are almost touching. "It was all to get back at the two of you and her."

"Then why did you kill Cal?" Declan draws Lukas's attention back to him while Tadd watches Bront, waiting for a signal he should take Lukas down, but Bront watches, his giant face impassive as he looks down at the scene below him.

"I killed Cal to hurt her. Her precious son was the only person in the world she cared about, so I took him out first. I was going to kill Egan next and try to frame her, but then I caught her alone, and it was too easy. And it worked out so well too." Lukas laughs as he turns to Egan. "Your temper made them suspect you. I didn't even have to try to frame you."

"But then you knew he would convince us he was innocent, so you killed him too."

"Bingo." Lukas smirks at Tadd. "And the two of you were going to be next. I wanted to wait a few days, but then you went into the Underworld, and I didn't know what you'd learned there, so I couldn't risk it. It would have worked too, if Tadd hadn't moved."

Declan's brow furrows. "What? We were both in the office when you got there."

Lukas rolls his eyes and speaks slowly, as though Declan is a small child who can't understand what he's saying. "I was going to kill your husband first. When I looked in through your windows to see where you were, he was working out and you were in the office. Only, he wasn't working out when I went in. You were both in the office."

"I'm not stupid."

"Really?" Lukas raises his eyebrows. "Could have fooled me." He turns back so he's facing Zeus, crosses his arms over his chest, and tilts his head up to look at Zeus's towering form. "There. Happy now? Anything else you need to know before you smite me?"

"I have a question." Adara moves so she's in front of Zeus and looks Lukas straight in the eyes. "Why didn't you tell me how you felt and ask me to remove the curse?"

"Ask you?" Lukas lets out a hollow laugh. "You would barely acknowledge my existence. And when you did? You told me no before I could even ask anything. How could I possibly convince you to remove it if the first thing you said to me was you wouldn't?"

Adara opens her mouth to protest, but Tadd steps forward. "He's right. You did the same thing to Tadd and me. We'd show up and you'd tell us you weren't going to remove it. Before we could even say hello, sometimes." He hates defending Lukas, even in this, but the way Adara automatically assumed they were there to talk about the curse got old quickly, especially once he and Declan had established themselves happily.

"Fine!" Adara huffs. "My attention was hard to get! That doesn't mean you had to kill us! Tartarus sucks!"

"It's supposed to, darling, that's the point." Hades says from his place behind them. "It's designed to be eternal torment. That wouldn't work very well if it was sunshine and puppies, now would it?" He crooks one finger, makes a pulling motion in the air, and all four shades return to his side as though they're puppets tugged on a string. "I think that's quite enough, don't you?"

"Agreed." Zeus extends a crackling lightning bolt toward Lukas. "Helios. For the crimes of murdering Athena, Eros, Aphrodite, and Hephaestus, I banish you to Tartarus."

219

"You can't!" Lukas blanches. "I'm not dead."

"Neither are the Titans." Zeus steps down off the dais, towering over Lukas, and throws the lightning bolt. It hits with a crack that drowns out Lukas's screams and shatters the marble beneath his feet. The air fills with smoke that quickly obscures everything, leaving Tadd, Declan, and Selene to fumble their way back to the safety of the daises.

Utter chaos reigns as the room fills with a primeval terror. Demigods draw their swords, gods cower, and anguished cries fill the room, stretching time until a heartbeat takes an eon and a second feels like eternity.

Then it stops, the sounds cutting off and leaving behind a silence that's almost as terrifying as the noise. Tadd reaches out, finding Declan's hand by feel and curling his fingers around it. He squeezes tightly as their fingers lace together, and they stand like that, drawing strength from each other as they wait for the smoke to clear.

No one moves or makes any noise until the last wisps of smoke fade away, revealing a pristine marble floor that bears no trace of the earlier chaos. Lukas isn't there, nor is he anywhere else in the room, and a quiet murmur builds as the gods and demigods realize Helios is no longer among them.

"Silence!" Zeus's voice booms through the chamber, commanding immediate obedience. No one says a word as he shrinks back to his normal size and turns to Tadd and Declan. "Give me the daggers." He curls his fingers around the bronze handles when they comply, and looks straight at Tadd. "I want the last one as well."

"You'll have it by the end of the day." Tadd suppresses the slight pang he feels at the command and nods. It's a gorgeous weapon, one he would love to possess, but Zeus's tone has made it clear it isn't up for discussion, and he's not going to try. Not after what the daggers were used to do. Someday, maybe, he'll try to get them for his collection, but it isn't a battle he can win right now.

He and Declan both step back to their places, leaving Zeus alone at the front of the circle. An awkward silence descends on the room, and it's almost reached the unbearable point when Hades steps forward.

"Well," he says, shoving his hands in his pockets and smiling around at everyone. "As fun as this has been, I think it's time for me to get back. I need to look in on my new charge. Make sure he's settled in uncomfortably and all that." He spins, spreads his arms, and heads toward the four shades standing at the foot of his dais. "Come along, now. Playtime's over."

"Wait!" Adara steps to the side and avoids Hades's arms. "We're going back?"

"Well, yes." Hades raises one eyebrow. "What, did you expect I was going to let you frolic around up here until someone took pity on you and made you a new body? You died. That means you belong with me."

"But—"

"No buts. The dead belong in the Underworld."

Adara turns to Zeus. "Can't you do something about this?"

"Yeah, man," Cal adds. "We're gods. This wasn't supposed to happen."

"But it did." Persephone steps forward and stands next to Hades, putting one hand on his shoulder for a moment. "I have to spend six months a year in the Underworld. Seth spends most of his time there. What makes the four of you so special that you should get out of it?"

"We weren't stupid, sweetheart." Egan crosses his arms and cocks his head to the side. "We aren't the ones who did something we weren't supposed to."

"Why should we be punished for Helios's mistake?" Sofia adds, putting her hands on her hips as she moves forward to join the others. "Persephone spends time in the Underworld because she broke the rules. We didn't."

"It's against the rules for you to leave now that you're dead," Persephone counters. "Do you think every mortal in the Underworld died when they deserved to? There are a lot of souls down there because other people messed up. Your situation is hardly unique."

"We're gods!" Adara's protest is echoed by the others.

"Not anymore." Hades holds out his hands palms up. "I'll tell you what. Behave, and I'll let you out of Tartarus. Maybe someday you'll even get into the Elysian fields."

"And you're going to let him do this?" Adara takes another step toward Bront. "You're going to let him drag us back down there?"

For a moment, Zeus looks genuinely regretful. "I promised. And Persephone is correct. The dead belong in the Underworld."

"There was a time—"

"We don't live in that time anymore, Aphrodite." Zeus's voice booms out over the room almost as loudly as it did when he was condemning Lukas. "Your fate has been decided."

"We don't deserve Tartarus." Sofia crosses her arms as she glares at Bront. "If we must spend the rest of eternity in the Underworld, surely we deserve to be judged as fairly as any mortal."

Bront nods and directs his glare back at Hades. "She has a point. Judge them like you would any mortal who comes before you."

Hades doesn't look happy, but he nods, whispers something in Tabitha's ear, and vanishes, taking the shades with him.

As soon as they vanish, Zeus looks out at the rest of the assembled gods and demigods. "Leave," he commands. "Return to your lives and forget about this place again." He holds up one hand to silence the protests. "We left Mount Olympus for a reason. That reason still holds. Unless you want to exist as less than a shade, be gone!"

He gestures toward the ornate doors, and they morph into the doors of the elevator that brought them all here. One by one, the gods and demigods pile in, never quite filling it, until only Tadd, Declan, Bront, and Selene remain. With a wave of his hand, Bront closes the doors and sends the elevator on its way. "Was there something else?" he asks, regarding the three of them with a tilted head and a cocked eyebrow.

"I am curious about one thing," Declan admits. "How did your bracelet end up underneath Egan's body, Selene? That was the main reason we thought you had killed him."

"I would have, if I'd had any proof he killed Adara and Sofia," she admits, casting a sidelong glance toward Bront. "But no. I did go talk to him this morning and tried to get him to slip up, but all I managed was to piss him off." The way she rolls her eyes says far more about her opinion on that than any words possibly could. "He grabbed my shoulders and shook me and threatened to do more if I didn't leave him alone. I guess my bracelet must have fallen off while he was doing that. I didn't notice until I got home." She smirks. "I thought catching the real killer was more important than retrieving my jewelry."

Declan pushes down the urge to roll his eyes. "Of course you did."

"It's probably good you didn't," Tadd adds before Selene can jump in with a sarcastic response. "Lukas couldn't have showed up too long after you left, and if you'd come back while he was there...."

Selene's eyes widen and her hand flies up to cover her mouth. "Oh. I hadn't thought of that." She rolls her eyes. "If I'd arrived while Lukas was there, I would have killed him. I'm not a weak little boy."

"Neither was Egan."

"And that's why Lukas took him by surprise," she says slowly. When neither Declan nor Tadd gives her the pleasure of a response, she lets out a soft sigh, tucks her hair behind her ear, and straightens. "You're right, it might have been bad. But probably, I would have shot him and Egan would have stabbed him and that would have been the end of it. We would both have been surprised, but I would've had the advantage while he was busy with Egan."

Tadd exchanges a glance with Declan, but neither of them says anything. It's odd having Selene talk to them as equals, but it's nice too, and after the day he's had, Tadd isn't willing to do anything to jeopardize nice, no matter who it comes from.

Tadd pulls the bracelet from his pocket, where he'd put it on their way to the Underworld. "Here," he says, holding it out to her. "We picked it up after Egan died. We were going to use it as evidence against you, but since we don't have to, you should have it back."

Selene slowly reaches out, eyeing Bront as she curls her fingers around the bracelet. It's almost as though she's reluctant to take it in front of him, but he nods at her as her fingers touch the shimmering metal, and she doesn't hesitate to take it after that. "Thank you."

"You're welcome."

"If that's all...?" Bront looks between the three of them with a raised eyebrow.

"I think so." Declan takes Tadd's hand again. "Unless you have something else?"

Bront tilts his head to the side, regarding them for a moment. "Thank you. All of you."

That is even stranger than Selene being cordial and thanking them, and Tadd isn't sure what to do with it. He manages a grin and a nod and hopes he doesn't look like too much of an idiot. Declan, at least, manages to say "You're welcome," and Selene bobs her head in agreement with that as they walk to the elevator.

DECLAN sinks down on the bed as soon as they arrive home, letting his head fall forward into his hands as he lets out a shuddering breath. "Zeus, that was...."

Tadd chuckles as he sits down next to Declan and rubs his hand up and down Declan's back. "Intense?"

"That's one way to put it." He lets out another deep sigh and lets himself fall back on the bed. "I feel like I ran around the world a few hundred times and all I did was stand in an audience chamber."

"After fighting for your life, taking a trip to the Underworld, finding another dead body, and spending the morning talking to old friends trying to pin a murder on the guy who died next." Tadd lies down next to Declan and turns his head to look at him. "It's been a busy day."

"It has." Declan rolls onto his side and stares at Tadd with a somber expression. "And fighting with you didn't help."

"Declan." Tadd reaches over and brushes a stray piece of hair back from Declan's forehead. "Can we forget about it? Please?"

"No." Declan catches Tadd's hand and presses it against his cheek. "I can't."

"You should. I have."

"No, you haven't."

Tadd rolls, pushing Declan onto his back and pinning him down by lying on top of him. "Declan," he says, frowning down at Declan's wide-eyed expression, "I get it, okay? You were tricked. Lukas wanted you to look at me so you wouldn't look at him. He wanted us fighting so we wouldn't think about him as a suspect."

"Yeah, but I shouldn't have doubted you, and—"

Tadd silences Declan with a finger over his lips. "You said it was only for a second, right?" He pauses and lets Declan nod, but doesn't pull his finger back. "And you already apologized a million times." He lets his voice drop an octave on the last two words. "I also know Lukas was right, and you really did have to ask or you wouldn't have been doing what Bront told you to do. Right?" Declan's nod is a little less certain this time, but Tadd ignores that and smiles softly. "Which means we're good."

Declan blinks when Tadd pulls back his finger. There are plenty of reasons they should talk about this more, no matter how much he doesn't want to. "But—"

"We're good." Tadd presses his lips against Declan's, silencing his protests before he can give voice to them. Declan squirms and tries to pull back, but Tadd tangles his fingers in Declan's hair, holding him still, and slips his tongue into Declan's mouth. He's not gentle as he slides his lips over Declan's and curls his tongue, but he puts everything he's feeling—joy that they survived mostly unscathed, relief that the whole ordeal is over, lust that he always feels after a battle, and love for the man lying underneath him—into the kiss. By the time he pulls back, they're both gasping for breath, and Declan looks up at him with wide, wonder-filled eyes. "Understand?"

"Yeah," Declan breathes as his lips curl up into a smile. "I understand."

"Good." Tadd lets his smile turn predatory. "Because I have other plans for the evening, and they don't involve mushy apologies. So unless you're too exhausted...."

"Fuck no," Declan whispers. He thrusts his hips up, showing Tadd how on board with the idea he is, and matches Tadd's grin. "Do your worst."

A slight growl is all the warning Tadd gives, and then he's mashing their lips together, slipping his tongue into Declan's mouth. He takes Declan's words to heart, not giving Declan the chance to do anything as he undresses them both with a thought and pins Declan to the bed, pushing his hands up above his head and holding them there. Declan strains against the hold, lifting his head to chase the kiss as Tadd pulls back, but Tadd smirks, makes a tsking noise, and dives down to suck at Declan's collarbone.

He moves all along Declan's neck and shoulders, nibbling and leaving marks everywhere his lips touch and eliciting the sweetest moans from Declan. Tadd's cock aches from the noises his husband is making, and Declan is hard beneath him, barely able to hold back as Tadd teases and licks. "Please, Tadd," he moans, rolling his hips up to rub their groins together and gasping as their skin touches. "Need you. Now."

"Yes." Tadd moves lower, releasing Declan's arms so he can slide his hands down the long, muscular torso stretched out in front of him. He presses his palms against Declan's hips, his fingers spread along the curve of Declan's ass, and looks up at him with heavily lidded eyes. "Mine."

"Yours." Declan bends his knees, offering his ass in a clear invitation. Tadd moves, taking it without pause. Later, he'll do this right, take the time to tease them both through exquisite pleasure before bringing them to climax, but right now, all he wants is to claim Declan, to retake what he almost lost, and to reassure them both they still belong to each other.

He stretches Declan quickly, one finger, then two and three as quickly as Declan's body can take it, and then he lines himself up and thrusts. It's not gentle or caring, but it is full of love and trust, and as

Tadd starts to move, making sure to hit the right spot every time, he looks straight into Declan's eyes, locking their gazes as he makes sure Declan knows he meant what he said.

There's nothing to forgive.

Declan grabs Tadd's arms and pulls him down for a kiss that expresses everything Tadd wouldn't let him say and then some. It says he's sorry and he wishes he had never doubted Tadd, but also he does believe Tadd. It reminds them both that despite everything stacked against them and the horrific, nightmare quality of the past week, they survived this intact and they're stronger for it.

They move together, rolling around on the large bed, their hands roaming over each other's bodies as their tongues dance and their hearts beat as one. Declan comes with a gasp, calling out Tadd's name as he throws his head back, his fingers digging into Tadd's shoulders. It's all Tadd needs to follow him over the edge, and he buries his face in Declan's shoulder as he comes, gasping out Declan's name as he shudders.

He falls forward, draping his body over Declan like a blanket and wriggling around to pull out. "I love you," he says, tilting his head up to press a kiss to the underside of Declan's jaw.

Declan curls his fingers around Tadd's chin, tips it up a little more, and kisses him softly on the lips. It's so gentle as to be almost chaste, but it's perfect. "I love you too."

They've both been reminded that isn't something they can ever say too often.

Later, when they're lying curled together, covered by their silky soft sheets, Declan turns his head to kiss Tadd's cheek and pushes himself up on one elbow so he can look Tadd in the eyes. "Do you think since Adara is dead, the curse is lifted?"

Tadd raises one eyebrow. "Does it matter?"

"I suppose not." He touches the tip of Tadd's nose with one finger, grins and tries to twist away. "I was curious. I mean, if Lukas really wanted to be free from it, he might have just been able to kill her."

"Let's not think about it, okay? You're not planning to run off and find someone else if it is, are you?"

"No." Declan slides his finger down over Tadd's lips, then lets Tadd suck it into his mouth and curl his tongue around it. "I was just curious, is all. I mean, the whole thing sucked, but I can't regret it, even after all this. I was wondering if we would have ended up together if she hadn't cursed us."

"Of course we would have." Tadd rolls so he's on top of Declan and kisses him soundly, his tongue curling around Declan's as he laces their fingers together. "Us? This?" He pulls their joined hands in, trapping them between their hearts, and grins that wide smile that never fails to make Declan's heart skip a beat. "It's fate."

NESSA L. WARIN lives in southwestern Ohio with a cat who graciously allows her to pay all the bills and demands pampering on a regular basis. She enjoys wine tastings and travel, and can easily get lost in science fiction or fantasy stories. She's a true geek, enjoys costuming, and can be found dressed up at at least one Renaissance festival and fantasy convention each year. When she's not having fun, Nessa works in Corporate America coordinating the production and mailing of marketing materials and wishing she had more time to write.

Visit Nessa's blog at http://nessa-l-warin.livejournal.com/and follow her on Twitter @nessalwarin. She can also be reached at nessa.l.warin @gmail.com.

Also from NESSA L. WARIN

http://www.dreamspinnerpress.com

Also from NESSA L. WARIN

the stars are
brightly shining

nessa l. warin

http://www.dreamspinnerpress.com

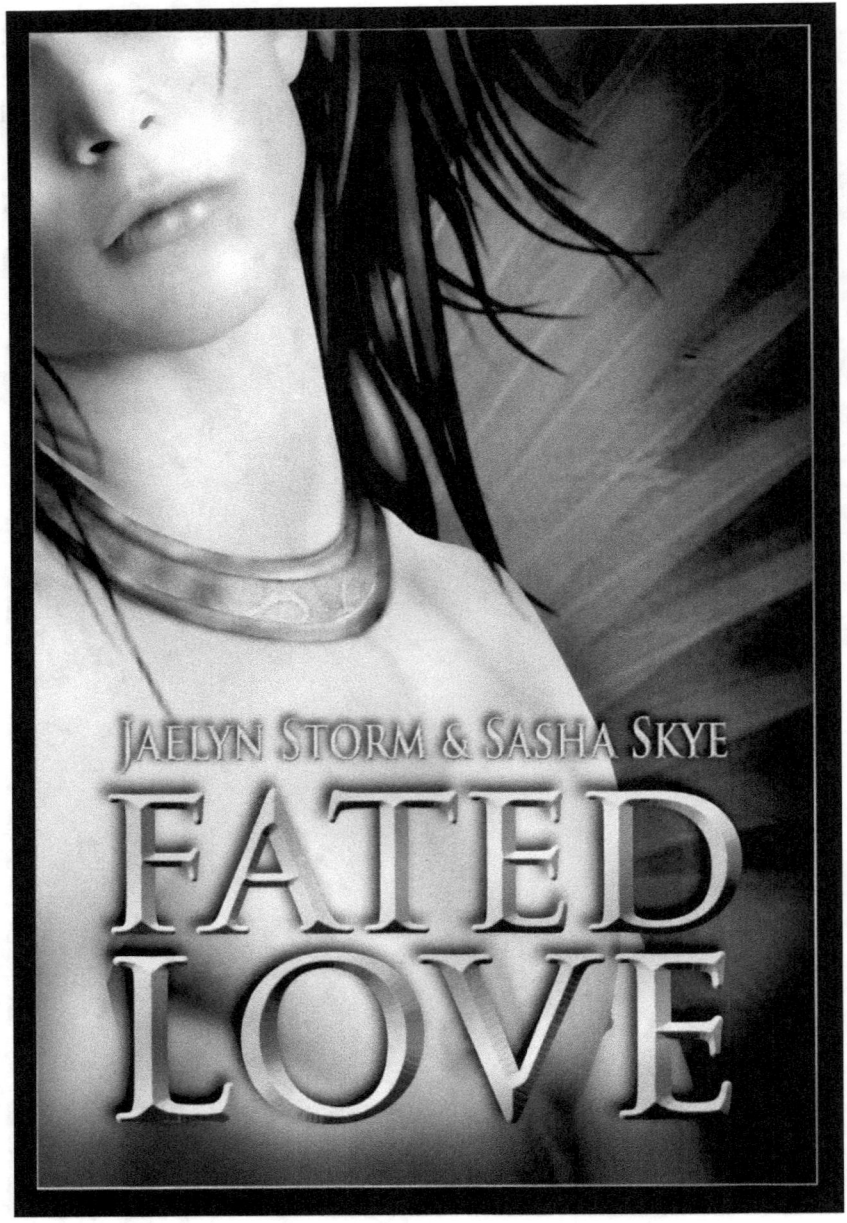

Also from DREAMSPINNER PRESS

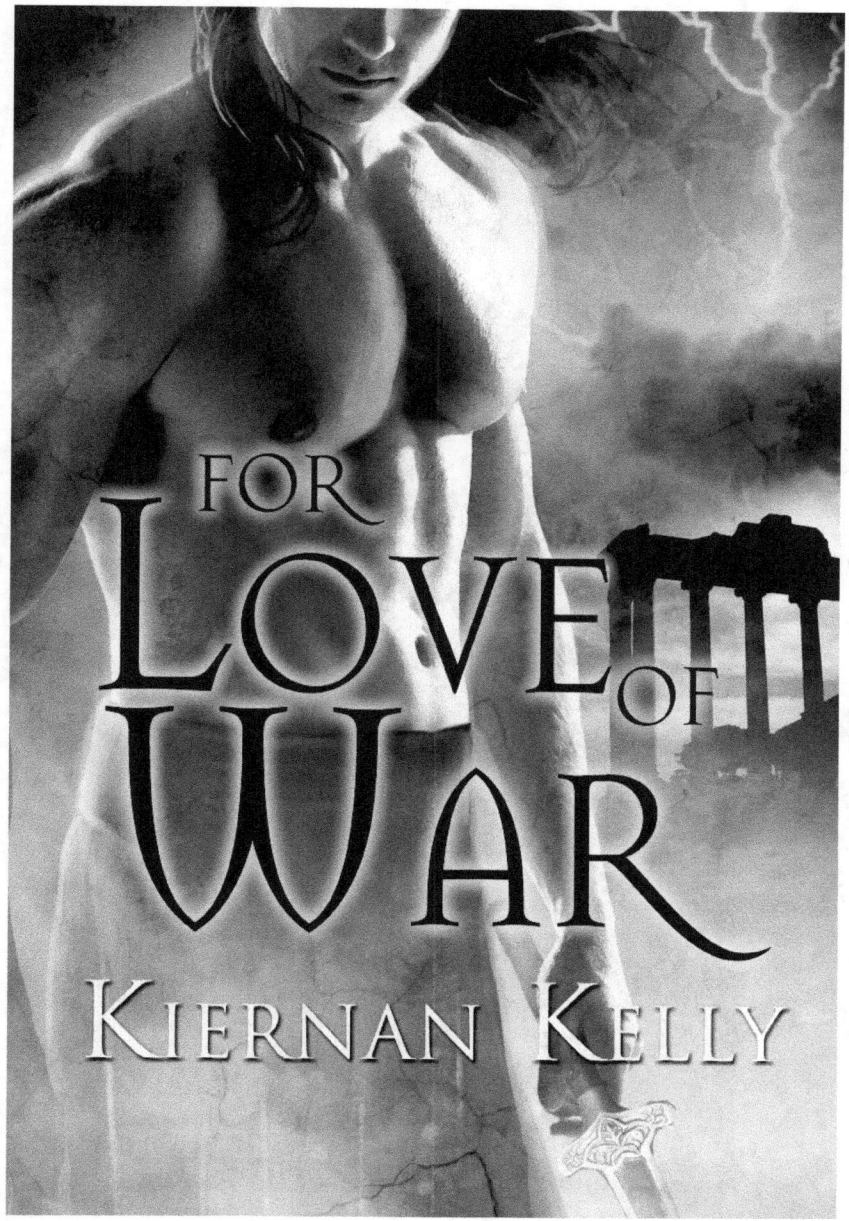

FOR
LOVE
OF
WAR

KIERNAN KELLY

http://www.dreamspinnerpress.com

www.ingramcontent.com/pod-product-compliance
Lightning Source LLC
Chambersburg PA
CBHW071308250626
47159CB00004B/1350